The Phantom in the Fog

RICHARD JAMES

First published by Sharpe Books in 2020.

3

For Ann & Bill.

CONTENTS

AUTUMN, 1892

"And have I not told you that what you mistake for madness is but over-acuteness of the senses?"

The Tell-tale Heart, Edgar Allan Poe.

Prologue

For the first three nights, he was restrained. In his mania, he wrestled with the straps, frothing at the mouth. Sleep eluded him for days. His restless limbs forbade it. Immediately upon his admission he had been assessed and sedated. It had done nothing to calm him, but rather robbed him of his capacity to fight his condition. Numbed by the medication, he found himself helpless against the visions that assailed him.

The severed head of a young woman stared at him with mismatched eyes. The wound at her neck dripped not with blood but water, her mouth agape in a silent scream. It sat on a wooden block. Incongruously, steam rose around it. As he stared in horror, he saw her face transform into one he knew well.

Anna.

He felt his throat dry. He struggled against his bonds, but the straps held him tight to his bed. He could feel the frame through the flimsy, filthy mattress beneath him.

She was trying to talk, her ghastly mouth moving up and down in a mockery of life. Her lips creased with the effort. Two words. He strained to hear. And suddenly, he fell into her eyes.

He was underwater. The cold felt as sharp against his skin as any blade. The rush of the river sang in his ears. He felt his lungs begin to burn. His coat twisted about him as the currents took him down. Improbably, on the riverbed beneath him, he saw a gallows. From this distance, it seemed an old rag hung from the noose. As he was pulled nearer, his lungs fit to burst, he could see it was a body. A young woman twisted in the water, her face bloated from the rope about her neck. He was frantic now, struggling in vain to get purchase on the water around him. As he fought against the instinct to breathe, he saw the girl's head turn towards him. He knew what to expect. Anna's face, her chestnut hair swirling about her in the eddies, seemed to shine in the ripples from the light above. But her eyes were dead. With the strange, lifeless movement he had once seen in a child's automaton, her mouth snapped open and closed as if in speech.

He strained to hear through the rush of water. Two words.

He was on Hanbury Street. He could feel the cobbles against his cheek as if he had been dropped from a height. Pushing himself up on his hands, he could see another figure lying in the dirt. Her clothes were tangled about her and she was covered in grime and blood. She lay like a discarded doll, her limbs contorted into impossible angles.

Sergeant Graves had him, holding him back with a strong arm around his shoulders. Somewhere, a woman screamed. His senses sharpened, he could hear the thundering of hooves and the rattle of a carriage receding behind him. She had just been hit. He could even see the impressions the hooves had left on her skin. Her face was bruised and bloodied. He shook off Graves' embrace and shuffled nearer, his feet as heavy as lead. And then, she sat up. She rested, suspended in the road as if she were nothing more than a puppet on strings. Her head twisted to face him. A hand was raised to beckon him, though he felt she was already devoid of life.

Looking around him, he could see London life proceeding. Traffic clattered past them in the road, the wheels flicking up mud to spatter his coat. Passers by, muffled against the cold, hurried past, oblivious to the scene by the kerbside. There was no sign of Graves. His heart was thumping in his chest. Anna was looking directly at him now. He could see blood on her face. Her jaw was slack and hanging at an unnatural angle. It had been broken. He had never before considered how she had died. Had she felt the weight of beast and carriage crush the life from her? Even in its broken state, her jaw began to move. Her chest heaved as if she had not expected to ever breathe again. He heard a rasp escape her. Two words.

He leaned towards her, marvelling at her beauty even through the filth that caked her. Through it all, he was robbed of speech. Her lifeless eyes stared blankly at him. Her flesh hung loose about her face. A hand clutching at his lapel, she whispered again. Two words.

"Join me."

He felt her pull at him. Suddenly caught off balance, he was pitched towards her, through her.

2

He was adrift.

All of time blurred into an eternal present. The void was a comfort. Soon, even the notion of self had gone. He was a point of light, the sum total of all his experiences focussed into a pure, white beam. And then, he was nothing.

Doctor Taylor sighed. He had been sorry to see Bowman back, but not surprised. In truth, he had barely recognised him. His face looked more drawn than ever, his eyes gazing in a sightless stare. Taylor had felt obliged to grant him his liberty all those months ago, but had been certain he would relapse with time. It seemed the way of things. Beds in the asylum were scarce and, despite the protestations of the matron, patients had to be let go as soon as possible.

Taylor read back through his notes. George Bowman had been presented for admission some seventeen months previously, exhibiting an extreme melancholia following the death of his wife. He had, after several bouts of a violent mania, eventually become a compliant patient. Only minor interventions had been required. Taylor ran his finger down the list of treatments. Chloral had been given in increasing doses to induce sleep. Cold water baths had been administered to cool the patient's anguish. Monitored confinement had kept him safe from himself and a course of leeches had eased the pressure on the patient's brain. Furthermore, a strict regime of regular mealtaking and exercise had brought him to a recovery of sorts. It had clearly been insufficient.

In his dormitory, Bowman was lifted from a chair to his bed. From all around him came the sounds of disquiet. The man in the bed next to him sobbed fearfully. A younger patient with a harelip rocked back and forth in his cot, a stream of abuse issuing from his lips. Somewhere, someone was laughing.

The orderly placed a pillow behind Bowman's head and bent for the straps. Lifting his eyes, he saw Bowman gazing back with pleading eyes. He was shaking his head. Casting a look to the door, the orderly saw Doctor Taylor standing, watching.

3

With a slight incline of his head, the doctor gestured that Bowman should be granted a night's rest without restraint. The orderly nodded his head in return, placing Bowman's hand back on his bed beside him.

Bowman settled back in his bed, nodding in thanks to the doctor at the door. Satisfied with the progress his patient had made, Doctor Taylor left the ward for the evening.

He had dutifully taken his Chloral at the allotted time, only to hide the chalky tablet beneath his tongue until the matron had gone. If she had recognised Bowman from his previous stay, she did not say. With the gas jets that ringed the room extinguished for the night, he spat the sedative pill to the floor. He tried to steady his breathing.

Bowman had forgotten how dark it could be on the wards. Far from the lights of the city, the only illumination came by way of the moon. The ward was home to perhaps two dozen patients in various stages of recovery. The men in these beds were judged to be the least likely to do harm to themselves or others. The drugs they had been administered with their evening malt had had the desired effect and now, with varying degrees of quietude, they had succumbed to sleep. Some gibbered constantly in their slumber. Barely formed words escaped from their babbling lips with a rising sense of urgency. One man by the door would periodically let out a ghastly cackle, as if he alone was privy to some private information that had implications for them all. Everyone else, it seemed, snored. The air was ripe with the attendant smells of many men pressed together under the same roof. Even with the windows raised behind their bars, the night air was too still to shift it.

Bowman felt remote from his actions. Reaching to the wall at the head of his bed, he calmly removed the wooden crucifix that hung there. Feeling in the dark, he located the nail in the wall and pulled. It came easily and quietly, pulling a little plaster after it. Wrapping it in his fist, he fell back to the bed and widened his eyes to see into the gloom. Rolling onto his side so as to obscure his hands from the night attendant at the door, he felt as if he were observing a scene in a play. He was entirely divorced from his physical self. He felt nothing at all as he pulled the rusty nail across the skin on his wrist. He had attended enough suicides to know it would be effective. The life would drip from him over an hour or so. Silently, the blood seeped into the mattress beneath him. Bowman realised he had not breathed for an age. As he expelled the air from his lungs, he felt his head begin to swim. Sweat pricked at his brow as he forced himself to attend to the matter at hand. Soon, he would join her.

As if from afar, he saw himself slicing into his other wrist. The resultant slick of blood shone a sickly black as the moon appeared from behind the clouds. He felt every muscle in his body relax. Craning his neck, he gazed out the window above his bed. He fancied he could see her eyes in the stars. His life oozed onto the sheets. Soon, he would be free of pain. He smiled.

Just as he felt certain he could smell her perfume, he felt a hand grab at him. Suddenly aware of the pain in his wrists, he was pulled to the present. He could feel his back sticking to the sheets beneath him. Gulping for air, he squinted into the darkness at the apparition before him.

A naked man stood at his bedside, grinning inanely. His white flesh hung loose from his bones, Bowman noticed in his delirium, particularly around his ribs. Wiry hair sprang from his body in tufts. Bowman recognised him as the patient from the bed opposite. A manic light seemed to glint in the man's eyes as he lifted Bowman's arm from the bed. With a cackle, he peered at the nail in Bowman's hand, seemingly enthralled by the spectacle. He flexed Bowman's fingers, watching in silent amazement as they opened and closed around the rusty metal. A string of saliva fell from his bottom lip. Dropping his gaze to Bowman's wrist, he noticed the blood. He took a breath as the smile faded from his lips. Bowman reached out to try and quieten the man, but the gesture only frightened him all the more. His eyes wide in panic, the poor unfortunate stumbled back from the bed and let out a scream.

Suddenly, chaos reigned. Seemingly as one, men sat up in their beds to join in the chorus, splitting Bowman's ears with their screams. Several patients took cover beneath their beds, their hands pressed firmly to their ears, rocking to and fro to find some comfort from the din. Others yet stood upon their mattresses and screamed all the louder as if it were some strange competition. The night attendant sprang to his feet. Uncertain at first what to do in the face of such a tumult, he elected to light the gas jets on the wall. As they sputtered to life, he was greeted with such scenes of disorder that, for a moment, he considered retreating from the ward entirely. Instead, he found the presence of mind to pluck the whistle from his desk and give a hearty blow. The shriek was almost lost in the din. Several patients had left their beds by now and were making their way to the naked man at Bowman's bedside, their hands outstretched towards him. The screams had pitched into hysterical laughter. Bowman sank back into his bed, his vision fading as he bled over the sheets. He felt he had stumbled upon a scene from Hell itself. A sudden panic rose within him.

Three other orderlies had arrived at the door, Doctor Taylor at their head. He stood for a moment in the melee, taking a moment to decide what best to do.

"Doctor Taylor!" the night attendant called. "This man is injured!"

Bowman suddenly realised the attendant meant him. The orderlies pushed through the throng to his bedside, Doctor Taylor doing what he could to calm the patients on the way.

"Matron!" he shouted over his shoulder, a note of panic in his voice. "We must sedate them! We will need Chloral and Laudanum!"

The matron stood at the door, a look of alarm on her fleshy face. Clearly having been roused from her own slumber, she had presented herself in her nightclothes, a coat thrown hastily over her shoulders.

"Now, matron!"

Spurred into action by the doctor's entreaties, she turned on her heels and fumbled with the keys to the medicine cupboard.

The night attendant was leading some of the calmer patients back to their beds. Even the naked man at Bowman's bedside seemed suddenly happy to oblige. Taking their cue from him, the other patients ceased their shrieking and an eerie calm descended upon the ward. It was as if nothing had happened. Doctor Taylor puffed out his cheeks. Such was the condition of many of the men in the ward, he knew this incident would barely be remembered come the morning. He gazed down at the man in the bed beneath the window.

The patient before him had succumbed to a fitful delirium, scratching at his wrists and letting forth great, heaving sobs. Then Taylor noticed the blood. Springing forward, he grabbed at the sheets and pressed them against the man's wounds.

"Bowman," he breathed, sadly. He leaned his weight against the patient's wrists as he turned to the orderlies. "We must get this man to the infirmary."

I: Hot Off The Press

Temperance Snell knew Ludgate and Ludgate knew Temperance Snell. His attire alone marked him out from the crowd. Only this very morning, he had pulled on a pair of garish mustard-coloured trousers that were so short they swung around his ankles. 'Half-masts', his fellow drinkers called them. His patterned spats were buckled loosely about a pair of fine leather brogues he had won in a bet. As he lifted his pint to his lips, he hooked a thumb into the pocket of his brocade waistcoat. It was trimmed with fur about the collar and fastened with shining silver buttons. A heavy, purple frock coat hung from his shoulders like a cape, and an ostentatious top hat was jammed on his head. He was never seen without it, nor without the ostrich feather that bobbed from the band about the brim. Finally, a tatty scarf was thrown about his neck. Catching his reflection in a mirror by the bar, Snell took a certain pride in the fact that no one colour was a match to another. He was a symphony of corduroys, velvets, cottons and silks. A sight to make all eyes sore.

Still only thirty-two, and having only spent time in a debtor's prison just the once, Snell had done well for himself. He loved to tell the story of how he had been discovered as a new-born on the steps to a nunnery in Southwark. It was partially true, at least, and far more romantic a tale than the truth of the matter. In fact, he owed his life to the dalliance of a nun with a gardener, come to tend the nunnery orchard. He was sent to the workhouse aged five and never knew the comfort of a mother from that day. No matter, he thought to himself as he downed the dregs of his ale, London had been mother enough for him. The city had taught him, fed and clothed him and even afforded him a little status. As a boy, he had learned the best places to escape a whipping from the workhouse masters. The wilds of Hackney Marshes had been his favourite haunt. There he had spent hours building dens, whittling sticks and learning to catch the geese that grazed there in the mornings.

He grew into a lanky lad, but he already had a magpie's eye

for the finer things. He had put his nimble fingers to work in the markets of Covent Garden and had soon amassed enough to start his own business lending money to the market traders when they were short. But he had overstretched himself. Just as he had begun to count himself a respectable man, he found himself on the bad end of a wager. Together with the failing of three or four of the traders who owed him money, it was enough to leave him penniless and in gaol.

Strangely, he had rather taken to imprisonment. He had found the other inmates to have generally fallen on hard times rather than being of the criminal class. There was even a gentleman among them, a Knight of the Realm, no less. Or so he had claimed. Sir Ranulph Fernsby delighted in telling tales of his downfall. He had, he would declare to anyone who would listen, invested in copper where he should have invested in steel, in amethyst where he should have invested in diamond, and in tea where he should have invested in sugar.

It was under Sir Ranulph's tutelage that Temperance Snell had learned to read and write. There was no greater gift, Snell came to realise, that any man could give another. The knight required nothing in recompense for such a service, beyond the company that Snell was happy to give.

The gift of learning served him well upon his release. Snell noticed how much of the world was suddenly open to him. He devoured books on history and commerce and, bit by bit, began to improve himself. Having secured employment at a local print works, Snell made his way up from a junior under clerk to manager of the print floor within three years. His wage meant he could afford a smart set of rooms near Ludgate Circus, a short walk from his place of work and, crucially, The Blackfriar.

Snell cast his eyes around the snug bar. The Blackfriar occupied a wedge of land on Little Water Lane, just north of St. Paul's Station. As a result, it was the most peculiar shape; narrowing at one end so that barely two men could stand shoulder to shoulder. Legend had it that the court of King Henry VIII had drunk there. Snell mused that it must have been a very small court indeed. Or, at least, most peculiar in shape. Downing the last of his ale, and noting that it tasted for all the world as if it had been brewed in the time of the bloat King himself, Snell tipped his hat at the barmaid and made for the door.

He took a rolled cheroot from his pocket as he stepped onto the street, striking a match against the heel of his shoe to light the soggy paper between his lips. Turning his collar up against the fog, Temperance Snell passed under the London Chatham and Dover Line that rose above him. A late train, invisible in the mist, thundered over him, seemingly shrieking in pain as its wheels struggled for purchase on the curve of the line.

The streets beneath the railway were ill lit. Snell kept to the middle of the road as he walked. He had learned to stay well clear of the arches and alleys once the sun had dropped behind the brickwork. They were home to the vagrants and pickpockets that teemed across the city by day and weren't above making a little extra by night. He could hear their chattering and cackling as he passed. As he turned the corner into Union Street, he was surprised by a bedraggled figure propped up against a filthy wall, his eyes rolling back in his opium-addled head. Snell cursed beneath his breath, partly in disgust and partly in pity. He was careful not to judge the vagrant too harshly. He knew that, had his own life but taken another road, he might well have found himself in such a condition.

Finally, Snell turned on to Waithman Street. Squinting through the fog, he could just make out the printing works ahead of him. Just as he expected, a single light burned from a middle window. Had the rain not been slapping against the cobbles beneath his feet, he might very well have heard the hiss and rumble of the printing press. Snell was pleased that business was booming. The public's appetite for adventures and stories featuring unsavoury characters and more unsavoury crimes had kept the printing works busy. An unexpected order for a new run of penny dreadfuls had seen Snell run the presses through the night. Printed on cheap pulp, they would be on their way to newsstands, shops and libraries as the sun rose, the ink barely dry on the page. Though happy with the income they provided, Snell disapproved of their contents. He had a feeling that the whole of London could be improved if only the populace tempered their appetite for the gory and, instead, fixed their minds on higher things.

By the time he reached the entrance to the printing works, the rain had turned the debris on the road into a filthy sludge. It had already made a mess of his spats. Reaching for the bunch of keys at his belt, Snell leaned his shoulder to the door and stepped gratefully inside. Swinging his hat from his head, he tapped the moisture from its brim and replaced it back upon a thatch of thick, blond hair.

"Gaunt!" he called as he stepped gingerly up the concrete stairs. "How goes it?" He was not surprised he could not be heard above the din. In two or three hours, the sound would be louder still. By then, the print floor would be full. Typesetters, printers and their apprentices would be hard at work to produce the morning's papers. The very walls would shake to the pounding of the presses.

As Snell ascended the steps, something in the rhythm of the noise made him break his stride. The regular hiss and whump with which he was so familiar seemed somehow discordant. Quickening his pace, he turned off the stairs onto the print floor.

The presses occupied a whole storey of the building. In the guttering light from the gas jets placed at intervals around the walls, Snell could see the variety of machines he had accrued over the last few years. Hand presses and pedal presses stood cheek by jowl with their modern counterparts, the great, hulking cylinder machines that were used for bulk printing. Snell had gone out of his way to purchase the older machines at a discount, recondition them and put them to work, thus freeing up the more modern presses to fulfil the larger contracts. It was a tactic that had led to a three-fold increase in profits. He even had a mind to purchase a colour press. That, he thought, was where the future lay. For now, all but one of the presses stood idle. Resting, it seemed, after their days' exertion.

As he cast his gaze along the print floor, the arrhythmic pounding of Gaunt's press bothered him. Perhaps a belt was loose or a flywheel too tight. Snell shook his head. It was unlike Augustus Gaunt to be remiss in his maintenance. He knew little of him beyond the fact that he was a nervous man but a hard enough worker. Snell had been happy to entrust him with the night's employment.

"Gaunt!" he called again. "How goes the order?"

The cylinder press that growled in the corner was driven by steam from the same furnace used to heat the building. Even in the chill of the October night, Snell could feel the warmth of the air around him. His nostrils thrilled at the familiar scent of ink and oil.

"Gaunt?"

It was odd that the man had not responded. Indeed, as Snell drew nearer to the machine, he could see no sign of Gaunt at all. Still, the irregular rhythm bothered him. The roll of the cylinder and the hiss of the pistons should have been in concordance, the one with the other. Snell often fancied himself as a conductor at a concert as he stood on the steps to his office by day. Each machine would play its part in the symphony of ratchet and steam, adding its individual rhythm to the beat of the whole. It was often all Snell could do to desist from raising his cheroot and waving it as if it were a baton.

Gaunt's machine, he could tell, was out of time. There was an extra bump as the cylinder turned, a wrenching of gears as they made their displeasure felt at some obstruction. Snell dropped his eyes to the machine. Where he should have seen the smooth procession of paper beneath the cylinder, he saw the body of a man laying face up across the paper tray. He knew at once it must be Augustus Gaunt. His upper torso lay sprawled across the platform, his twisted legs dangling ungainly across the floor. The cylinder jumped in its moorings as it spun. Holding his hand involuntarily to his mouth, Temperance Snell could see the obstruction clearly. It was Gaunt's head.

As the cylinder beat repeatedly against Gaunt's skull, Snell could see his skin had begun to peel away. His hair was congealed with a sticky mixture of blood and ink that seeped from the printing table to the floor below. Snell felt his stomach lurch. Breathing quickly, he leapt for the machine's controls. He spun the taps to cease the flow of steam and slowly the drum came to a stop. He felt his feet sticking to the floor as he approached Gaunt's body, blanching as he realised he was walking in the poor man's blood.

Snell was at a loss. "What to do?" he breathed. Peering closer in spite of the horror of the situation, he could see the unfortunate man's face was entirely disfigured. "Augustus?" he whispered, tentatively reaching out a hand. Nothing. Gaunt was clearly dead.

Detective Inspector Ignatius Hicks didn't much like the look of the man in front of him. His gaze rose from the man's too short trousers to the ostrich feather in the brim of his hat. No matter what the man had to say for himself, it was clear the inspector had already made up his mind. He was not to be trusted.

"You say the machine was still operating?" Sergeant Anthony Graves was standing immediately to Hicks' left, a notebook in his hand.

Temperance Snell nodded, the feather in the brim of his hat bobbing in agreement. "Just as I left it at seven of the clock."

Graves had joined Inspector Hicks at the printing works following a late night at the Yard. Providence had ensured that he had been walking down the stairs to the reception hall when the desk sergeant called out.

"Ah, Sergeant Graves. You'll do."

Graves' heart had sunk. He had hoped to be on his way home. He was investigating a case of fraud under the instruction of the newly advanced Detective Superintendent Callaghan. It was beginning to take its toll. The muscles in Graves' back felt tight and his eyelids heavy. He yearned for nothing more than to climb aboard the hansom cab that awaited his appearance outside Scotland Yard and the promise of a hot bath at his rooms in Stanmore. At first, Graves had considered simply walking on, as if he had not heard Sergeant Matthews' entreaties. Casting a glance around him, however, he saw the cavernous reception room was otherwise empty. It had clearly been a quiet night for Matthews. Sergeant Graves envied him for it. With a sigh, the sergeant turned his heels to the wooden desk in the centre of the room. Graves had looked the desk sergeant up and down as he approached. As ever, he had presented himself as the very model of efficiency. Graves could tell that even Matthews' hair had been smoothed down with just the requisite amount of pomade; no more, no less. Behind the desk, Graves was amused to see loose pens and pencils tied up neatly with string. Folders of paper were labelled and marked for reference. A place for everything, and everything in its place.

"There has been a suspicious death near Ludgate Circus," the desk sergeant began. "A man crushed by a printing press."

That detail alone had been enough to excite Graves' curiosity. He could never help himself but take delight in the more gruesome aspects of his employment. It was something he had struggled to explain to his colleagues, most of all to his erstwhile superior, Detective Inspector Bowman.

"Why should a man not take an interest in his work?" Graves had responded once. "It is to be applauded in almost every other walk of life, why not this?" He remembered Bowman's moustache twitching with uncertainty upon his upper lip. "Besides, it is a reminder that I am alive," the young sergeant had continued, "and that I am lucky to be so."

Graves remembered Bowman had nodded thoughtfully and sighed to himself. An odd response, he had thought.

"Is there no man else that can attend?" Graves asked Matthews as he rubbed at his face with a hand.

Matthews waved a pen before him. "There is no man else but you." He was struggling to hide a smirk.

Graves sighed again. "Am I to have no one to accompany me?" Rather than fearing for his safety at such a late hour, Graves was merely concerned that he would miss some detail or other due to the fog that addled his tired brain.

"There is already an officer in attendance," Matthews had said, knowingly. He had made a pretence of reading the name from the ledger on his desk. "Detective Inspector Ignatius Hicks."

It was enough to rouse Graves from his torpor. Almost at once, his blue eyes regained their lustre. "Hicks?" he roared. It was just the response Matthews had hoped for. "Tell me the address at once."

And so, Detective Sergeant Anthony Graves found himself on

the print floor of Gibson and Son, Printers.

"And where were you between seven of the clock and when you discovered the body?"

"All the workers here frequent The Blackfriar," Snell replied. "And I am no exception."

As he made a note of Snell's whereabouts with the stub of a pencil, Graves took a step back from the press. Two police constables had been tasked with removing the unfortunate man's body for inspection by Doctor John Crane at Charing Cross Hospital.

"There'll be no sense in asking anyone at The Blackfriar," Hicks wheezed through the fug of his pipe tobacco. "The ale there is enough to make a man insensible within minutes." He regarded Snell through hooded eyes.

As the two constables lifted Gaunt's body onto a stretcher, Graves took the opportunity to peer closer. The man's head was a mess of ink, blood and bone. What features he had left had been smeared across the face.

"Are you sure," Graves began, carefully, "that this is, indeed, Augustus Gaunt?"

Snell nodded again. "I am certain of it. The build of the man." Snell gestured weakly with a hand. "The clothes."

Graves nodded to the constables to move on with their load. As he followed them to the door with his eyes, he glanced around the room. The street side was adorned with large, arched windows that would, no doubt, afford ample opportunity for natural light when the sun rose. Ventilation, too. Graves took a breath.

"What time is it now?"

"'Tis just gone five," Hicks hissed impatiently. He was clearly in a hurry to be done.

"I was of the impression that printers' works started early, on account of the morning papers." Graves turned to Snell, his blond curls dancing about his head.

"That is so," Snell confirmed. "They start their shift at four. By rights, the men should have been here an hour ago."

"Then where are the workers?" the sergeant asked, suddenly aware of his companion shifting uncomfortably beside him.

15

"Inspector Hicks suggested they be sent home upon their arrival."

Graves' eyebrows rose as he turned to the portly inspector beside him. Hicks' great beard seemed to bristle with indignation.

"I saw no sense in having everyone here," he flustered, clamping the bit of his pipe between his teeth. "They would surely have hampered our investigations."

Graves ran his fingers through the curls on his head. "Inspector Hicks," he began, trying to keep calm, "just how do you think questioning those of the workforce who knew Augustus Gaunt would have hampered our investigations?" He jabbed at his notebook with the lead of his pencil. "Any one of them might well have furnished us with just the detail we need."

Hicks planted his hands on his hips, defiant. "Except," he roared, "that it is already clear to me just how that unfortunate man met his end." The bluff inspector clearly enjoyed the silence with which his assertion was met. He crossed his arms across his broad chest, ready for the entreaty to continue. Eventually, and against his better judgement, Graves acquiesced. "Very well," the sergeant sighed. 'You have our attention."

Hicks looked for all the world like he was winding himself up. He puffed out his chest and seemed to grow and inch in height as he prepared to deliver his monologue. "It is true," he began, theatrically, "that I am no expert when it comes to the printing press - "

Graves couldn't help but snort. He was well used to Hicks' theories. They were often based on nothing more than gut feeling and supposition. They were rarely on the mark. The best policy, Graves had learned, was to let the inspector burn himself out before getting back to the facts in hand and continuing the investigation proper.

"But," Hicks was continuing as he paced around the machine before him, "let us suppose Gaunt's death was an accident." He peered closer to the press, scrutinising the cylinder and the various plates and wheels. He nodded in satisfaction as if he understood their innermost intricacies. "There appear to be no guards around the more dangerous parts."

"There is no need for them," Snell interjected in earnest. "Gaunt and every man that works here knows their own particular press. They are well trained."

"No doubt." Hicks returned to his place beside Graves. "But let us say Gaunt was careless."

"In point of fact," Snell began again, "he was he most conscientious of all my - "

"Let us *say* he was careless," Hicks boomed. "Who would bear the blame?"

Snell blinked. Sergeant Graves narrowed his eyes. Just what was Hicks insinuating?

"Mr Snell," Inspector Hicks continued, "we have now in this country a slew of laws designed to protect the working man." Graves noticed a sneer in Hicks' voice as if, in fact, he considered those very laws to be wholly unnecessary. "As the manager of this printing works, I believe your proprietor would hold you responsible for the safety of your workhouse." Hicks leaned in so close, that Snell could feel the inspector's breath on his face. He fought the urge to cough.

"Mr Gibson has the utmost faith in me."

"Of course he does," Hicks soothed. "But I should imagine even he would prefer his manager went to the wall due the accidental death of an employee, than risk his own neck."

Temperance Snell gulped. "There is something more." He suddenly cut a pitiful figure in his too-short trousers. "Something I have not yet divulged." Hicks' eyes sparkled at the prospect. "Ah. Here we go," he smirked.

"As I stood over Gaunt's body," Snell began, "I had the feeling I was not alone." "Aside from the unfortunate man who lay dead before you?" Hicks asked, crassly.

Snell nodded. "As I looked round, I saw a figure by that farthest wall." He pointed the length of the print floor beyond the machines. "Only fleeting, but definitely a man." Hicks looked around. "Then where did he go?"

"I gave chase through that door and down the stairs beyond,

17

but   could   not   get   near   him."
Hicks harrumphed, unconvinced.

"Could you tell us at least what he was wearing?"

"That's the oddest thing of all, Sergeant Graves." Snell had lowered his voice, as if ashamed at the admission. "For all that I could see, he was wearing a cape and top hat." Snell gnawed at his lip in a gesture that gave Graves to understand he was, even now, holding something back in the description of the man.

Hicks could control himself no more. "This is preposterous!" he roared. "It sounds more like he was dressed for the opera than to kill a man!"

Snell shrugged. "P'raps he was."

Hicks shook his head in exasperation.

Graves flicked over a page in his notebook and continued to write. "You gave chase, you say?"

"Through here," Snell nodded, walking the length of the room to the door set in the farthest wall. He flung it open, leading the two detectives into the stairwell beyond. Steadying himself with a hand against the bannister, Hicks puffed with the exertion and reached for his pipe.

"Just as I reached the top here, I saw him run out the door at the bottom," Snell continued.

"But you still had not seen his face?"

"I had not." Snell evaded Graves' questioning look.

"What the blazes?" Hicks' sudden cry made Graves jump where he stood. Snell looked at the portly inspector with barely concealed contempt. Hicks was slowly lifting his feet from the floor in a strange dance. "The floor's sticky."

Striking a match on the bannister, the portly inspector reached over to a gas jet on the wall and, turning the spindle at its base, brought it to flickering life. The three men dropped to their haunches to survey the floor beneath Hicks' shoes.

"Blood," breathed Graves.

"Footprints," acknowledged Hicks, pointing back the way they had come.

"And two sets at that," said Graves, pointedly. Snell looked beyond the door and back into the print room. Two tracks of bloody footprints led from where Augustus Gaunt had lain prone on his press.

"See?" he said in triumph as he rose.

Hicks' shrugged. "They lead down the stairwell."

"It is just as I said," breathed Snell hurriedly as he led the way down. "I pursued the man down these steps and into the yard beyond."

The two detectives followed him down, Graves keeping his eye on the two sets of prints on each step. Even in his haste, he could tell the shoes were of markedly different sizes.

"Just as I reached this step," Snell continued, "I heard the door to the yard being thrown open, and I knew I had him."

"Then it was not locked?" Hicks raised his eyebrows.

"It is the one thing I regret," Snell admitted, sadly. "It fell to me to lock this door after the last delivery. I failed to do so."

His shoulders slumping, Snell pushed at the door at the bottom of the stairwell. Hicks almost stumbled into the yard in his haste to see. The small, open courtyard beyond was crowded on either side with the backs of the tall buildings that surrounded the print works.

"There's not another door gives out onto the yard," Hicks noted, pointedly.

"It is the sole preserve of Gibson's printers," Snell explained. "Paper is delivered here twice a day and the final publications picked up in the morning."

"Then where did your man go?" Graves was looking about him in the gloom. With the fog hanging in the air and the sun yet to rise, he found it difficult to see. Even the odd lamp in the occasional window gave off nothing more than a diffuse halo of light.

"Not through the gates, that's for sure." Snell led them to the entrance to the yard. The gates were firmly locked and bolted. "Nor over them, neither." He pointed up to where the top of the gate met the lintel over the entrance. Even in the dark, Graves could see there was no space where a man might escape.

"Then just where do you propose this mystery assailant went?" Hicks puffed furiously on his pipe, his hands planted firmly on either side of his wide hips.

Snell swallowed. "I can only assume he went up." Squinting into the drizzle, he lifted his eyes up to the rooftops.

"Are you suggesting he scaled the walls?" Hicks was clearly having the most enormous trouble believing anything the man said.

"Not at all, inspector. He would not have had the time." Snell had a look of defiance about him. "I am suggesting he jumped."

Graves' jaw hung slack as he peered up into the rain. The buildings around him were five storeys high. A man would have to possess superhuman powers to clear such a height. Peering back at the man before him, he was convinced that Snell was certain of the truth of his story. He was also convinced he was holding something back.

As the three men walked back to the printing floor, Hicks saw that the two constables had returned from their duties.

"Take this man away," he barked, gesturing towards Snell with the stem of his pipe.

"Upon what grounds?" Snell protested as the two men approached.

"On the grounds, sir, that you are a murderer, sir!"

Sergeant Graves had heard enough. "But what of Mr Snell's insistence that there was a witness?"

"We only have his word for that." Hicks swung his arms wide to indicate the vast, cavernous space around him. "There were none others here that could corroborate that fact."

"Of course not!" pleaded Snell, exasperated. "It was the middle of the night."

"And that," said Hicks, sounding a note of triumph, "is the most convenient fact of all."

Graves was striding to the stairwell where Snell had insisted he had given chase. "Then how do you account for the two sets of footprints? It is clear Mr Snell was following another, just as he insists."

Hicks paused for thought. "It is clear Mr Snell fancies himself a clever man," he sneered, rubbing his belly. "I should imagine it would take quite a feat of intellect to rise to so responsible a position in life." Hicks looked the man up and down. Snell gave himself away, he thought. It was there in his outrageous attire,

20

and the way he held himself. Hicks had seen such men before and despised them. He had all the markings of one who was attempting to reach beyond his natural station in life. The man before him blinked.

Hicks continued. "I should imagine it ran something like this." Graves sighed. Hicks was treating the whole affair as if it were no more than a game. Hicks watched Snell carefully as he spoke, keen to see if any of his assertions found their mark. "Aided by the fact that there was no other witness at so late an hour, he concocted the story of an interloper, even going so far as to make two sets of footprints with the poor man's blood."

Graves' eyes widened. "Two sets of prints?" He threw a look of apology to Snell.

"It would be a simple enough matter to find another pair of boots," Hicks concluded, triumphantly.

There was another silence as Sergeant Graves considered the implications. Snell was opening and closing his mouth in desperation.

"Then where is the second set of boots?" he spluttered. He was clearly at his wits' end.

Hicks took the pipe from his mouth and pointed the stem at the unfortunate man. "That, Mr Snell, is the very question that my constables shall turn their efforts to answering, just as soon as they have escorted you to the cells of the nearest police station."

II: The Visitation

For the first week after the incident, he had been placed in a room on his own. An attendant was set to watch him day and night. He was restrained again as he had been upon his arrival, and his only visitors were Doctor Taylor and the matron. The latter would do little more than shake her head and 'tut' at his condition. Bowman was sure she wished him ill and would feign the swallowing of the chalky tablets she dispensed.

Through it all, Anna was beside him. Sometimes he would lay his head upon her lap, sometimes stroke her hair. In the dark of the night, he would beg her forgiveness. She would quieten him with a look and rock him to sleep. He was conscious in these moments of calling her name aloud. Conscious, too, of every utterance being made a note of in the attendant's notes. These, in turn, were poured over by Doctor Taylor and the matron with much shaking of heads.

For the following weeks, time had no meaning. Bowman learned to measure out his days by the meals he had taken. A thin porridge was served in the morning, followed by a thick broth for dinner and stewed meat for supper. There was as little variation in the menu as there was to his routine.

Soon, he was judged safe to release from his bonds. As he sat upon his bed, rubbing at his ribs where the restraining jacket had chafed against his skin, he was surprised to see two orderlies carrying some furniture through the door.

"Am I not to return to the ward?" Bowman enquired, quietly. After weeks of little communication, he was surprised by his own voice. It sounded thin and reedy. He swallowed.

"Orders from the superintendent," one of the orderlies announced. He was a rotund man with too thin a head for so round a body. "Ours is not to reason why."

Bowman blinked. He had a memory of his last stay at the asylum. Then, he had been under the impression that he had received preferential treatment at the request of some outside force. It seemed it was so again.

A rickety chair was tucked under a small table beneath the

window. A shallow, china basin and jug were positioned next to a rough towel. Bowman scratched at his chin. He doubted he would yet be allowed a razor and strop.

So much of Colney Hatch was familiar to him. He even recognised several of the inmates. On his way to the refectory of a morning, he would acknowledge the salute of an old man with a head of unruly, white hair.

"Mornin' yer Majesty," the man would bark. "Fine day, ain't it?"

Bowman had learned to humour him with a smart nod of his head. In truth, the man frightened him. Was Bowman destined for such a condition? On the days when he was beguiled by illusions, it certainly felt so.

He ate his food carefully, being sure to see others on his table finish their bowls first. He would study them for any ill effects in the minutes immediately after. Finally satisfied he would come to no harm, he would lift his own spoon to his lips and eat.

Some days, he would gouge feverishly at his skin as if it would release his anguish. When he was seen scratching in the queue for the baths one morning, he was hauled to one side to have his nails pared and warned that any repetition of the action would see him forced to wear thick gloves. He felt foolish. Mostly he felt without worth, devoid of value. He felt less than himself.

July tipped into August and then September. A blazing summer came and went. Soon, the ghastly events in Larton that had led him again to the gates of the asylum were as distant as the city that crouched low on the horizon. If Bowman remembered them at all, it was as if through a gauze, the images diffuse. Occasionally, they would resolve into something sharp and painful; the stinging cold of the water where it was intended he should drown, his muscles in spasm as he struggled to breathe. Soon, it was as if Colney Hatch was all he had ever known. His world entire was contained within its walls.

He found himself often in the asylum's library. Large and airy, it had been converted from a drawing room with the addition of many shelves groaning with books. It was an eclectic collection that had been donated over time by various charitable institutions. Here, Bowman could lose himself for an hour or two amongst the works of Milton or in The Cartographical Study Of The Ancient Rivers Of London. There was barely ever another reader save a young man who had started to appear more often. He would sit at a table by the fireplace with a newspaper spread out before him. At first, Bowman mistook him for a member of staff such was his trim appearance, but he soon learned from the man himself that he had been a patient here for several months.

"You're the detective," the man announced one afternoon. Bowman had positioned himself in the autumn sun that streamed in through the windows, painting everything it touched with a russet gold. By way of reply, he sought to bury his head even further within the pages of The Brothers Karamazov. He had read the same paragraph perhaps five times now, the words somehow failing to make any impression upon him.

"I'm glad you have found the library," the man continued, seemingly unconcerned by Bowman's lack of response. "It is perhaps the only place in the whole asylum where there is no noise."

Bowman cocked his head. The man was right. Positioned out on one of the wings of the building, the library was far from the wards. Even the grounds beyond the window were out of bounds to patients.

"My name is O'Reilly," the man persisted with a half-smile.

"Bowman."

"I know," O'Reilly nodded. "I followed your case in the newspapers last year." He held up his own paper before him, as if by way of confirmation. "The details were rather salacious."

Bowman winced. His memories of Jack Watkins' headlines in The Evening Standard were all too vivid. He had devoted many column inches to Anna's accident and Bowman's first stay in Colney Hatch. Indeed, upon his release, Watkins had shadowed his investigation into the affair of the frozen head in the River Thames. He had been none too sympathetic.

"I am to leave at the end of the week," continued O'Reilly.

Bowman looked closely at the man. He was close shaven and smooth-skinned. His eyes shone with a quality Bowman had not seen for many weeks. Hope.

"There is a lodger in my rooms at home, and I must wait for him to leave." Bowman noticed O'Reilly rocking gently as he spoke. "I wonder if they would take my place here as quickly."

Bowman allowed himself a wry smile. "Are you recovered?' he asked, tentatively.

There was a pause. O'Reilly lay his newspaper on the table before him. "You are asking for yourself, are you not?"

Bowman swallowed.

"Perhaps you have a hope that if I am recovered, you too may find your way to such an outcome?"

Bowman smoothed his moustache to cover his agitation. He knew the man was right.

"I am recovered," said O'Reilly, simply. "And I hope that gives you comfort. I have been here for some eleven months, but only really myself since the spring." O'Reilly gestured at his regulation jacket and shirt. "I am most anxious to wear my own clothes again."

"Do you have employment waiting?"

O'Reilly bit his lip. "I should imagine not. I am a tutor, you see. I cannot see any sensible parent allowing me near their charges now." He shook his head, resigned. "No. I shall use the allowance I am awarded upon my release. Once that is gone, I must throw myself upon the Fates."

Bowman felt for the man. Despite O'Reilly's outwardly cheery demeanour, the inspector thought he detected a hopelessness about him. It was there in the biting of his lip, and the way in which his eyes could not rest for long upon the same object. If O'Reilly had sought to offer him hope, he had in fact offered Bowman nothing more than the picture of a man in a desperate state. Feeling suddenly uncomfortable, Bowman excused himself from further conversation and turned his attention back to The Brothers Karamazov.

"Bowman!"

He was startled to hear his name called across the airing courts to the allotment where he worked. Stripped to his shirtsleeves in the sudden warmth of an October afternoon, he had been tending a bed of marrows. They crowded for comfort around tall clusters of Brussels sprouts. The earth was rich and dark but stony, and Bowman had made it his occupation to clear the larger stones from the loam. Much of the other produce had been harvested in the preceding days for fear of the first frost. He looked up from his toil, his moustache twitching in irritation at the interruption.

"George," Doctor Taylor called as he neared. Bowman blinked at the use of his Christian name. "Put down your spade, George," the doctor continued. "You've done a good day's work there." He nodded approvingly at the soil beneath Bowman's feet. "Matron will be pleased."

Bowman could almost see him making a mental note. "I do not dig to please the matron," he mumbled. He felt like a child.

"Quite so," the doctor nodded. "Quite so." He gestured at the spade again. Resigned, Bowman lifted the blade to plunge it again into the earth then leaned on the handle, expectantly. He could only assume the doctor meant to discuss some change to his medication.

"You have a visitor," Doctor Taylor beamed.

The very notion seemed an impossibility. Bowman shook his head, certain he had misheard. "A visitor?" he stuttered, running his hand across his head. He was suddenly fearful. Looking nervously about him, he could see that others on the allotment had ceased their work to listen. "I did not think we should have visitors," he whispered.

"I believe it will do you good," the doctor assured him. "Though I would be grateful if you would keep the matter from the matron." He shot a look to Bowman, who smirked in response. "You are to meet them in the superintendent's reception room."

Bowman's eyebrows rose almost comically on his forehead. Just who would warrant such ceremony? Retrieving his jacket from the stump of a tree, he followed the doctor wordlessly back to the main building. Stamping the mud from his boots at the door, he turned towards the superintendent's rooms.

In contrast to the peeling paint of the corridors and halls where Bowman spent his days, this part of the asylum was smart and fresh. The only part of Colney Hatch accessible to the public, and then only rarely, time and thought had clearly been spent in deciding how best the building should present itself to the world. No bars were fixed to these windows, mused Bowman. There was even paper on the walls.

Doctor Taylor had left him to walk on alone now, and Bowman was surprised to see the superintendent himself standing by the open door to his reception rooms. Athelney Wilkes had affected an even more officious air than usual. He stood ramrod straight, his eyes peering from the deep orbits of his skull as Bowman approached.

He felt more nervous with every step. Try as he might, he just could not guess who his visitor might be. He had no family to speak of. He hoped to God it was not Graves. Catching his reflection in a window as he passed, he knew he could not bear to be seen in such a condition by his sergeant. His hair was sprouting in tufts upon his head. His skin was pale and blotched. Swallowing hard, he acknowledged the superintendent's beckoning hand and turned into the room.

His breath caught in his throat at the sight of her. There, sitting primly at a chair by the fireplace with her hands upon her lap, sat a woman Bowman had thought never to see again. At the sound of his approach, she turned her delicate features from the fire. The inquisitive eyes and subtle cleft in her chin were unmistakable.

"Hello, Inspector Bowman," began Miss Elizabeth Morley with a smile. "Sergeant Graves said I should find you here."

III: A New Broom

Inspector Hicks was very appreciative of the view from his new office. He had sat upon his windowsill so many times now that the wood had taken on a greasy sheen. As he drew on his pipe, his attention wandered absently along the Victoria Embankment beneath him. A keen October wind had whipped along the river, sweeping away the fog before it. It threatened to dislodge many a fine hat and caused many a coat to billow about the wearer's legs. Those that were brave enough to venture out found themselves leaning into it to make any headway at all. Even the pigeons seemed almost to give up on their efforts, allowing themselves to be blown haphazardly this way and that. Powerful gusts stripped the trees of their autumn leaves that gathered in drifts against the river wall. Hicks saw a vagrant had made a bed of them, sinking into their soft embrace as if they were a fine feather mattress. The inspector was glad he had thought to light his fire.

Turning into his office, he looked at the cluttered collection of ephemera and detritus that littered every surface. A collection of pipes was scattered upon the bureau. Papers were strewn across his desk. His heavy astrakhan coat was thrown carelessly across the chair. Even the page from the Chiswick Herald hung askew in its frame on the wall where Bowman's wretched map of London had once hung. It included an article of which Hicks was most proud, detailing the successful recovery of a priceless artefact from a thief in Chiswick. He had to admit the journalist's description of the case and his part in it was most flattering.

"Detective Inspector Ignatius Hicks," the article proclaimed, "is to be congratulated upon the perspicacity and professionalism he deployed in the face of a most heinous crime." Hicks allowed himself a smile as he read the words aloud. There were further paragraphs that treated upon the assistance lent to him by Sergeant Springer of Chiswick Police Station, but Hicks regarded them as mere hyperbole and not worthy of any special attention. He was happy enough with the headline - 'SCOTLAND YARD INTERVENES TO SOLVE

THE CHISWICK ROBBERY' - and the rather flattering picture of him holding the recovered Traubenpokal of Heidelberg. Lost in the contemplation of his own particular talents, Hicks barely noticed the knock on his office door. Suddenly roused, the inspector flung his coat to the floor and eased himself into the chair behind his desk. It creaked in complaint as he settled his bulky frame. Reaching quickly for a pen and a few sheets of paper, he gave as good an impression as possible that he was busy.

"Enter!" he called at last.

Sergeant Graves stood at the door, his eyes narrowed with suspicion. He had still not got used to there being a new occupant in Bowman's office. Where once he might have expected to be greeted by the sight of the gaunt inspector gazing thoughtfully across the Thames from the window, he was now confronted by a mountain of a man with a great beard who, even now, was adding to the already noxious atmosphere with the smoke from his pipe. Hicks held up a hand as if to tell Graves he had almost completed his work. It was a pantomime of course, Graves knew, one in which he was now an unwilling participant. Just as Hicks made a jab at his paper as if to put a full stop to his sentence, the portly inspector realised he had been holding his pen upside down. Without the slightest embarrassment, he simply laid it down upon the desk and turned his eyes upon the young sergeant in the doorway.

"Ah, Graves," he boomed. "What news from the Royal Armitage?" His eyes twinkled with mischief as he spoke.

Graves sighed. He had been hard at work all morning on the fraud case that Detective Superintendent Callaghan had presented to him. In truth, it was a struggle. Callaghan had made him all too aware of the lack of resources that would be at his disposal, but he had not reckoned on being left entirely to his own devices. The evidence concerning a case of fraud at the Royal Armitage Bank was contained within twelve boxes of closely written text. Once or twice, Graves had caught himself almost falling asleep at his desk.

"I am making progress," he lied, his usual spirits deserting him for the moment. "And you? What of the case at the printing works?"

"I am to question Mr Snell this very afternoon," Hicks responded, cheerfully, "in the company of Sergeant Mahoney at Cloak Lane Police Station." He sat back in his chair, counterfeiting a tiredness at the enormity of the work before him. "I will have it all wrapped up by this evening." He scratched at his head with a smile. He had no doubt there would soon be another article proclaiming his success to grace the wall above the bureau. "It is my hope to present the case as being closed by the end of the day and to tell the Detective Superintendent himself."

"Then you may tell him of your intention to do just that," Graves replied. He was only just able to refrain from rolling his eyes at the hubris on display. "Callaghan has called for us both."

Hicks was out of breath by the time they reached Callaghan's office. Resting against the doorframe, he gestured that Sergeant Graves wait a moment for him to catch his breath before knocking. The two men stood aside as a young constable passed them, then Inspector Hicks nodded that Graves should proceed.

Detective Superintendent Callaghan's office could not have been a greater contrast to Hicks'. In comparison, it seemed a haven of taste and orderliness. One entire wall was given over to the display of a collection of books. Kept behind latticed glass cabinet doors, Graves could make out titles alluding to the history of the Roman Empire and the economics of Ancient Greece. Copies of De Brett's peerage were arranged cheek by jowl with treatises on the criminal system of medieval Europe and dusty volumes dedicated to the precepts of English Law. A pair of exotic plants stood in shining copper pots at either side of the fireplace, their fronds spreading like the fingers of a hand to the ceiling. Dark, mahogany furniture stood at intervals about the room. Here, a small coffee table with a bevelled top inlaid with gold, there an overstuffed ottoman strewn with tasteful cushions. The walls were adorned with pastoral scenes and pictures of Callaghan himself. Two portraits in particular stood out, the first a picture of Callaghan as a young man in military attire sitting on a horse before a dusty background. The other, clearly a recent acquisition, showed him sat behind the very desk Graves could see him at now. It was quite unlike any office Graves had set foot in before. The young sergeant could see the door to another room stood slightly ajar by the window. Perhaps, he thought, the Detective Superintendent even had his own private bathroom.

The man in front of them sat in a sober, black morning suit, his elbows resting upon the desk, making steeples of his fingers. He had a full head of hair, pomaded so that not a strand was out of place. A fine pair of mutton chops graced his granite features. His cool, grey-blue eyes gave nothing away.

Detective Superintendent Patrick Callaghan was enjoying the fruits of his recent advancement. The affair with the Kaiser at London's docks and Callaghan's part in the villain's capture had led to him being looked upon favourably by the commissioner. He had been glad to leave the Special Irish Branch behind him, its image tarnished by the actions of Ichabod Sallow and others of his ilk. "Let them all hang," Callaghan had thought upon receiving news of his promotion. Now, from his lofty office in the very heart of Scotland Yard, the Special Irish Branch seemed a grubby little outfit, not worthy of a man of his calibre.

He regarded the two men before him with steely eyes. Graves resented him his new position, he knew, but was too sensible a fellow to give voice to his feelings. Perhaps the sergeant thought Inspector Bowman should have received the rewards now bestowed upon the Detective Superintendent. Though what good they would have done him, Callaghan couldn't guess.

The superintendent cleared his throat. "Gentlemen," he began portentously, "you may have noticed a change has come over Scotland Yard in recent weeks and, in particular, over your department."

Hicks nodded, seriously. Graves bit his lip.

"We must make progress against the tide of crime," Callaghan continued, his features inscrutable. "We must be more active, more decisive and be seen to be so."

Graves held his breath. He had indeed noticed a change at the Yard. Whilst the young sergeant always kept in mind that the police were servants to the public, he had been aware of a growing faction who believed themselves to be masters over them. There was a new culture that held the public in contempt. That culture, it seemed, had no greater representative than the man sat before him.

Callaghan smoothed his hair with a hand. "The commissioner wishes to publish figures." He almost sneered at the word. "They are to detail our successes every month and they shall be released for all to see."

Graves heard Hicks snort beside him. Casting a glance his way, he noticed the portly inspector rolling his eyes at the news.

"We are their servants, after all," Graves said, carefully, finally giving voice to his thoughts.

"Indeed we are," hissed Callaghan, none too convincingly. The detective superintendent rose from his desk to stare at a picture on the wall above the fireplace. It was a portrait of David and Goliath, painted in the Renaissance style. David was crouched low, his slingshot aimed at the mighty giant before him. It was clear to Graves which of the two characters Callaghan identified with most. "And to that end," the superintendent was continuing, "the commissioner considers we must throw them the occasional scrap from the table." He smirked at his analogy as he turned back into the room. "If we must publish figures, then so we will, but those figures must rise, month on month." He folded his arms across his chest.

"Very wise, sir," agreed Hicks. He caught Graves' eye and gave a none too subtle wink. Graves sighed.

"Now, I don't know quite what you have been used to - " Graves swallowed as Callaghan continued. His implication was clear. "But I will reward results." He leaned in closer. "Frankly," he breathed, "I do not care if corners are cut to achieve them."

Graves could not help but speak up. "Inspector Bowman was keen to follow the correct procedures in the pursuit of a case, sir."

Callaghan nodded, a wry smile playing over his lips. "Indeed he was, Sergeant Graves." Graves was sure he saw the superintendent share a look with Inspector Hicks. "And much good it did him."

The young sergeant struggled to control his temper. "I believe Inspector Bowman is still on the payroll, sir." His blue eyes blazed in defiance.

"That much is true, for now." There was another look to Hicks. "Just how much detecting do you think can be done behind the walls of a lunatic asylum?"

The room was suddenly thick with silence. Graves turned to Hicks, but the portly inspector dared not return his gaze.

Callaghan took the moment to sit at his desk again, leaning forward in his chair to reach for a particular sheet of paper from a wire tray. "Ignatius, what progress has been made at the printing works?"

Graves was certain he saw Hicks blush at the use of his first name.

"Great progress, sir," he boomed. "I have apprehended the manager, a Mr Temperance Snell, on suspicion of murder."

"Snell insists there was another man present at the scene," Graves interjected.

"That is a subterfuge." Hicks waved his great paw of a hand as if he were swatting at a fly.

"To what end?" Graves spluttered.

"To save his own skin!" Hicks scoffed.

"And the footprints?"

"Fake."

"Sir," the sergeant began in earnest as he turned back to the man at the desk, "I would like to investigate the printing works further, to learn more of the man Snell saw last night."

"*Claims* to have seen," Hicks corrected him, raising a finger of admonishment.

"I would like to question the other workers, too."

"A waste of time," Hicks concluded.

Graves looked at Callaghan in exasperation. The superintendent had clearly enjoyed their exchange. Callaghan waved the sheet of paper before him. "And what became of this mysterious assailant? Your report does not say."

"Because sir, rather tellingly, Mr Snell could not say." Hicks rolled his eyes again. "Beyond saying he jumped the surrounding buildings."

Callaghan nodded, his steely eyes narrowing in thought. "Sergeant Graves," he continued at last, "I would like you to leave this matter in the capable hands of Detective Inspector Hicks." Graves noticed he took particular pains to emphasise Hicks' rank. "He already has a suspect in the cells and is clearly in anticipation of a result following an interrogation."

Hicks nodded emphatically, his great beard jutting proudly from his chin.

Graves took a breath. "Respectfully, sir," he began, choosing his words with care, "I feel a broader approach to the case might be of benefit."

"But might take longer," added Hicks, pointedly. "Surely, the last to see the victim alive must be the prime suspect?"

Graves' blue eyes widened, aghast. "What leads you to that conclusion?"

Hicks puffed out his chest. "Experience, Sergeant Graves."

Graves sighed. He could remember no investigation, whether accompanied by Hicks or not, where that had proven to be the case.

Callaghan nodded in agreement. "A broader approach will take time, Sergeant Graves. Time we can ill afford." Graves felt the man was drawing toward something of a conclusion. "Besides, you have the Armitage case to attend to. I should have thought that was more than enough to keep a man busy."

Graves dropped his gaze to the floor in defeat. "It is, indeed," he said quietly.

Callaghan rose again. "Then do not let us keep you, sergeant. I am sure you have much to occupy you."

There was another silence in the room. It was suddenly clear to Graves that his bluff companion was not to be dismissed with him.

"Yes, sir."

As Graves turned to leave the room, he saw Callaghan lean over the desk towards an ornate cigar box. As the young sergeant closed the door to the office slowly behind him, he noticed the detective superintendent retrieve two cigars from the humidor and hand one to a grateful Inspector Hicks.

IV: An Uncomfortable Meeting

Bowman's instinct was to turn immediately from the room and leave Miss Morley in the chair by the fire. His heart raced under her beatific gaze. He felt his palms begin to sweat. The fingers on his right hand began to shake. He had been at Colney Hatch an eternity, he thought, or at least too long to remember the intricacies of social discourse. He did not know where or how to begin. He felt suddenly ashamed that she should visit him in a place like this. He swallowed hard, the memory of their last meeting in his office at Scotland Yard suddenly vivid. He had so much explaining to do.

His chair was placed almost exactly opposite her. As he took his seat, he was suddenly conscious of how he looked; aware he was at least a stone lighter than when they had last met. Aware, too, that he was shaven headed and dressed in the asylum's own regulation clothes. His unruly moustache twitched on his upper lip.

She was speaking, he noticed, though whether or not it was to him he could not tell. The air between them was thick as water and her words seemed not to travel. His limbs were heavy as lead. He could hear the rush of his blood in his ears. Looking around, he saw that Athelney Wilkes had shut the door behind him. Bowman was alone with the woman. So, she was talking to him. He lifted his eyes to the ceiling then dropped them to the floor, anything to avoid her gaze. Still she was talking. Her speech was indistinct, but Bowman could discern the gentle rise and fall of the cadence in her voice. They were soothing words, he could tell.

"Why are you here?" he heard himself say. He was startled by his abrupt tone and took the opportunity to look at her for the first time.

Elizabeth Morley seemed bright as a shaft of light as she shimmered on her chair. Her hair had a lustre that was only surpassed by the glow in her skin. Her eyes sparkled. Bowman was shocked by her sheer vitality. Was all the outside world so vivid and so full of life? She was looking at him kindly, which made her presence all the harder to bear.

"Why, I came to see you were well," she soothed.

"But," Bowman stammered, "to such a place."

Elizabeth gave a laugh, her hand rising to her neck in a gesture that Bowman found startlingly familiar. "Why not in such a place?" she smiled.

He was at a loss. He had not thought that anyone would wish to see him in so diminished a state. She leaned forward on her chair. For a moment, Bowman feared she was about to put her hand upon his knee.

"I came as a friend," she whispered. Bowman swallowed again.

"I wish that you had not," he said, plainly.

With a gentle nod of her head, Elizabeth rose and walked to the window. The view beyond was of the gravel drive that swept across the front of the building. She could see patients in the grounds. Some stood staring into the middle distance, she noticed. Others busied themselves tidying the fallen leaves with wheelbarrows, brooms and spades. Here and there, an orderly stood in supervision.

"There was a time," she began quietly, "that you came to me in a time of trial."

Bowman frowned. His memory of their initial meeting was quite different. As he recalled, she had presented herself to him at Scotland Yard. Lacking the energy to contradict her, he let her continue uninterrupted. "I needed a guiding hand upon the death of my father." She turned to him. "You were that hand, inspector." She held his gaze for the longest time. He had forgotten just how forward she could be. "I have often thought of the time we spent in each other's company." Bowman shifted in his chair. "I believe you were sent to me." Elizabeth took her seat again, her hands in her lap. Bowman noticed her skirts billow about her as she sat. "Perhaps I have been sent to you."

There was a silence in the room. Was she expecting a response? Bowman cleared his throat.

"You are followed by ghosts, Inspector Bowman," she said suddenly. Shocked at the assertion, Bowman looked around him, half expecting to see his wife standing at his side. Could

Elizabeth see her? In truth, Anna had not appeared to him for weeks. Was she with him still but beyond his seeing? The thought appalled him.

"I have learned much since our evening at The Empire Rooms." Elizabeth was sitting back now, a cloud of thought passing across her face. "I saw my father that night, it is true, but I learned that ghosts are often best left in their own realm."

Though it seemed a lifetime ago, Bowman recalled the evening only too well. The anticipation of the crowd, eager to commune with the souls of their dear departed, the strange sight of Madam Rose and her assistant Khy processing through the centre of the room to begin their performance and the wisps of smoke that were used to signify the presence of the spirits. Most of all, he remembered the disappointment he had felt at Elizabeth's total commitment to the proceedings. He was shocked at her gullibility, but there was something more. Bowman thought back to the light that had shone from her eyes in The Empire Rooms. He had envied her, he realised now. Envied her for her certainty, for her utter, unswerving belief. With a start, Bowman realised he had no such belief in anything, and had not done so since Anna had died.

"Perhaps it is time you left your ghosts behind you." Elizabeth levelled her gaze straight at him. Bowman held his breath. "How have they been looking after you?" she asked, breezily.

Bowman raised his hands instinctively to his shaven head and regretted it at once. "Tolerably," he lied. He saw her flinch as her eyes flicked to his wrists. He cursed himself for his carelessness. The wounds had healed but still the milky trace of a scar could be seen on each of his arms. He had not thought to cover them.

"And the food," she continued, as much to ease her own discomfort as his. "I should imagine they feed you well?"

Bowman nodded. "Miss Morley," he offered, quietly, "you have not caught me at my best."

"I had to come," she interjected, a note of sudden urgency in her voice. "When Sergeant Graves told me all that had happened, of your visions and of your - " she paused, searching for the right word, "*troubles* at Larton, I knew I must come."

Bowman's moustache twitched. Not for the first time, he wished Sergeant Graves had been a little more circumspect.

"In truth, inspector," Elizabeth continued, hesitantly, "I was somewhat confused."

Bowman held his breath, convinced Miss Morley was drawing closer to the real purpose of her visit. She had dropped her eyes to her hands as she spoke. Bowman noticed she was toying with a ring on her little finger, twisting it this way and that in her anguish.

"When we last met at Scotland Yard," she almost whispered, "you told me you had accepted a position in the West Country."

Bowman gulped. How he wished to be anywhere but in that room.

She lifted her eyes to meet his. He dared not look away. "Did you not take up the post?"

Bowman gnawed at his lip. He felt his neck burning beneath his collar. His shirt felt suddenly too tight. "Miss Morley," he began, "you must forgive me." And now the admission. The moment had come, he knew, when he must make an honest account of himself and his actions. In truth, he was grateful for it. He took a breath. "I was not in my right mind." The words were out in the world. Bowman felt his body relax as if unburdened from some invisible load.

Elizabeth reached forward to clasp at his arm. He could feel the warmth of her touch through his sleeve. Guiltily, he thrilled to it.

"Then you are surely in the right place," she said.

Bowman forced himself to show no emotion. She must imagine every room in the asylum to be like this, he thought. He looked around at the plush furnishings and the wallpaper, the pictures on the walls and the potted plant by the window. A simple chandelier hung from an ornate rose in the centre of the ceiling. The whole room spoke of a domestic calm. What could she know of the medications, the treatments, the therapies?

As Elizabeth sat back in her seat, Bowman gave voice to a thought that had been bothering him. "Miss Morley," he began, "why were you at Scotland Yard?"

She rose again, blushing at the question. Her hand went to the pearls at her throat. "A silly thing, I am sure," she laughed, "but I thought I might get help from the police."

"In what regard?" Bowman sat forward on his seat, suddenly eager for information.

Elizabeth Morley placed her hands on the back of her chair and gathered her thoughts. "You never did meet my brother, did you, Inspector Bowman?"

Bowman shook his head. "I do not believe you even mentioned him."

"Oh, that is quite possible," Elizabeth flicked a stray strand of hair from her eyes. "Roger is something of the black sheep of the family. For the last two years, he has been in India and so left me to attend to father's affairs upon his death."

Bowman remembered their conversation in Scotland Yard's properties room when Elizabeth had come to collect her father's effects.

"He came in his own time, but not before the funeral. And so he was too late to see his father buried." From the sudden steel in her voice, Bowman guessed it was a bone of contention between them. "He has, for the last three months, taken a position as the owner of a brewery in Holborn."

Bowman raised his eyebrows.

"He had hoped to brew a beer that would prove most popular amongst the more fashionable in London." A smirk showed Bowman exactly what she thought of the matter. She turned to face the inspector square on. "Just three days ago, Inspector Bowman, an employee died as the result of a most improbable accident."

Bowman's moustache twitched almost comically at the revelation.

"He had been left to work on his own and was found drowned in a mash tun, a vessel used to steep and heat the grain with water."

"And so you made your way to Scotland Yard?"

Elizabeth nodded. "Where else?" she asked, plainly. "Of course, my brother, ever eager to avoid confrontation of any kind, refused to consider it as a crime at all." She shook her head with a sigh. "Yet, there is a detail that I find most compelling,

39

and I wished to present it to the detectives at Scotland Yard."

"And did you so?"

Elizabeth threw her hands up in exasperation at her own actions. "I did not! At first, I met Sergeant Graves. He recognised me and, when I asked after you, he told me of your - " she gestured around the room, "*whereabouts*. I'm afraid I was more concerned with seeing you than in pursuing my own silly little hunch."

"What was the detail that troubled you so, Miss Morley?"

Elizabeth Morley thought how best to proceed. "On the night of the accident," she began, "I happened to be passing the brewery in a cab. I was on my way home from a meeting, you understand. At the Hampstead Spiritualist Church."

Bowman nodded.

"As we turned into Southampton Street, I saw a figure run from the building." Miss Morley had closed her eyes as she spoke, as if the gesture would summon the spirits of her tale to life. Her hands rose before her as she described the scene. "He was dressed in a cape and top hat, but had so agitated a demeanour that I knew he had been up to no good. Aside from the workers, there was no reason why anyone else should be at the brewery so late, and I did not recognise him as one of them."

"Did you recognise him at all?"

"I did not. He had wrapped a dark material where his face should be. A scarf perhaps." Her eyes snapped suddenly open. "All these facts together made me suspicious of the man, and so I bid my driver follow him."

Bowman couldn't help but be impressed. "Where did he go?"

"Do you know Holborn at all, inspector?"

Bowman confessed he knew it a little. He blinked away the memories of a woman lying, strangled, in the dirt.

"Even at so late an hour, Southampton Street is busy enough. Still, the driver had no trouble in keeping pace with him." Again, Elizabeth Morley closed her eyes. "We crossed over High Holborn into Little Queen Street, where a small road cuts off to the left. It is in fact a builder's yard. A dead end."

"So, you had him?"

Elizabeth's eyes snapped open. A look of amusement played

about her pretty features. "You would expect so, would you not, inspector? In point of fact, the man had completely disappeared."

"In what sense?"

Elizabeth let out a laugh at Bowman's eager questioning. "In every sense! There is only one way in to George Yard and one way out, and that was blocked by the hansom in which I rode. There is no way the man could have doubled back upon himself."

"Then perhaps there were doors into the other buildings around the yard?" Bowman was intrigued.

"There are none. The school that backs onto it has built a wall across to prevent entry. What tenants there are must now go via Twyford Buildings. There is no other explanation but that the man disappeared."

Bowman shook his head. "But that is not possible. There must be a rational explanation."

Elizabeth's eyebrows rose. "I would agree, inspector. Although we may debate what is and what is not rational."

Bowman narrowed his eyes, remembering the zeal with which Elizabeth Morley held her particular views. "Then what would be your explanation, Miss Morley?"

Elizabeth paused and leaned in close, her voice almost a whisper. "The supernatural, Inspector Bowman."

Bowman let her words hang in the air, unanswered. He didn't even allow himself a nod of understanding.

Elizabeth Morley straightened again. "It was only the next day when my brother told me of the poor man's death, that I reasoned the creature I saw must have been responsible."

"Creature?"

"Surely no mere man could have scaled those walls in the instant before we were upon him? One moment he was there, the next he was not."

Bowman was alarmed at her fervour. She seemed quite serious in her assertions. "You think he climbed the walls to escape?"

Elizabeth shook her head. "Oh, no, inspector," she said emphatically. "That would have taken far too long. I most assuredly would have seen him." Again, she lowered her voice. "I believe he jumped."

Bowman sat back in his chair, afraid that he had been taken for a fool. Did the poor lady really believe what she was saying?

"Miss Morley," he began, "despite my current predicament, you must not think me completely mad."

Elizabeth looked suddenly hurt. "Of course not, inspector. And you must not think the same of me."

Gathering her skirts around her, she rose at once, the interview clearly at an end. Bowman had the sense that she had said all she had needed to say. Why she had felt the need to say it to him, he could not be sure. Perhaps she had thought he would believe her.

Just as she reached for the door handle, Elizabeth Morley turned to face the man at the fireplace. "Your wife is with you, Inspector Bowman," she said, suddenly.

Bowman almost looked around again. Could she see her? It was preposterous, of course. But yet -

"The dead are always with us." Elizabeth was nodding slowly. "Just as my father is always with me. I feel him in the breeze, see him in the clouds."

Bowman sat stock still. "If it brings you comfort, Miss Morley," he said gently, "then I am happy for you." He meant it.

Her face lit up with a smile. "Grief is just love, Inspector Bowman. The love you want to give but cannot." He felt tears prick behind his eyes at her words. Elizabeth was nodding at the simplicity of the thought. She lifted a finger as if this were the most important lesson of all. Perhaps it was, thought Bowman. "Grief is just love with no place to go."

With a final tilt of her head, Elizabeth Morley said her goodbyes, opened the door with a soft click, and made her way into the corridor beyond.

V: Mob Rule

Detective Sergeant Anthony Graves could feel a headache coming on. He had stared at so many pieces of paper and attempted to decipher so many cryptic scrawls, that his vision was beginning to swim. Pushing himself away from the desk, he pinched the bridge of his nose and let out a sigh. Even on such a blustery day, he would not wish himself here. Graves was naturally a creature of action. To be stuck in the office for hours on end was anathema to him. He looked around the room for anything to distract him. It was possessed of a high ceiling, but still the space felt oppressive. Every inch of wall was given over to shelves of documents and files, each carefully tied and labelled in a clear, officious handwriting. It seemed that every piece of paper that had ever passed through the Yard had ended up here. It was a repository of minutiae that was groaning at the seams. The banded red brick and white granite home of the Metropolitan Police Force had barely been in service for two years and already it was not fit for purpose. Nowhere was its deficiency of space better exemplified than here, the records office, situated on the first floor immediately above the entrance hall. What little room there was between the shelves had been stuffed with papers. Boxes filled the spaces under desks and between chairs. Looking around, Graves could see two or three others stationed at desks about the room. The watery light from the large window overlooking the Thames fell upon furrowed brows and ink-stained fingers as his companions in tedium leafed their way through various documents with barely disguised boredom. Graves was certain that any one of them would rather be anywhere else.

Puffing out his cheeks and tapping his pencil on the desk, the young sergeant resigned himself to returning his attention to the bundle before him. It was a pile of evidence relating to a supposed fraud underway at the Royal Armitage Bank. It was Graves' job and Graves' alone to get to the bottom of it. There had been a push in recent years to get more officers on the street, so that they may be a visible reassurance to the public. Together with Callaghan's professed desire for results, it was a policy that left precious few men to do the office work. Graves sighed again. He hoped this wasn't a sign of things to come. He had joined the Force in search of a little excitement and had relished the life it had afforded him thus far. If the pile of papers before him was a glimpse into the future, he was not sure it was for him. To compound it all, Graves was sure he could hear a commotion in the reception hall below. Sergeant Matthews must be having a busy day, he mused with a wry smile.

Before him lay reams of evidence, reports and summaries of reports. Graves rubbed his eyes to clear them. It wouldn't have surprised him at all to find those summaries had also been summarised. Taking the top piece of paper from the pile, he traced the text with a finger. At least, he sighed again, this one was legible.

It was a promissory note, he saw, for redemption at the Royal Armitage Bank. Like all the other documents he had looked through and puzzled over that morning, it was also clearly forged. This particular note promised to the bearer a sizable sum from the account of a Golightly Holdings upon submission at the bank's Chancery Lane branch on the seventeenth day of October, Eighteen Hundred and Ninety Two. Graves scratched behind his ear. That was today's date. The note, according to the supporting paperwork, was found in a raid in Cheapside some weeks before. The name Royal Armitage had been enough for it to make its way to this particular file. Now, all Graves had to do was discover its connection to the other collected evidence. Mostly promissory notes similar to the one in his hand, they had been found all over London in the preceding months. There was even evidence of them having been traded at exorbitant prices on the black markets of the capital city. At least two people that Graves had heard of had been murdered for them. These innocent little bits of paper held within them the power of life and death. It was a sobering thought that made Graves shudder as he turned to the next file, the incorporation documents of Golightly Holdings itself. It comprised trust deeds, memorandum and articles of association. A note was attached to each with the single word FORGERY written in forbidding block capitals. Shaking his head at the noise emanating from the room beneath him, Graves was about to delve further into the pile of papers before him, when he heard a commotion at the door.

Grateful for the distraction, Graves turned to see Sergeant Matthews clutching at the door frame, trying to recover his breath.

"Sergeant Graves," he panted, "you are needed downstairs."

With the door ajar, Graves could hear the fracas more clearly. It sounded for all the world as if Scotland Yard were under siege. Occasional shouts echoed up the stairs and Graves could just make out the words 'scam' and 'fraud' booming from the floor beneath.

"Is there no one else who can provide assistance, Matthews? I am busy with the Armitage case." He indicated the papers strewn upon his desk.

"And that," said Matthews, recovering, "is precisely why I called upon you."

Graves had often seen the reception hall busy, of course, but never so busy as this. Looking over the heads of the mob as he ascended the stairs with the desk sergeant, he could see yet more people streaming through the entrance in search of justice. Almost to a person, they waved bits of paper above their heads. Graves saw two or three constables in their uniforms trying in vain to keep order.

"This is Detective Sergeant Anthony Graves," Matthews shouted above the din. "He is investigating the fraud at Royal Armitage Bank." If he had meant to calm the crowd, he failed. The noise became even louder, and Graves was suddenly besieged by angry faces. They shouted at him in their ire, demanding reparation for the wrongs they perceived had been done to them.

"I spent a hundred pounds on this piece of paper," boomed a particularly angry man with a red face. "And it's not worth a penny!" Graves opened and closed his mouth almost comically as he sought for a response.

There were cries of agreement from the throng, the noise

amplified by the high ceiling above. A woman held her child aloft. "How can I feed my Ernie? I spent my savings on that note and now I have nothing!"

Graves raised his hands to calm the crowd. "I need one person and one alone to speak for you!" he boomed. The mob calmed enough for one man to speak and be heard without shouting. It was the man with the red face.

"We have come from the Royal Armitage Bank in Chancery Lane." There were ominous murmurs of agreement. "Each one of us has a promissory note which we have purchased in recent months."

"My broker vouched for them personally," interjected an elderly man with a haughty air, "and now my savings are gone."

"Shocking!" called a younger man in an ostentatious coat. He, too, waved a familiar piece of paper in the air. "I was advised to plough my entire year's profits into this scheme, and now I have nothing."

"Each one of us," the red-faced man continued, "has a promissory note to collect a substantial sum from Golightly Holdings today, but upon presentation at the Royal Armitage Bank, they barred the doors against us!" There was a roar from the crowd. Graves waited for the noise to subside before he continued.

"You have all come from the bank?" he marvelled, his eyes wide. There must be at least a hundred angry people crammed into the reception hall with more joining by the minute.

"We have!" the elderly man boomed above the din. "And much good they have done us!"

Another wave of discontent arose in the room.

"We were each promised a share of funds dependent upon the price we paid for entry to the scheme and how many more we recruited."

"I recruited four of my neighbours," interjected the woman with the infant child by her side, "and in each case I passed their money on to Golightly Holdings. I was promised a hundred pounds for my pains upon presentation of this note, but the bank is barred against me!"

Graves sighed as the room around him descended into a

pandemonium of opprobrium. The Royal Armitage's name was spat as if it were a curse, and the sergeant noticed that one or two of the crowd had seen fit to tear up their promissory notes.

"I want to know what Scotland Yard is going to do about it!" yelled the young man in the flamboyant coat.

Graves ran his fingers through his curls. Looking to Matthews for support, he noticed the desk sergeant had slipped away through a door to the relative safety of the lost property stores. There was nothing for it, Graves reasoned, other than a visit to the bank. The young sergeant puffed out his cheeks in exasperation. It seemed he was to work alone all day.

VI: An Examination

The meeting had left Bowman feeling out of sorts. Doctor Taylor noticed a marked change in the inspector's spirits over the ensuing days. It was there in the slope of his shoulders, the dark shadows beneath his eyes and the shuffling gait with which he navigated the labyrinthine corridors of the asylum. At meal times, he barely ate at all, content to simply move the food about his plate with a fork. He eschewed any attempts at conversation. At night time, it was observed, Bowman lay still upon his bed, eyes wide open, his arms by his side. Doctor Taylor no longer had any concerns that Bowman would again attempt to take his life, but still there was enough of a change in the inspector's behaviour that he sought to bring the matter up in the next weekly meeting with the matron and Athelney Wilkes.

"I do not think the meeting was beneficial," he began, his notes in his hands. "In many ways, I should say it served only to set his progress back by several weeks." He slapped the notes down on his lap. "In short, it was a mistake."

The matron harrumph. "Just as I said it would be." She pursed her lips and folded her arms across her bosom. Not for the first time, Doctor Taylor noticed the buttons on her uniform struggled to contain her. The matron was a large woman, of that there was no doubt, but any patient looking to find motherly solace in her would be disappointed. She looked to the superintendent, her eyes gleaming in triumph.

"Thank you, matron." Wilkes tapped his long fingers on the windowpane where he stood, gazing out into the gardens and grounds that surrounded the building. Fierce gusts of wind pressed intermittently against the glass. As he watched, he saw three orderlies pursue a patient across the lawn. The patient was dressed only from the waist up. With his arms flailing about him, he hid behind the trunk of an ancient cedar tree. He was discovered in due course, the orderlies aided in their search for the man by the sound of his wild laughter. It was an irony, mused the superintendent wryly as the wind thumped against the window, that while many of those within the building were desperate to get out, it seemed the elements were intent on getting in. Wilkes straightened the tie at his collar and removed his spectacles.

"Is he a danger to himself or others?" he asked.

"I would judge not," the doctor replied.

The matron scoffed again. "It was your judgement that led him to this pretty pass in the first place."

"It is our intent," began the superintendent as he turned from the window, "that each of the patients in our care might one day return to the outside world, there to prove themselves happy and useful citizens. The road might well be strewn with rocks, but it is our place to help them navigate their way."

"Will he recover?" The matron fixed her withering gaze upon the doctor.

"I believe so." Doctor Taylor nodded vehemently. "And it is to that end, that I wish to make a request on his behalf." He cleared his throat nervously as he consulted his notes. "I should like the patient to avail himself of the services of an Alienist."

"The man is suffering from nothing that a strict adherence to medication and routine will not remedy," the matron snapped. "If those two precepts had been followed to the letter, I dare say he'd be in a finer position today."

"In the main, they have been followed," the doctor replied.

The matron's eyes grew wide and her cheeks flushed. "In the main?" She shook her head as if in disbelief. "It is not in any patient's interest to follow rules *in the main*. They must be followed *precisely*."

The superintendent had been following the argument intently. He pulled the chair out from behind his desk and sat. "Why might such a course of action prove beneficial to Bowman in particular, Doctor Taylor?"

"There are many in our care who are beyond help." The doctor eyed the matron carefully for her reactions as he spoke. "Those who have been born with some defect of the brain that prohibits a natural and healthy development. It is our duty to care for such needs as they have, whilst fully realising that any hope of a standard recovery is minimal. There are others whose condition may be attributed to the profligate use of drink or drugs. In those cases, we may provide some solace by way of insisting upon abstinence throughout the duration of their stay." He shifted on his seat as he warmed to his theme. "And then there is a third category of patient. Those whose misfortune has been predicated upon an event or circumstance beyond their control. George Bowman is such a one. Indeed, he holds himself to be responsible for the event which first brought him here. The death of his wife in brutal circumstances."

The superintendent nodded. "We are both familiar with Bowman's case notes, Doctor Taylor. What makes you think he might benefit especially from the attentions of an Alienist?"

Doctor Taylor continued carefully, only too aware of the matron bristling by his side. "I believe a strict regime and the medications we provide will only take George Bowman so far. He might, indeed, present himself as being recovered within a very few weeks but, with the kernel of his mania unresolved, he could very well be back with us again in due course." He reached for the bag at his feet. "We cannot keep failing the man."

The matron's eyebrows rose upon her head. "He has been treated the same as any other patient in his condition."

Doctor Taylor nodded as he withdrew a small square of cardboard from his bag. "And therein, perhaps, lies his problem." He stretched across the desk to hand the card to the superintendent. Athelney Wilkes slid his spectacles down his nose, the better to see the name printed there. The doctor pressed on. "There are some interesting ideas on the continent concerning the treatment of melancholia predicated upon trauma. This man is the foremost practitioner. He is from Paris but has premises on Harley Street." If he had hoped to impress the matron with the mention of so prestigious an address, he had singularly failed to do so. She twitched where she sat. "He comes highly recommended," the doctor concluded.

The matron rolled her eyes. "And what may a Frenchman do that we cannot?" she tutted.

Wilkes had heard enough. "Engage this man, Doctor Taylor," he commanded as he rose. "And have him report back to me on the success or otherwise of the intervention."

For the second time in a week, George Bowman found himself in a room he hadn't seen before. He had been called after his breakfast by one of the orderlies and ushered down a quiet corridor. Bowman noticed the tiles on the walls were cracked or missing. Paintwork peeled from the low ceiling in tiny flakes to gather against the skirting boards in drifts. The glass in every other window seemed cracked or missing entirely. Bowman guessed he was being led away from the communal areas of the building, heading towards the laundry rooms in the east wing. He didn't think to question why. Since Miss Morley's visit he had felt like a vacuum, devoid of spirit and lacking in agency.

"You are to wait in here." Gesturing that Bowman should enter, the orderly closed the door after him. Bowman heard his footsteps recede back up the corridor beyond.

For the first time in many weeks, the inspector was alone. The smell of the damp air stung his nostrils. His eyes flitted almost instinctively to the only source of natural light in the room. He sighed. The window set high in the wall was barred to prevent escape. He tried the door, only to find it locked from the outside. Looking around him, Bowman saw the wall opposite the window was given over entirely to a set of shelves upon which was arranged a collection of dusty boxes. Each was labelled with a name and a date. 'Marmsby, A,' read one. '11.07.91 No Next Of Kin.' Bowman moved to the next one along. 'Timpson, D. 04.10.89 No Next Of Kin.' With a shudder, Bowman realised they contained the clothes and personal effects of those who had died, friendless and alone, in the asylum. He counted at least thirty such boxes. Turning from the shelves, he walked to the only other furniture in the room. Two chairs stood facing one another several feet apart. A panic rose within him. Was he to receive another visitor? Almost unconsciously, he raised a hand to smooth his moustache. Trying to steady his breathing, he sat in a chair, stamping his feet against the cold. Just as he was beginning to wonder quite why he had been led here, he heard a key turning in the lock.

His heart suddenly racing, Bowman kicked over the chair as

he rose and backed away towards the window. The door was opened to a crack just wide enough to admit a head. Bowman saw a trim moustache positioned above a pursed, almost effeminate mouth. Dark eyes peered into the room from behind a pair of wire-rimmed spectacles. A long, lean nose seemed to act as a scout before them. The man's hair was swept back from his forehead and kept in place with an oil so pungent that Bowman could smell it from the window.

"Monsieur Bowman?" the man enquired in a splendid French accent. Bowman swallowed. "You are the patient?" the man snapped.

"Yes," the inspector gulped. "I am George Bowman." He noticed how strange it was to say his own name. He didn't find it entirely convincing.

"Bon."

With a curt nod, the man entered the room and, Bowman noticed, immediately seemed to fill it. He was an odd shape, almost tapered. His broad shoulders and pigeon chest seemed to shrink down to a pair of spindle legs.

"Aristide Aubertin," he announced as he placed his bag onto the nearest chair. "From Paris." A prominent Adam's apple bobbed at his throat as he spoke.

Bowman's first thought was that there had been some mistake. He had never, he was certain, met the man before in his life and could not imagine why he had been granted so strange an audience. He scanned the figure before him for any clues. His bag was medical but his demeanour and, moreover, his dress were most certainly not. Aristide Aubertin dripped jewellery. Rings were perched on every finger and chains hung at his wrist and neck. Bowman was almost sure he could hear the man rattling as he moved. He wore a suit of bold stripes and a waistcoat of brushed velvet. The overall effect, thought Bowman, was of a man who dressed as he pleased and did not concern himself with what others may think of it.

"Why am I here?" the inspector asked, at last.

The man paused at the table. "When a man asks such a question of a man such as I," he replied, "it is not what he means at all." He lifted his head to look Bowman squarely in the eye.

"He means, 'what are you going to do to me?'"

Bowman fidgeted where he stood.

Aubertin gestured to the floor. "The patient will pick up the chair and take his seat."

As Bowman bent to the floor, he kept the man carefully in his sights. He was pulling strange instruments and papers from his bag.

"Tell me, Monsieur, just how long have you had the affliction?"

Bowman sat. "Which one?" He smirked at his own response.

"Specifically, that." Aubertin had pulled himself up to his full height to point at Bowman's right hand. As it rested upon his knee, it was quite clear there was a tremor in his index finger. Suddenly ashamed, Bowman snatched it from view.

"Many months," he mumbled.

The Alienist nodded thoughtfully, then turned his attention to the implements on the table. "This is not your first stay at the asylum, is it not?"

"It is not."

"This is typical," Aubertin sighed. "The patient was released before the incubation period was over."

Bowman blinked. "Incubation?"

Aubertin picked up a set of joint callipers and held them to the light, loosening a screw on the handle. Bowman noticed him periodically flick his gaze to the inspector's head as he spoke.

"Did you ever, as a child perhaps, call your name beneath the span of a bridge?"

Bowman was taken aback by the man's unusual line of questioning.

"The sound comes back to you, hmm?" Aubertin was chuckling. "An echo, n'est pas? But, if the arch is big enough, there will be another echo a second later. And then, perhaps, another."

Bowman swallowed.

"You were released only after the first echo. Now, you hear the others." He straightened the implements on the table before him. "The patient will remove his clothing to his undergarments."

53

Such was the note of assurance in the man's demand, that Bowman couldn't help but comply. Slowly, his head bowed, he hung his jacket and trousers on the back of his chair. All the while, the Alienist studied the tools of his trade. Bowman saw slides of glass and some small phials and dishes. Curiously, a fine-toothed comb was laid next to an empty envelope. Standing only in his long johns, the inspector felt the cold of the room more keenly.

"The patient will sit." Without question, Bowman sat. Aristide Aubertin sprang suddenly towards him and held his head still by the chin with his left hand. In his right, he skilfully manipulated the callipers about Bowman's skull. With a deft movement of his fingers, he was able to increase the size between the blades to precisely measure the width and depth of the inspector's head. "Any meaningful event," he muttered as he went about his work, "may leave an echo behind it. We may feel it in the mind for some time. Perhaps a lifetime." Aubertin placed the callipers on the table to note the distance between the blades in a notebook. "And sometimes, in the body, too. I am concerned with the search for the somatic seat of mental disease. Its cause may be exhibited in the body and its functions, if only we know where to look. To that end, I have constructed the Five Pillars Of Observation. Firstly, the skull!" Aubertin held the callipers before him. "Any sign of trauma to the skull may be pertinent." He bent to scribble the measurements into his notebook.

"Next we must turn to the skin." Aubertin reached for a magnifying glass. His face a mask of concentration, he lifted the sleeve on Bowman's arm and scrutinised the skin around his elbow. He made strange, clucking noises with his tongue that Bowman could not interpret. Evidently having found something of interest, Aubertin lunged for the table and retrieved a small, glass slide and Petri dish. He scraped the glass against Bowman's skin, being careful to collect the resultant flakes of dried skin in the dish. "Any imbalance in the body's function may be observed through the skin," he breathed, excitedly. "Any dry areas or redness may speak volumes as to a man's mental condition." Aubertin tutted at the faint scars on his subject's wrist.

Bowman felt utterly subservient. He was a thing to be studied, no more. An object of scientific curiosity. He had a mental image of a butterfly pinned to a board.

A lid placed carefully upon the dish, the Alienist dragged a comb through the tangle of Bowman's hair. He tapped the flakes into the envelope and sealed it carefully with a fold of the paper. This done, Aubertin moved to the window. "Next, the muscles," he announced, turning into the room and lowering his spectacles to observe his subject. "The patient will twice walk the length of the room."

Bowman was beyond any sense of self-consciousness. He had, over the previous months, become so used to following procedure and regulation that he complied without question. Rising unsteadily to his feet, he shuffled from one end of the room to the other. Through it all, he felt Aubertin's eyes upon him.

"The patient will be seated and spit into this phial." Aubertin had placed a funnel into a small, glass bottle which he held directly beneath the inspector's lips. Bowman spat.

"I will order that for the next two weeks, your urine, faeces and all excreta be collected and stored for my personal examination." If the man expected any response, he did not show it. Indeed, it seemed to Bowman that he had ceased to see his patient as anything other than as a thing of scientific interest. Aubertin screwed a cap on the bottle and placed it carefully in his bag. As he stooped to gather up his implements, he turned to his subject with a strange gleam in his eye.

"Lastly," he proclaimed, "the brain, which of course I cannot study until your death." He carefully gathered up the last of his medical ephemera in his bag and snapped it shut. "Unless," he continued, "you would permit me to extract it now?" He held Bowman's questioning gaze. Clearly hoping that his attempt at humour might have been met with more appreciation, the Alienist shook his head. He pulled up his chair with a shrug and sat directly opposite his patient.

"Doctor Taylor," he began, suddenly matter-of-fact, "has been good enough to share with me your case notes." Bowman nodded. He had become used to every private thing being made public. "The regime here has been one of moral management." Aubertin sat up straight, his hands placed on his knees. "That is to say, they have provided for you everything you need in terms of food, clothing and relative comfort." Bowman winced. He hardly thought he had been living in comfort. Aubertin spread his arms wide. "But what of the body? The brain?" He tapped furiously at his temple before taking a breath and leaning in, conspiratorially. "I have in my cabinet in Paris," he whispered, "over one hundred specimens of the brain, left to me for my researches." Even in his numb state, Bowman felt himself shudder at the thought. "I have learned much of how lesions, tumours and a thickening of the skull may leave one susceptible to melancholia or bouts of mania."

Aubertin sat back, clearly ready to pronounce judgement upon his patient. "My diagnosis is this. That you are suffering from a general paralysis of spirit as the result of trauma. This unfortunate event has left its mark upon the brain in the form of a lesion which I have no doubt will one day make itself plain *post-mortem*." Bowman blinked at the implication. "I have observed a staggering gait," the Frenchman continued, "difficulties in conversation, physical ticks and muscular weakness. I read, too, that you experience frequent delusions and have a propensity to alcohol." He observed Bowman carefully as he spoke. "It is your masculine self in crisis, your spirit in decline. In withdrawal, if you like." Aubertin sucked in air between his teeth. "Without prompt intervention, first your spirit will fail, and then your body. They are intimately linked. When all is finally beyond repair, the patient may last only a few weeks."

Bowman stared. Far from Aubertin's words causing alarm, they brought a comfort. Death held no horror now, only the promise of relief.

"Doctor Taylor made mention of a recent visitor."

Bowman blanched at the memory of Elizabeth Morley sitting by the fire, her very presence an affront.

"He made note of a mental decline since the visit." Aubertin leaned forward again. "A question. Did your visitor have any link to the event that caused your trauma? The death of your wife?"

Bowman's moustache twitched. Of course he knew. Doctor Taylor's notes would be thorough, of that he had no doubt. They would have detailed the circumstances under which he had first been admitted to Colney Hatch in May of last year. They would have included, no doubt, a report on the death of his wife beneath the wheels of the carriage on Hanbury Street and his state of health upon admission. There would be lists of treatments and medications. Perhaps his every conversation had been noted. Of course he knew.

"She did not."

"Ah. She has no connection to anything in your past?"

Bowman cleared his throat. He found the man's line of questioning particularly intrusive. He was a patient here, he reminded himself, not a criminal. "I have only very recently got to know her, and then very little."

Aubertin frowned. "That is most odd. It seems you had the most severe physical reaction to her visit. Perhaps there is something of which you are not yourself aware?" Aubertin left the question hanging in the air as he rose to his feet. "Aside from the actions I have already detailed, there is one other course of therapy that I shall myself oversee." Bowman noticed the Alienist thumbing his lapels in an attempt to look authoritarian. "You will, from this evening and every day, undergo a course of Galvanic Therapy." Bowman suddenly felt his fingers begin to twitch. "It is quite a simple procedure," Aubertin continued, clearly aware of the tremor's sudden reappearance. "And quite efficacious." Suddenly, he was all bustle, grabbing at his bag from the table and moving towards the door. "The patient will now dress himself," he announced, abruptly. With that, Aristide Aubertin snapped the door open and made his way from the room.

VII: A Visit To The Bank

The Royal Armitage Bank had stood upon its present site for seventy years and received its royal charter just twenty years later. The building itself looked proud of the fact, the coat of arms above its portico polished to a shine. A smart colonnade ran along the front of the building and its windows were crowned with decorative lintels, giving it more the air of a palace than a financial institution. Granite carvings stood in alcoves along its facade, each representing gods of fortune or abundance from the world's myths and religions. Pluto stood alongside Lakshmi, Fortuna next to Horus. Each of them gazed down from their lofty perches. Their feet rested on a line of white Portland stone that ran the length of the building and displayed the bank's motto in carved letters; 'Absque argento omnia vana'. Without money, all is in vain.

The building stood proud amongst its prestigious neighbours. Offices, courts and societies had all made their home here, some many centuries ago. Imposing Georgian buildings jostled for space with more modern developments. A marvel of Victorian Gothic architecture, the Public Records Office stood guard almost opposite. It was clear the Royal Armitage Bank and its directors felt themselves very much at home amongst such august company.

On an ordinary day, the doorman would nod in greeting and hold the door for a steady stream of customers. Once inside, they would be greeted by a large airy reception hall panelled with wood. More statues stood here and there as if to direct them to the correct counter for their enquiry. Had they cast their eyes upwards, they would be greeted by the sight of a large frieze painted in bold colours. It depicted the temple of Solomon the Wise and, in particular, the Biblical king himself, seated upon his golden throne.

On an ordinary day, the customer could have chosen to make use of the comfortable leather chairs placed strategically about the room to peruse the latest financial papers or exchange gossip with their broker. On an ordinary day, there would have been space for all. But today, it seemed to Detective Sergeant Graves as he pulled up in a hansom, was not an ordinary day. Firstly, his cab was forced to stop short and drop him on the corner with Fleet Street, such was the throng of people crowded at the bank's entrance. Secondly, as he approached on foot, he saw the doorman was standing in front of a closed door, his arms folded in defiance of the mob.

"Looks like your friends are here before us," called Graves over his shoulder. At Scotland Yard, he had thought it prudent to elect one of the crowd to act as spokesman on their behalf and so the red-faced man had accompanied him on his journey. Whilst in the hansom, he had introduced himself as Bartholomew Sprogget, a shipping clerk from Bermondsey.

"I was approached at a shareholders' meeting," he had elucidated as they rattled through The Strand. "I have long held shares in Capel Coffee and am active on the Board." Graves noticed Sprogget's face lost much of its hue as he spoke. Perhaps it was a relief for the man to unburden himself before one who was keen to listen. Reasoning that to record the details in his notebook would prove folly in the swaying carriage, the sergeant determined to commit the salient points to memory.

"I was approached after the meeting by a representative of Golightly Holdings. I forget his name for now," the man huffed, "but I was struck by his trustworthy nature."

Graves nodded to encourage the man in his tale.

"He told me Golightly Holdings had many assets abroad and counted many successful companies among its portfolio of interests." Sprogget sighed as he sat back in his seat. With the early morning drizzle having exhausted itself, the cool air upon his face was clearly acting as something of a calmative. Graves was beginning to feel sorry for the man.

"I was persuaded to part with my dividend for a promissory note to be redeemed at the Royal Armitage Bank this very day." Sprogget ran his fingers through his hair as he recalled the events. "I know it sounds so very improbable, Sergeant Graves," he keened, "but the man was so dashed convincing."

"May I ask," began Graves, carefully, "how much you bought the note for?"

Sprogget gave a sardonic laugh. "For the sum of five hundred pounds!" he announced, seemingly suddenly aware of the ridiculous nature of the deal. Graves was aghast. He would be lucky to earn such a sum in five years. "I was told I would be recompensed two fold if I recruited other shareholders to the scheme."

Graves raised his eyebrows. "At a cost, I assume?"

"Naturally," Sprogget nodded, sadly. "Each new member was to pay five hundred pounds into the Golightly account. And of course, they were encouraged to recruit more members, too. The greater the number we recruited, so the greater the share of the Golightly fortune we were promised."

Graves' eyes grew large as he stared into the streets around them. Such a system, he knew, was unsustainable. Those at the very top would benefit hugely from the money paid in by each member, while those further down the chain, Sprogget included, would lose everything. As the hansom clattered onto Fleet Street, the young sergeant mused that crime had very many faces, indeed. Though this was no murder or assault such as he had become used to investigating in his time as a detective sergeant, the consequences of the crime could be just as devastating.

"This promissory note," Sprogget proclaimed, holding the piece of paper before him, "was to fetch me over a thousand pounds." He lowered his hand and looked suddenly forlorn. "It is, in point of fact, the most expensive piece of paper I have ever owned."

With that, the man spoke no more, but sat for the rest of the journey in silence. There was much he had left unsaid, thought Sergeant Graves. Just why had such an obviously astute man, who had no doubt spent his professional life dealing with things financial, fallen for so transparent a scam?

"Just how many people bought into Golightly Holdings?" Graves was aghast as he shouldered his way through the crowd to the door.

Sprogget was behind him, following gratefully in the sergeant's wake. "Hundreds, I would think," he called. "We have each been played for fools."

They made their way through the mob with much cajoling. There were cries of "Shame!" and demands to be permitted entrance from all around. A fight had broken out on the fringes of the crowd. Once or twice, Graves was conscious of treading on feet in order to make progress.

"Watch yer step mate!" cautioned a particularly burly man in a bowler hat. "There's no use hurryin', anyhow. They've locked the doors against us."

As the two men drew nearer to the bank, they saw the doorman had retreated further into the portico. In his smart uniform of navy blue frock coat and pillbox hat, he looked the very picture of stern implacability. His bottom lip, however, betrayed him. Graves noticed it quivering as he approached.

"I am Detective Sergeant Graves of Scotland Yard," he announced as he retrieved his identification papers from his coat pocket.

"I don't care who you are," the poor man replied, haltingly, "just get this lot to go away." His arms folded across his chest, he clutched at his coat with trembling fingers as he spoke.

Graves raised his voice above the din. "Let me inside, then get yourself to Holborn Police Station. Have them send some constables to disperse the crowd."

"These people have a legitimate grievance," Sprogget added from his side. "They won't go quietly."

"Then maybe they'll be persuaded to give their details to the sergeant at Holborn," offered Graves, not unreasonably. "I've no doubt it'll all come to me at Scotland Yard." He sighed inwardly at the thought of yet another evening sat before a pile of evidence.

The doorman nodded his assent and reached into his pocket with a shaking hand. As he reached for the lock, there came a cry from the throng. "He's letting us in!" A triumphant cheer rose into the air. It fell to Sergeant Graves to disabuse them of the notion.

"There will be no entrance for any one here," he called, raising his hands to quell the noise. "The bank will remain closed for the day."

The cheers of triumph turned to a grumbling despondency.

"What of my money?" shouted a man from the crowd. "I've lost a year's wage on this note!"

"I've lost double!" came another. Now everyone waved their papers in the air, keen to elucidate just how much they had lost in the pursuit of riches.

"Each one of you will have your say!" Graves soothed as best he could.

"We don't want our say, we want our money!"

Graves gnawed at his lip. He knew financial redress was unlikely, to say the least. Sensing his companion's discomfort, Bartholomew Sprogget stepped forward.

"We must trust this man to get to the bottom of it," he said, "but we must also face facts." A stillness came over the assembled throng as they listened. "Like you, I paid for a note on the promise of future reward. I may even have recruited several of you in my cause." He scanned the crowd, certain he recognised one or two faces among it. "We have been played for fools," he said, quietly. "And we have paid a price for it." There was much shuffling of feet and shaking of heads as the doorman gave the sergeant and his companion egress to the bank. As the door slammed shut behind them, the two men heard another roar from the crowd as the doorman ran off to find help at Holborn.

Inside, it was another world. The tumult on the street was muffled by the great oak door and the rarefied atmosphere of the reception hall seemed quite at odds with the noise outside. Motes of dust danced lazily in the air. Graves saw the staff sitting at their desks as expected, but the leather, wing-backed chairs opposite them were unoccupied.

"Why the devil did he let you in?" The reedy voice belonged to a man so thin, Graves thought he might break if faced with the least resistance.

"I am Detective Sergeant Graves of Scotland Yard," Graves began, reaching for his papers out of habit.

"Then you are no use to me in here," the man interrupted. "You should be out there, arresting every last man Jack of them." He gestured vaguely beyond the door with one hand while laying the other across his temple. It was as if he had found the whole exchange rather tiring.

"Under what charge?" Graves teased.

"Common assault, if their behaviour towards my staff is anything to go by." The man gave a haughty sniff.

"They only want what is theirs, by right," Sprogget breathed. Graves could see the man's face flushing red again. He placed a hand upon his shoulder to calm him and turned to the austere gentleman before him.

"You are the manager?"

The man sniffed again. He rather gave the impression, thought Graves, of being haunted by a most disagreeable smell. "I am the director of the Royal Armitage Bank," he said with pride. "Maximilian Hackenburg." He stiffened as he introduced himself, only just stopping short of clicking his heels together by way of a salute.

"Perhaps there is a more appropriate place for our discussion," Graves suggested.

Hackenburg cast a look to his staff. To a man, they leaned in at their desks, the better to hear the conversation. Upon seeing their director turn to face them, they each counterfeited being busy about some business at their ledgers.

"Perhaps you are right," the director demurred, and he led the two man into a corridor off the main hall, the soles of his shoes tapping on the parquet floor. Looking down, Graves wasn't sure which was the most highly polished. "We pride ourselves upon our discretion, Detective Sergeant," Hackenburg said as he walked. "The last thing we need here is a scandal." Taking a bunch of keys from his pocket, he stopped to unlock a gate that stretched the width and height of the corridor. Once the men were through, their journey continued.

"You have at least a hundred people at your door," hissed Sprogget, impatiently. "Looks like you have a scandal already."

Here, there were no windows and the lighting was more subdued. The decor, far beyond the public's gaze, was more muted. No portraits hung from the walls, and no statues stood guard. The paint on the wall was an institutional grey and the floor was of an inferior wood. Selecting another key, Hackenburg unlocked a door marked 'Strong Room'.

"Wait here," he barked, only to disappear into the strong room and close the door behind him before either man had a chance to peer inside. Within moments he had returned with a folder tucked under his arm. Graves noticed that the director was careful not to allow him even the merest sight of what lay beyond the door. Turning the corner, he led the two men further down the corridor. Taking the keys again, he showed them into an impressive wood panelled boardroom with windows along one wall that gave out to the street beyond. A long table stretched the length of the room, with eight or nine upholstered chairs arranged along either side. A portrait, no doubt of one of the bank's founders, hung above the fireplace opposite a picture of Queen Victoria herself. Perhaps, mused Graves as Hackenburg ushered the men in, the prime positioning of the founder's portrait as the focus of the room gave an indication as to where the directors' loyalties lay.

Sergeant Graves pulled a notebook from his coat pocket, licking the point of his stubby pencil as he sat. Sprogget remained standing at his side. Graves could see him flexing his fists involuntarily as he stood.

"Tell me of your morning, Mr Hackenburg," began the young sergeant. "What precisely happened here?"

Hackenburg shrugged. "My staff were ready for a perfectly uneventful morning. I was breakfasting at the Atheneum with a rather noteworthy shareholder, when we were interrupted by Hembury." Graves looked up from scratching at his notebook. "He is one of the two boys we employ to run errands at a penny a day," Hackenburg clarified. "He told me that, as soon as the doors had opened, the bank had been besieged by customers, each of them eager to cash in their promissory notes for their part in Golightly Holdings." Hackenburg rubbed his hands together as he spoke. "I hailed a cab and got here as quickly as I could. By then, there was already a sizable mob upon the streets and so I ordered that the bank's doors be closed."

"That mob," said Sprogget at Graves' side, "only want what is theirs. And I count myself as one of them."

"Ah, yes," Hackenburg nodded. "I remember your face. You were particularly vocal, as I recall."

Graves stifled a smirk at the remark.

Sprogget reached for his note and slapped it upon the table. "This bank owes me a thousand pounds."

Hackenburg raised his eyebrows at the sum but was otherwise unmoved. "No, sir," he said, coolly. "Golightly Holdings owes you a thousand pounds. Or at least, they would if they were still solvent."

There was a silence as the import of the director's words sunk in.

"They are bankrupt?" Sprogget was clearly trying very hard to keep a rein on his anger.

"Oh no, sir," Hackenburg continued. "The account was closed upon Mr Golightly's death and all the money held in the account withdrawn."

Graves lay his notebook on the table before him, his pencil beside it.

"Who withdrew the funds, Mr Hackenburg?" he asked, carefully.

At this, Hackenburg pulled out a chair and sat at the head of the table. He opened the folder before him with his long fingers and withdrew several sheets of paper. "All the information is here. Upon the death of Mr Golightly himself, the business was dissolved and the funds withdrawn. It is, as far as we can see, all above board." He rested his hands on the desk, clearly in the belief that there was to be no further argument.

"Above board?" echoed Sprogget, his voice trembling with emotion.

"When did Golightly die?" asked Graves.

"On the thirteenth day of this month, according to the death certificate produced upon closing the account." It was clear that Hackenburg saw nothing untoward.

"The man died just four days ago?" Sprogget's face was flushing again. "How convenient!"

Graves attempted to soothe him with a look. "Is it not curious," he continued, turning back to the director, "that the funds were withdrawn so soon before the presentation of so many promissory notes?"

"That may be your opinion, Detective Sergeant," Hackenburg

said, calmly. "But, as far as I can see, the Royal Armitage has done nothing wrong in this instance."

"Surely you have an obligation?" seethed Sprogget.

"To whom?" replied Hackenburg.

"To the people at your door who have found themselves the victim! If they are reduced to such circumstances as I have been, they will be left in a very sorry state, indeed."

Graves turned his eyes to his companion and noticed Sprogget's face had fallen to an expression of despondency. For the first time, Graves wondered just what his initial outlay of five hundred pounds had meant to the man. Now it was clear that it was a loss from which he would find it difficult to recover.

"My wife is very ill, Sergeant Graves," he explained, quietly, "and her treatment expensive." He looked down as he spoke, his voice barely a whisper. "I had hoped my investment in Golightly Holdings would pay for the medication and equipment she needs to sustain her." Graves noticed his bottom lip beginning to quiver. "I called in all my debts and prevailed upon my own bank to lend me the money for my promissory note. But now I have lost everything, and the bank will be expecting the repayment of their loan, plus interest." At last, Sprogget looked up, fixing the director of the Royal Armitage Bank in his gaze. "And I would wager every man at your door has just such a story."

Graves blinked. It seemed hundreds of people had been taken advantage of; the very people who could least afford it. He marvelled how the perpetrators of this particular scam could sleep at night.

Hackenburg swallowed hard in the face of Sprogget's story, but was insistent in maintaining his innocence. "We were presented with all the details required to close the account, including the death certificate, the notice of cessation of trade and the account to which we were to direct the funds. The latter, of course, is held to be private in law, but the other certificates are here for you to see." With that, he slid the folder towards Sergeant Graves who leafed carefully through the papers within.

"Cessation of trade?" he repeated, his blue eyes narrowing. "Just what did Golightly Holdings trade *in*, Mr Hackenburg?"

"Misery," interjected Sprogget, sadly. "They traded in misery."

"That, sir," the director sniffed, "is no business of ours."

Graves had turned his attention to the death certificate secreted in Hackenburg's folder.

"Did you or your staff ever have dealings with Mr Golightly or his representatives?"

"Only when the account was opened some three months ago," Hackenburg confirmed. "We met with his secretary."

"Perhaps the very man who approached me," Sprogget breathed.

"Perhaps," agreed Graves. "This death certificate appears in order," he continued, "but as Mr Sprogget here has intimated, the timing of Mr Golightly's death is convenient, to say the least."

"Not for me, nor the others at the door," Sprogget opined.

Graves scanned the document in his hand. "Perhaps I should call upon Mr Golightly's doctor. He is here listed as Doctor Frederick Samson." He turned to the bank's director. "Mr Hackenburg, I would urge you to make enquiries as to the whereabouts of this Doctor Samson."

"Urge?" Hackenberg was suddenly suspicious.

"Indeed," Graves continued, slowly. "It would be a shame to tarnish your no doubt auspicious career with a charge for obstructing the police in their duties."

Hackenburg blinked as he thought. "I will see what I can do," he said at last.

Finally, Graves reached inside to withdraw the last piece of paper.

"Mr Golightly's Last Will and Testament," Hackenburg declared. "As I said, Detective Sergeant, all is in order."

Graves angled the note to the window, the better to read its contents. "I, Thomas Golightly of Hollington Street, Kennington do make this my last Will and Testament as follows. I hereby give, devise and bequeath unto my physician Doctor Frederick - " Graves stopped mid sentence and flicked his eyes to the death certificate on the table. He heard Sprogget gasp audibly beside him and, looking up, noticed that even Hackenburg looked unsettled. Graves cleared his throat and continued. "Doctor Frederick Samson, The sum total and all consolidated annuities now standing in my name in the Books of the Royal Armitage Bank and also all my money and securities for money of what nature or kind soever and wheresoever the same shall be at the time of my death and I do appoint and constitute the said doctor sole executor of this my last Will and Testament hereby revoking and making void all and every other will or wills at any time heretofore made by me and do declare this to be my last Will and Testament In Witness whereof I the said Thomas Golightly have unto set my hand and seal this twenty sixth day of August in the year of our Lord one thousand eight hundred and ninety two."

There was a silence.

Finally, Graves pushed his chair back from the table and rose to face his companion. "Mr Sprogget," he began, "it is doubtful you will ever see your investment again." Graves noticed the man's shoulders sag. "The most I can promise," he continued, "is that I will endeavour to bring those who have preyed upon you to justice." With that, the sergeant thanked the director of the Royal Armitage Bank for his time and turned to the door. The whole unfortunate episode and the many victims that the perpetrators had left in their wake had put Graves in mind of another victim of another crime. It dawned on him that, as Inspector Hicks was concentrating his energies upon Temperance Snell over the death at the printing works, he was neglecting entirely any investigation into the victim, Augustus Gaunt. Stepping from the bank back onto Chancery Lane, Detective Sergeant Graves took his leave of Bartholomew Sprogget, realised he was but a ten minute cab ride to Cloak Lane where Snell was being held, and resolved to make amends.

VIII: Cloak Lane

Detective Inspector Ignatius Hicks was never happier than when he had a fork in his hand. The fact that he had just impaled the fork in question deep into a particularly juicy pie made him happier still. Under instruction from Detective Superintendent Callaghan to proceed with his interrogation of the print works manager at Cloak Lane Police Station, he had decided to fortify himself first at The Silver Cross before continuing. Harris, the landlord, had been happy enough to welcome him from behind the bar. Trade was quiet on these cold autumn mornings, and Harris was happy enough to entice the inspector with one or two choice items from the menu.

"The beef is from the butcher across the way," Hicks had droned, his lank hair falling about his ears. "You'll find none fresher. He takes delivery every morning."

Hicks had smiled appreciatively. "Then a beef pie will suffice." He had tapped a pump handle on the bar. "And a pint of porter to wash it down."

Now, as the bluff inspector hung his hat on a hook on the chimneybreast, he regarded the chairs before him. The one nearest the fire, he knew, had been Bowman's favourite. He saw no reason now to stand upon ceremony. Drawing the chair towards him, he squeezed his bulk onto its well-upholstered seat and let his hands rest on the arms. If he felt any discomfort at occupying the seat of a colleague who had found himself in such dire circumstances, he did not show it. As he stretched his legs out in front of him and awaited his refreshment, he let his thoughts wander to something that had been bothering him.

All along Whitehall, the road had been busy with carts and pedestrians going about their business. Hawkers gave full voice to their wares as they sauntered hopefully towards Trafalgar Square. An omnibus had clattered crazily towards Westminster, its team of horses sweating despite the autumn cool. As Hicks had emerged from Horseguards' Avenue on his short walk from Scotland Yard to The Silver Cross, he had paused to look behind him. Just as he turned, he was sure he had noticed a figure dart from the throng to duck into an alcove nearby. He stopped twice more on his journey and the same had happened again. If Hicks knew one thing above all else, it was to trust his instincts. He was being followed. If the inspector had been more lissom in his constitution, he might have considered quickening his step. He had thought of leading his pursuer through the maze of alleys and streets around Whitehall but reasoned that it would be to no particular benefit. Concluding that his stalker would make himself plain in good time if that were his wish, Hicks had pushed at the door to The Silver Cross and made his way to the bar.

"Beef pie. Porter."

Harris' sudden appearance at the table served to rouse the inspector from his reverie. The landlord's leathery face betrayed concern as he slid Hicks' meal towards him.

"How is Inspector Bowman, sir?" he asked. "I miss his custom."

"I expect you do," Hicks chortled. He raised his jug of porter before him. "I shall do what I can to make up the shortfall." With that, he drained his drink in one, the whiskers of his moustache trailing into his tankard as he drank. Giving a great, satisfied belch, Hicks slammed the jug back onto the table, gesturing that Harris should refill it. "I think it only fair and decent I raise a glass in the absent inspector's honour," he beamed.

Harris looked as if he might pass comment on the remark, but instead he gave a curt nod and retreated to the bar with the tankard.

As Inspector Hicks wrestled with his pie, he endeavoured to keep an eye on the road outside the inn. The overnight rain had retreated, leaving a grey sky and muddy streets behind it. The bravest souls were venturing forth without their hats, but most were muffled up against the October weather. A keen wind was whipping down Whitehall. It snatched playfully at scarves and coat tails as it passed, like an errant child escaped from the admonishing gaze of its parents. Just as he lifted a particularly juicy bit of beef to his lips, Hicks noticed the fire in the grate blaze all the brighter as the door was thrown open. The gust of wind was such that the inspector's hat was blown from its peg. It rolled dangerously near the hearth. Bending to retrieve it, Hicks brushed the dust from the rim and blew a cobweb from its crown. Turning back to rest it safely on the table by his plate, his eye was drawn to a large envelope that had clearly been placed before him as he had looked away. Glancing quickly up that he might see who had left it there, he was greeted by the sight of the door swinging shut on its latch. He looked around the saloon to the bar. Harris was busying himself carrying barrels from the cellar. What few customers he had were talking amongst themselves in the farthest corners. Hicks was sure none of them had moved. Reasoning that he was too late and, more to the point, too slow to give chase through the door, Hicks reached for the envelope and slid it slowly towards him. There, written in a large, neat hand in capital letters was a single word. 'SNELL.'

Cloak Lane Police Station was home to the fourth division of the City of London Police Force and occupied a large building between College Hill and Queen Street, just a quarter of a mile north of the Thames. It rose over six storeys, its austere facade accentuated by a granite lintel above its wide entrance. At its apex, a bearded head glowered down at those who had the temerity to ascend the steps beneath.

Formed just over forty years ago, the Force's jurisdiction stretched across the square mile of the City including the Middle and Lower Temples to the east and Farringdon and Cripplegate to the north. Comprising, as it did, many of the most troublesome wards in the capital, it was, as the desk sergeant was wont to remark, 'enough to keep a man busy'.

Sergeant Mahoney was a burly fellow with a mop of thick, red hair and keen eyes that, as soon as Detective Inspector Hicks was through the door, had already made an appraisal of the man. He was the sort, thought the sergeant, to demand attention, but today he would have to wait his turn. A long and shambolic queue had formed at his desk. As soon as Mahoney had relieved the night watch and thrown open the great oak doors that gave out to Cloak Street, he had been besieged by members of the public. Some were drunk and looking for shelter in the cells, others came with an intent to report crimes of varying degrees of seriousness. One elderly gentleman had queued for half an hour solely to report that he felt his daughter had been rude to him. He wished to know what action he could take whilst remaining within the law. Mahoney had advised the old man to go home and consider the fact that he would, in all likelihood, be reliant upon his daughter to care for him in his encroaching infirmity. A wife and her three children had appealed to the sergeant to help them find refuge from an abusive husband and father. The youngest child was only a babe in arms, and the poor lady looked exhausted from clutching the thing to her breast as she stood in line. The sergeant's only recourse was to instruct a constable to accompany the woman and her charges to a house of refuge in Cheapside. In truth, he did so with a heavy heart, cognisant of the fact that, unless the poor woman returned to her husband, her children at least would be bound for the workhouse. At last the queue thinned, and Mahoney was able to concentrate his energies on the large fellow with the pipe who had been loitering impatiently at the door. With his great, matted beard and food stains down the front of his coat, Mahoney had already decided what must be done with the unfortunate fellow.

"There's a Baptist Mission House not three streets from here," he announced. "They might have a bed for you. There's no room in my cells for a man who's fallen upon hard times."

Hicks blinked furiously, his jaw opening and closing in his indignation. "I need no Mission House," he boomed. "And I am far from having fallen on hard times." His hands shook as he reached into an inside pocket for his identification papers. "I am Detective Inspector Hicks of Scotland Yard," he proclaimed, pompously. "And I wish to see a man in your cells, not bed down in them."

Mahoney perused the paper in Hicks' hand with a studied intensity before raising his eyes to the portly inspector's bearded face. Before the sergeant, stood the most unlikely man to be a Scotland Yarder as he could imagine. Still, he reasoned, his identification seemed genuine enough.

"Take me to Temperance Snell," Hicks commanded. With a sigh, Mahoney ducked out of sight behind his desk, only to reappear clutching a set of keys. Hicks tucked his paper back into his coat and followed the sergeant to an alcove in the corner. From there, he was led down two flights of stone steps to the basement floor. Hicks leant against the wall to catch his breath, only to see Mahoney eyeing him suspiciously from the corridor ahead. Chastened, Hicks prised himself from the brickwork and joined the sergeant in front of the furthest cell. There, in the furthest corner through the bars, sat Temperance Snell.

"Thank you, sergeant, that'll be all." Hicks dismissed Mahoney with a wave of his hand. For a moment, it seemed Mahoney was about to offer something by way of a reply. As Hicks raised his eyebrows expectantly, the sturdy sergeant evidently thought better of it and ambled back to the stairs.

"Inspector Hicks, I hope you are here to release me."

Hicks turned to face the forlorn figure in the cell. With his sloped shoulders and haggard expression, Temperance Snell seemed half the man he was when the inspector last saw him. His colourful clothes which only yesterday had lent him a certain bravado, now mocked him with their jolly hues. A lack of sleep had left his eyes red and his skin sallow.

Hicks struck a match against the bars to light his pipe. Puffing at the bit to coax the flame, he took his time with his response. "If you think I bring anything but bad news in that regard," he said at last, the smoke from his pipe rising to obscure his face, "I am afraid you will be disappointed."

"I have not even been allowed to communicate my predicament to my wife," said Snell, sadly. "She will wonder where I am."

"As well she might." Snell was putting on a fine performance, thought Hicks. If he was not in possession of the most incontrovertible evidence that he was guilty of Gaunt's death, he might well have felt sorry for the man. "Perhaps there is much that she does not know." Hicks narrowed his eyes. Whether he was considering the prisoner before him in the light of this new evidence or whether he was irritated by his own pipe smoke, it was difficult to tell.

"Why do you keep me here?" Snell had sunk onto the low bunk that served him as a bed and a chair. It was the only furniture in his otherwise sparse cell.

"Because I believe you to be a danger to the public." Inspector Hicks pulled a chair of his own from further down the corridor and eased his large frame into the seat. Snell heard the chair creak ominously as the inspector sat. "I would not let a murderer free to walk among them."

"Murderer? You speak of Augustus Gaunt?"

Hicks nodded, slowly. "I do. It is clear to me, Mr Snell, that you are responsible for Gaunt's death." He puffed lazily on his pipe, watching Snell carefully for his response.

"But what of the man I saw?"

The bluff inspector rolled his eyes. "Nothing more than a fantasy."

"I give you my word - "

"That a man with a top hat and cloak killed Augustus Gaunt by trapping his head in the press?" Hicks raised his voice, incredulous. "That he then made his way into the yard and jumped a five storey building?" He allowed himself a sardonic chuckle at the very idea. "There is not a shred of credibility about your tale."

"But, why?" Snell blinked. "Why would I wish him dead? I knew little of the man beyond his work on the print floor."

Without breaking the man's gaze, Hicks reached dramatically inside the folds of his coat. "I did not say you wished him dead. Only that you caused it." Slowly, he withdrew the envelope he had found at The Silver Cross.

"What is that?" Snell peered through the bars in an effort to see.

"This is a collection of reports that have been lodged in recent years concerning your running of Gibson & Son Printers."

"I know of no such reports." Hicks thought Snell looked distinctly worried. "Where did you get it?"

"That is of no matter. Suffice it to say, they make for very interesting reading." With an effort, Hicks crossed one leg over the other and balanced the envelope on his knee. Craning his neck, Snell could clearly see that his own name was hand-written on the front in large capital letters. Slowly opening the envelope, Hicks was determined to make the man in the cell sweat. He held a sheet of paper up to the light afforded by the window behind him and made great play of reading its contents to himself. Despite being in the basement, the windows looked out onto the road outside, but from low down. They had afforded Snell a curious view during his incarnation as disembodied legs, visible only from the knee down, had hurried past. Finally, Hicks deigned to share the matter of the report with Snell.

"On the twenty-first day of August, Eighteen Hundred and Eighty Nine," the inspector read aloud, "a Hardwicke Manningthorpe lost a finger to an unguarded guillotine." He dropped the paper to gauge Snell's reaction. A look of concern had clouded his face. "On the seventeenth day of June, Eighteen Ninety," Hicks continued, "Thomas Bloom lost the sight in one eye following the dislodging of an ill-fitting wing nut." The inspector shook his head as if the paper alone was enough to seal Snell's fate. "On the thirtieth day of December that year, Franklin Marston lost an arm to a paper roller. Unable to work thereafter, he was thrown upon the mercy of the workhouse."

Snell was suddenly at the bars, a look of desperation on his face. Spittle flew from his mouth as he reached to snatch the papers from Hicks' hand.

"How do you know all this?" he rasped. "Where did you get those reports?"

Hicks shot him a look. "You do not deny them?"

Snell clung to the bars, his head hung in silence.

"In each case," Hicks continued, "you managed to turn the blame upon the unfortunate workers themselves. You claimed they had been negligent in their duties or heedless of procedures designed to keep them safe."

Snell lifted his head. "I wasn't even present when Marston lost his arm."

"But it happened on your watch. And I should imagine Mr Gibson was far from pleased." Hicks returned the paper to its envelope and tucked it back inside his coat. Rising from his chair, the portly inspector walked to the window. A tinker's cart rattled past. All Hicks could see from his vantage was the hooves of the nag that pulled it, the bottom half of the wheels to the cart itself and the ragged trouser ends, ankles and bare feet of the wretch who attended them. "I know little of the printing trade," he admitted, generously, "but I should guess the works manager would be held responsible for the safety of his work force?"

Snell nodded sadly, and rubbed his eyes with the back of a hand. The smoke from Hicks' pipe had by now infiltrated every corner of the little cell. As he turned back to face the prisoner, the inspector was either oblivious to Snell's discomfort or did not care. "You spent three years in a debtors' prison, did you not?" Hicks tapped at the envelope with a fat finger.

Snell blinked. Hicks watched as a bead of sweat formed on his forehead.

"And yet you neglected to inform your employer of the fact."

Snell swallowed. "I did not wish to prejudice his opinion of me."

"What opinion would that be? That you are a bankrupt? A criminal? You did not think he should know?" Hicks puffed out his cheeks, as if in exasperation at the notion.

"I wish to make my way in the world, Inspector Hicks, like any man."

"At any price, it seems."

Snell rose from his stool and walked closer to the bars, his head cocked at a curious angle. "Inspector Hicks," he began, "I am not the man you think me to be. You look at me and see a product of the criminal classes. A murderer, perhaps." He hooked his fingers into the pockets of his waistcoat. The fur trim and silver buttons seemed ridiculous in his current, sparse surroundings. Snell leant against the bars. "Each man's birth is but an accident, and none can be blamed for how they entered this world. It is how he leaves it that is of import." Snell's eyes locked onto Hicks', suddenly unafraid. "I made peace with my early years long ago. You may say I was dissolute, a bankrupt, and all that was true. But that is not the Temperance Snell that stands before you. I have fashioned myself anew, despite my humble beginnings. The man you see before you, inspector, is one of good repute and a fair mind. I have risen far and fast, and intend to rise higher still." Snell's chin jutted forth, proudly. His eyes were suddenly wet with tears.

Snell could not have known that the portly inspector was beyond being moved. Hicks slumped back into his chair, stretched his legs before him and scratched at his great belly. "I would put it to you, Mr Snell, that the order of events was something like this." It was as if he had not heard a word his prisoner had said. "You were drinking in The Blackfriar as you have attested, having left Gaunt at the press to complete an order."

"All this is true." Snell threw up his hands in defeat. He knew exactly what Hicks' conclusions would be, despite having little or no evidence to support them.

The inspector was enjoying himself. He clearly liked nothing more than a captive audience. "Upon returning to the print works, you discovered Gaunt as we saw him. And you panicked. Rather than be held accountable for the latest in a long line of accidents, you concocted the story of a mysterious assailant."

Snell had lowered himself onto his bunk. "If all this is true, why would I have fabricated such an incredible story?" He spread his hands wide before him.

Hicks leaned suddenly forward on his chair, jabbing towards Snell with the bit of his pipe to punctuate his words. "Because, Mr Snell," the inspector snarled, unpleasantly, "you like to hold yourself above the ordinary man. I am sure it gives you a particular pleasure to tweak the authorities by the nose and lead them a merry dance. Your little subterfuge has proven to be ill-advised."

Snell's eyes glinted with a mischievous light. "Sergeant Graves did not seem to think so," he said, innocently.

Hicks harrumphed. "What Sergeant Graves does or does not think is entirely his own affair." The disdain in his voice for his young colleague was clear.

"In fact," continued Snell, sensing that his mention of the young sergeant had hit home, "he listened most intently as I related the details to him again only this morning." Hicks was brought up short by the remark. He heaved himself forwards and rested his great hands on his knees. "You have seen Sergeant Graves?" he huffed.

Snell nodded. Suddenly, even in his most desperate condition, he felt a degree of control. "He wanted to know more of Augustus Gaunt." He noticed Hicks' eyes narrow. "He seemed of the opinion that the key to his death might lay in his private history or relationships."

"What did you tell him?" Hicks seethed.

"Only the little I know," replied Snell, emboldened. "That Gaunt had a dubious past." Snell broke Hicks' gaze, guiltily casting his eyes to the floor. "Like me, he chose not to tell his employer."

Hicks held his pipe aloft in triumph, his great beard quivering before him. "Ah! That was a hold you had over him."

"I did not see it like that."

Hicks nodded. Perhaps there was more to this Snell fellow than met the eye. "What was his history?"

"He professed to having escaped justice on a technicality for his part in a robbery."

"But still you gave him work?"

"Perhaps I saw myself in him. He proved a most skilled craftsman."

Hicks was barely listening. Instead he seethed inwardly that Graves had taken it upon himself to interview the man, against the explicit intrusions of his superior. Hicks would be certain that Detective Superintendent Callaghan knew of Graves' insubordination.

"Just what else did you tell the good sergeant?" Hicks almost spat the words. It was Snell's turn to toy with his interlocutor. "There was one more detail concerning the man in the stairwell," he admitted. He lowered his voice so that Hicks had to lean closer to the bars to hear. "When you hear it, perhaps you will understand why I haven't mentioned it before. I withheld it because it is so fantastical that I feared it would render my whole story unbelievable."

78

Hicks harrumphed loudly, clearly beyond trying to hide any disdain for the man behind the bars and his tall tales. "Go on," he thundered.

"As the man reached the bottom of the stairs, I was a flight or two above him. He looked up, straight towards me."

"Then you did see his face?" Hicks' eyes lit up at the news. Snell might just have backed himself into a corner. If he fabricated an identification of this mysterious man, it would be a simple matter to debunk his story.

"That's just it, Inspector Hicks." Snell turned on his bunk so that he sat square on, facing the inspector. "The man had no face, just a black void where a face should be." Hicks' eyes narrowed suspiciously. Just what was Snell playing at? "All I could see were his eyes," he continued, a slight tremor in his voice betraying his discomfort. "And that is the most curious thing of all. As he turned to look at me, inspector, I saw that his eyes were glowing a vivid green."

IX: An Extraordinary Remedy

Bowman had learned to welcome the Chloral. Perhaps he had come to crave it. He was certain it had been added to his food to begin with, in an attempt to remedy his reluctance to take the sedative in tablet form. Now, it was delivered subcutaneously. The matron withdrew the needle from his forearm and loosened the tourniquet just beneath his elbow. She had taken it upon herself to deliver the drug in person, morning and evening. Within moments, he felt his heart rate slowing. His breathing became shallow and his eyelids heavy. He looked at the world as if through a haze, the room about him appearing suffused with a lethargic mist. His limbs felt heavy. Since his attempt at self-murder, he had become too fragile for the physical world. Like some beast from the furthest depths of the sea, he had risen to the surface and found it intolerable. Much safer to stay in the deep, dark abyss of the soul. There was a comfort in his lack of agency. The Chloral soothed him.

Later, as if through thick, distorting glass, he watched as two orderlies wheeled a contraption into the room. Though he could make no sense of its purpose, he could see it was a chair of some sort, with thick leather straps hanging from the frame. Without a word of explanation, he was lifted onto the contraption and secured. He hadn't the energy or the will to object. Then, he was moving. The chair was wheeled through the door and into the corridors. They were quiet at this time of the evening, with most of the more troublesome patients sedated for the night. The rattle of the wheels on the flagstones echoed off the cracked tiles around him. The gas jets fixed periodically to the walls lent their sickly pallor to the cold air. Bowman could see his own breath rising before him but could feel no cold. In truth, he could feel nothing. The odd, incoherent babble of frantic speech drifted through the doors to the wards as they passed. Once, a scream pierced the air, only to decline into a nervous, high-pitched laugh. Bowman was aware of the rushing of staff towards the source of the sound; the flapping of coats and hiss of urgent whispers. None of it concerned him. His eyes were closing.

There was a strange, metallic taste in his mouth. Even the rattle of the cage doors failed to rouse him as he was pushed into the large, hydraulic lift at the end of the corridor. Ostensibly for the use of staff only, Bowman had periodically seen patients being wheeled in and out in chairs similar to his. He had never thought to wonder where they might be being taken.

It was a quick, almost noiseless descent to the basement. The flickering gas jets lent an ethereal air to the corridor, their flames dancing on the arched ceiling above. Most of the rooms off the bare brick corridor were used for storage. Hastily scrawled signs denoted what lay within. 'Medicines', read one. 'Restraints', read another. Bowman saw boxes of clothing and bundles of bedding arranged on sturdy shelves or laid in deep trunks. The last room of all had a more sinister sign attached to the door. As Bowman was wheeled into the dingy cell, he could just make out the words 'Electrical Room.'

Aristide Aubertin waited within. In an apparent concession to his surroundings or an attempt to appear more professional, he had tied an apron around his waist. As Bowman's chair was wheeled into position, the Frenchman busied himself at his apparatus.

"How is the patient?" he asked, pleasantly. Bowman could say nothing. Noticing his words were wasted on the man in the chair, Aubertin turned his attention to the two orderlies who shifted nervously where they stood. "I have not seen you before," he said slyly.

"We normally work the grounds," offered one, bravely.

"But the weather's turned," the other continued. "So we've been assigned indoors."

"Then, behold the greatest wonder of the Modern Age!"

The orderlies blinked. The man before them seemed more showman than doctor.

"Could you please be certain to apply the brakes?" With a curt nod, one of the men who had accompanied Bowman into the bowels of Colney Hatch bent to make the chair secure.

"He has been sedated?"

"He has," the orderly nodded.

"Are the restraints taut about the arms and legs?"

The orderly nodded again.

"Tres bien." Aubertin seemed satisfied enough to begin. Reaching for a pair of long-bladed clippers, he walked behind the chair to commence his work. As the orderlies stepped aside, Aubertin hacked at Bowman's hair with abandon. It fell to the floor in clumps. Soon, the inspector's skin was clearly visible through what hair remained. Aubertin was careful to cut especially short at the crown.

Content with the results, the Alienist walked back round to his equipment. He cleared his throat. "You will notice certain *paraphernalia* around you. You need not be concerned, these are merely the tools by which I will administer treatment. Much as a surgeon might make use of a scalpel, a barber the scissor or a fisherman the rod, so I will utilise the power of electricity to do my work." He seemed pleased with his analogies. "There is an artistry, of course."

With Bowman in his stupor, it wasn't immediately apparent just who Aubertin intended as his audience. The two orderlies looked awkwardly to one another as he continued. "The transformative power of the electric current resides within the battery." Had Bowman been in any way cognisant of proceedings, he might have noticed Aubertin gesture to a large wooden box resting on a trolley beside him. It was perhaps two feet long and a foot deep. With its lid resting open, it was possible for the orderlies to see spools of wire emanating from a central unit. A handle was fixed to the outside of the box with a row of switches placed alongside. Two wires protruded from either side, one attached to a small, metal tube, the other to what looked to be a rubber diaphragm. Aubertin was warming to his theme. "Melancholic paralysis is but the reaction to the modern world. The loss of self amongst the scale of industrial development." He gave a beatific smile. "How apt, then, that man's mental salvation may lie with a product of that industry. The discovery of electricity. Since Monsieur Franklin flew his kite into the storm, professional men of medicine have been seeking a way to turn this most natural of phenomena to a curative." Aubertin puffed out his chest so that his apron looked like it might tear. It was clear he considered himself just such a professional. He paused, dramatically. "Voila!" he announced, picking up the two metallic electrodes. "The tools of my trade." He chuckled to himself, his Adam's apple bobbing up and down at his collar. Placing the electrodes back on his trolley, he bent to the floor to retrieve a large bottle of water. "The patient's shoes will be removed," he announced.

As the Frenchman poured the liquid into a bowl, the younger of the orderlies bent to untie Bowman's laces. His shoes removed, Aubertin lifted the patient's feet and slipped them carefully into the bowl.

"Acidulated water," he explained as he rose. "It is the medium by which the current will enter the body."

Turning to his table once more, he made sure the rubber skull cap was attached to its wire then stretched it over Bowman's head, being careful to align the electrode with his crown.

"Electricity in Nature has the power to split trees," he proclaimed gleefully. "It may set a forest ablaze. Here," he tapped the battery, "it is tamed." Carefully dropping the metal tube into the bowl at Bowman's feet, Aubertin ran his fingers back along the wire to be sure that it wasn't tangled. "Through careful application of the current to discrete areas of the patient's brain, he may soon recover his old self. The process is most successful."

The younger orderly frowned. Aubertin's use of the word '*may*' had not gone unnoticed.

Bowman had observed all this as if from afar. The very air about him seemed thick as soup. Shadows blurred around him. They left a trail in their wake; after-images that hung in the air as they moved. Not for the first time, Bowman felt he was among ghosts. He guessed one of them must be Aubertin. His peculiar deportment and accent had made enough of an impression upon Bowman just two days before, that he recognised him easily through the Chloral-induced fog. His mouth drying, Bowman attempted to lick his lips. He found a plug had been tied there to keep his teeth from closing. He felt no alarm, more a detached interest. He was conscious of his feet being in water. Try as he might, he could not fathom why. The sound of Aubertin's voice, though seeming distant, had awakened the spark of a memory deep within Bowman's brain. As one may blow gently upon an ember to reignite a flame, so Bowman coaxed it forth from the fog of his mind. He held it delicately before him and it became a flower. Carefully prising the petals apart that he might see the bud of a thought within, he held his breath. There it was. He saw it as if from the side of his eye. He dare not look straight at it for fear of it disappearing beyond sight. A memory of something Aubertin had said during his examination. The Frenchman had suggested a link between Elizabeth Morley and the events that led to Anna's death. He had been wrong, of course, but there was a link to something else; something further back. Something Elizabeth had said that day resonated deep within the inspector's memory. He reached for it in his mind, this kernel of a thought. He grit his teeth against the bit between them as he strained for it. Just as he had it within reach, he saw Aubertin turn a lever on a box and throw a switch. And the world fell away.

X: Making Headway

"Sergeant Graves, this is a surprise."

Doctor John Crane stood in his dissecting rooms at Charing Cross Hospital, his spectacles half way down his nose. "I was expecting Inspector Hicks." Doctor Crane's Scottish burr betrayed more than a hint of suspicion.

"Inspector Hicks has been detained on other matters pertaining to the case," Graves lied. "He has sent me in his stead."

"Indeed?" Crane raised a quizzical eyebrow. In his dealings with the Metropolitan Police Force, he had often found the detectives he had met to be rude, demanding and lacking in understanding. But not Graves. In truth, he had a liking for the eager young man before him, and was actually rather relieved not to have to spend time in Hicks' company. He found the bluff inspector to be obstreperous, insolent and belligerent. Crane fancied that Hicks considered himself the centre of the universe. He counted himself lucky to have escaped his orbit for another day.

"Then you are here to see Augustus Gaunt?" The doctor removed his spectacles to clean them on a cloth. He bent as he did so, and Graves was treated to a fine view of the man's balding head, shining beneath the few strands of white hair that had been combed across in an effort to disguise it.

Graves nodded. "I am." As ever, the room around him was lined with shelves that groaned with strange medical implements. Diagrams hung upon the walls in between, charting the systems and processes of the human body, some in the most exquisite detail. Graves was always particularly struck by a picture of the human circulatory system that hung by the door. Its network of veins and arteries reminded Graves of the veins on a leaf or the meanderings of water courses such as one might see on a map.

"You may hang your coat by the door," the doctor barked, replacing his spectacles upon his nose.

Graves retrieved an apron from a hook and tied it about his

waist. It was markedly cleaner than the doctor's own which was stained with yellows, browns and reds of indeterminate origin. He looked, thought Graves, like a butcher at his block.

As soon as he had entered the room, the sergeant's eye had fallen upon the body beneath the sheet. He had shivered with a macabre thrill that, if he had been asked to do so, he might have found difficult to explain. He had, in his career, discovered a latent interest in the human body and its workings. He viewed any opportunity to learn more of its secrets, particularly in the presence of the doctor before him, as an opportunity not to be squandered.

He followed Crane to the table and waited patiently while the doctor pulled on a pair of rubberised gloves.

"I have done the best I can to clean the poor fellow up," Doctor Crane said, ghoulishly, "but he's still not a pretty sight." He looked even more bird-like as he stood, poised, at the table. His hands were held before him in the manner of claws, ready to pluck the sheet from the body on the slab.

Graves nodded that he was happy to proceed.

Slowly, almost theatrically, Doctor Crane rolled the sheet down the man's body until it was presented before them in all its naked glory. Augustus Gaunt was lying on his back, his hands by his side. His flesh, noticed Graves, was already possessed of a sickly blue pallor, tending towards yellow at the extremities. There was a faint whiff of decay in the air, mixing as it rose with the scent of whatever preservative fluids Doctor Crane had employed in the course of his work. It was a vaporous, chemical odour that caught in the back of Graves' throat. He fought hard against the instinct to cough. He caught Doctor Crane's eye and offered him a smile.

"Don't let me stop you."

Doctor Crane nodded. He had always enjoyed Graves' interest in the more macabre side of his work.

The man on the slab was of stocky build, Graves noticed, and was inordinately hairy about the chest and shoulders. "He would be a difficult man to overcome," he mused aloud.

"Unless he was taken by surprise," the doctor replied, pointedly. Crane rested his bony fingers alarmingly close to the man's head. Graves dropped his gaze to Gaunt's skull.

Doctor Crane had, indeed, been busy. Where once there had been a mash of blood, hair, bone and brain, was a face that was almost recognisable. The sergeant couldn't help but peer closer. The action of the cylinder drum upon the poor man's head had disfigured his skull entirely. His features seemed to have slipped their moorings and come to rest on one side of his face. A split eye was crowded against the bridge of his nose which was, in turn, spread across his right cheek. His mangled jaw hung at an alarming angle, so much so that Graves feared it was no longer attached at all. The man's entire upper teeth, he noticed, were broken, though whether as a result of the punishment they had endured on the press or through some previous altercation, he could not tell.

Doctor Crane stood in silence as Graves took in the grisly sight before him.

"The subject is a man in his mid forties," he began at last, his Scottish vowels suddenly clipped and professional. "Prior to his death, he was in generally good health. There is evidence of trauma to the man's right femur but that may have happened during adolescence. As a result, he may have walked with something of a limp. Aside from that, he is almost unremarkable in every way."

Graves raised his eyebrows. "Almost?"

The doctor took a breath. "It is no doubt tempting to conclude his death was as a result of the injuries to his skull."

Sergeant Graves looked up. "It was not?" he asked, his eyes wide.

Crane shook his old head, meaningfully.

"Then why put him in the press?"

Crane held a finger before him, as if lecturing a student in the dissecting theatre. "Why, indeed, Sergeant Graves?" He was plainly determined to make the young man think for himself. "Perhaps in the hope of putting the police off the scent?" Crane let the question hang in the air with the scent of embalming fluid.

"So you have found something else?" Graves' eyes were ablaze with excitement.

"If you would be so kind?" Doctor Crane indicated that Graves should station himself at Gaunt's feet. With a heave, the doctor sought to turn the body with a display of strength more fitted to a man half his age. Gaunt's arms slapped against the table as he turned, and Graves reached out to untangle the poor man's legs. They felt cold and heavy.

"Might I draw your attention to this?" Crane was extending a finger. Graves joined him at the table's head to see that he was pointing at a wound in the back of the man's neck. "This is what killed Augustus Gaunt."

Sergeant Graves squatted on his haunches, the better to see the wound. It was a puncture that seemed to extend some distance into Gaunt's neck. "How deep does that wound go?"

Crane lifted his finger again and poked it, as deep as he could, into the wound. He held it up for Graves to see. The tip was covered in blood to the depth of about an inch.

"This deep," said Crane simply. He wiped the blood on his already grubby apron. "The wound has been made by an instrument applied with such force as to separate the first two vertebrae at the top of the spine, the atlas and the axis."

Graves blinked up at the doctor from his position. "A blade?"

Crane was thinking. "Perhaps."

"How quick was his death?"

Doctor Crane adjusted his spectacles on his nose as he spoke. "Instantaneous, I should say."

Sergeant Graves rose and shook the feeling back into his legs. "Then it would seem our murderer knew exactly what he was doing."

Doctor Crane nodded in agreement. "The wound is most…" he searched for the word. "Precise."

Graves reached beneath his apron to draw out his notebook. Leaning against the table, he made a note of the salient points with the stub of a pencil as the doctor removed his gloves.

"You can be sure the wound was made before the damage to his skull?"

"I am most certain of it," Doctor Crane snapped. "Those two vertebrae have been disfigured due to an almost surgical blow from behind. The damage wrought by the action of the press was made from the front."

Graves nodded, thoughtfully. "This seems like a targeted attack." Doctor Crane stared blankly back at him as he spoke. "It is too much to imagine that such a murder, in such a place at such a time with such an implement is entirely random. This man was known to his killer." He snapped his notebook shut. "This smacks of an act of retribution or revenge. The killer took the time to seek him out, wait until he was alone, then strike in such a way that his death was assured, before attempting to cover up the fact." Graves blinked. He chose to say nothing to Doctor Crane concerning the mysterious assailant's supposed method of escape.

"You have gone beyond my remit, Sergeant Graves," the doctor asserted. "But I should say your theory is certainly supported by the facts as I see them."

Graves nodded thoughtfully, then moved to retrieve his coat from the door.

The shops and streets off The Strand flashed past. To save himself getting wet, Graves had hailed a brougham to Scotland Yard. Turning Doctor Crane's findings over in his mind, he gazed sightlessly through the carriage window. Even in this most inclement weather, the road was teeming with the flotsam of the city. Passers by did their best to sidestep one another in the throng. Those with business to be about walked with purpose, their heads down against the fine drizzle. Those with nowhere to go meandered aimlessly in the road, risking their life among the passing horses, carts and carriages. Hawkers stood on every corner, shouting their wares in defiance of the weather. Graves felt the wheels skid beneath him as the brougham fought to navigate the ruts and troughs on the road. Once or twice, he heard the horses give a whinny of alarm, only to be chivvied along with a smart crack of the driver's whip.

He felt he was getting to know Augustus Gaunt a little better, although that in itself brought him no nearer to knowing his murderer. The detail of the weapon was telling, Graves mused. Not a knife, perhaps, but a sharp prong. Such a distinctive tool of death. Graves' thoughts turned to Temperance Snell who he had seen languishing in his cell in Cloak Lane that very morning. With his slight frame, he certainly didn't seem the sort who could have overpowered Gaunt easily, no matter if he was taken by surprise. Surely, he would exhibit some injury, no matter how slight, where Gaunt might have lashed out in a fury?

As Graves gazed through the window, he saw the sign of a public house flash past. A thought crystallised in his mind. He recalled Snell admitting the workers at Gibson's print works drank at The Blackfriar on Queen Victoria Street. Graves reached up to pull the window down and call up to the driver, blinking at the rain thrown into his face. To know a man's mind, the young sergeant reasoned, you must start with where he drinks.

The rain had settled into something that wasn't quite drizzle or mist, but something in between. Graves cursed as the brougham rattled away, splashing water at his ankles from the puddles on the road. Queen Victoria Street was so rutted that pools of dirty rainwater now made up almost the entirety of its length. Those drivers that knew the hazards skilfully avoided the pits in the road and, in doing so, undoubtedly saved their carriage's wheels and their horse's hooves. Those not so familiar with the road found themselves veering from one side to the other as their carts and carriages were thrown off course. Graves even noticed a case fall from the top of a smart landau, jolted from its straps as the carriage bounced along the road. A young urchin ran to retrieve the luggage and chased the landau down the street, no doubt in hopes of a reward for his exertions.

Sergeant Graves seemed immune from the discomfort the weather caused to those around him. Collars were turned up and coats buttoned against the rain. No one loitered in this weather. Instead, all was bustle. Graves, however, rather liked the feel of it upon his skin and he stood for a moment to feel it settling on his face.

At last, he walked the few yards to The Blackfriar. It was so distinctive a shape that Graves paused a while to take it in. It seemed tapered, as if it had been cut from a larger building and deposited here. Graves was put in mind of a slice of cake, an image that made him smile. Looking about him, he saw that he was surrounded by railway buildings, small factories and builders' yards. Just across the road, he could see the backs of the wharves that butted up against the Thames. He was so close to the river here, that he could smell it. Around him, the streets were busy with traffic. Even in this weather, it streamed towards Ludgate Circus, where it would turn east to The Strand, west to St Paul's or continue ahead to Farringdon. It was one of the more pleasing things about his profession, mused Graves as he approached the public house, that he could be set down almost anywhere in London and know his bearings at once.

Pushing at the door, the sergeant found himself in a gloomy saloon bar with a low ceiling and dark wood panelling on the walls. A pall of blue smoke hung in the air and the sweet, sweaty tang of beer pricked at his nostrils. The Blackfriar was quiet. Two men slept at a table nearest the window, leaning up against each other for support. A string of drool hung lugubriously from the older man's lip. A mangy dog lay on the hearth by the fire, risking his fur being scorched by the fierce flames that fizzed and spat in the grate. The only other customer was a large woman who sat nursing her gin by the bar.

Graves leaned against the counter and ordered a pint of India Pale Ale from the barkeep. He was a young man with a surly expression. Clearly annoyed at having to actually do some work, he hoisted himself reluctantly from his stool where he had been casting his eye over a newspaper and reached up for a glass.

Graves looked at the woman beside him. She had a kindly face with a dimpled chin and rouged cheeks. She had been careful enough with her makeup that the skin on her face blended seamlessly with that on her neck, which seemed to Graves to be a very special skill indeed. A large mole had been painted just below her left eye and her red hair was piled high on her head into an unruly bird's nest of a bun. With his pint presented before him, Graves cast his eyes to the piano in the furthest corner. It had been positioned just where the pub was at its narrowest.

"Tempted?" the woman asked. Graves turned to her. A pipe

was clamped between her teeth. As she drew upon it, the sergeant couldn't help but notice the woman's large bosom heaving against her bodice. "By the piano, I mean," she cackled. Her voice was low and gravelly.

"I came for a quiet drink, but I could turn my hand to a tune if called upon." Graves smiled his most winning smile and the woman was conquered at once. With his dancing blue eyes and blond curls, she had never seen anyone look so cherubic.

The woman extended a fleshy hand and blew smoke between her teeth. "I'm Flora," she announced. "But most round here call me Big Flo."

Graves shook her hand and tipped his head in greeting. "Anthony Graves," he said, cheerfully. He was guessing she wouldn't be quite so talkative if she knew he was a detective sergeant with the Metropolitan Police Force. With most of her customers put to work in the surrounding manufacturies and yards, she was clearly biding her time until the evening.

"What brings you here?" Flo downed her gin as she spoke, leaving a greasy smear of lipstick on the rim.

Graves thought fast. "I'm a reporter with The Standard," he lied.

"Ah," Flo nodded wisely. "Then you'll be here for more than a quiet drink." She turned to the barman who had just that moment lifted himself back onto his stool. "Come on, Albert, shake a leg." She shook her empty glass before her as if ringing a bell. With a rolling of eyes and much muttering under his breath, Albert obliged in pouring her another gin.

"You're here about the print works murder."

"It's true," admitted Graves as he sipped at his ale. "Did you know Augustus Gaunt?"

"I know 'em all dear," Flo cackled. Her laugh turned to a low, rattling cough that saw her grabbing at the bar for support. "Gaunt was the stocky fella. Big hands." Her eyes twinkled. "Such a shame how he came to so rotten an end."

Graves took his notebook from his pocket. "Do you mind?" he asked, innocently.

"Course not," Flo replied, puffing on her pipe. "Long as you don't mention no names."

Graves nodded. "How long had Gaunt been drinking here?"

Flo sucked the air between her teeth. "Well, he moved here a couple of years or so ago, I reckon." She drew upon her pipe, sending plumes of noxious smoke into the air about her. "Or, at least, that's when he started drinking here."

"Do you know where he lived?"

Flo eyed him with mock effrontery. "I will tell you where he lived, so long as you don't ask how I know."

Graves nodded with a smile.

"He had a bed in a doss house on Fleet Lane. Shared the room with three others."

Graves scratched at his notebook as she spoke, keen to commit every detail to paper.

"And where was he before he came here?"

"Camberwell way, he told me. Then Holborn, then here. He just moved wherever the work took him." Flo's eyes shone as she thought of him. "He had his pride, you see. Would always rather work, unlike a few round here I could mention." She flicked her eyes to the two men sleeping by the window.

Graves allowed himself another smile.

"He was keen to make good of himself," Flo continued, "after a brush with the law some years ago."

Graves looked down at his notebook at the remark, affecting nonchalance as best he could. "Brush with the law, you say?"

Flo paused in response, then reached for her drink. Downing it in one draft, she slammed the glass down on the bar, pointedly.

"I'd love to say more, dearie," she twinkled, "only me mouth's a bit dry."

Graves smirked and nodded to Albert. Flo watched in silence as the reluctant barman filled her glass, then nodded appreciatively before continuing. "There was a robbery some years ago that turned bad. Farringdon way, I think it was." Flo tapped the spent tobacco from the bowl of her pipe and let it fall to the floor.

Graves was thinking hard as he scribbled at his notebook. The case sounded familiar. "Warwick Lane," he said, inadvertently.

"Oh!" exclaimed Flo in surprise. "You know it?"

"I remember the articles in The Standard," he bluffed.

"I'm not surprised," Flo replied. "It was big news for a while. A constable was killed, along with the owner of a jewellery shop."

Graves nodded. He did indeed remember it. The jeweller had stumbled across a thief one morning as he opened his shop and promptly called the police. He was discovered by the burglar and held hostage until the constable's arrival, whereupon he was killed and the policeman attacked. There had never, thought Graves, been so senseless a waste of life. The policeman had died of his wounds some days later, without ever being able to give evidence or identify the perpetrator.

"It was a bad night's work and no mistake." Flo was looking at the young sergeant carefully as she spoke.

"Are you saying," Graves said slowly, "that Augustus Gaunt was the thief?"

Flo seemed reluctant to continue. "There's many a man that says so," she said quickly. "But I wouldn't like to say."

Graves could tell she was annoyed with herself. "But I am sure he was acquitted."

Flo tutted. "The coppers had nothin' on him."

"Then how do you know all this?"

Flo sat in silence for a while. When she spoke at last, it was with a voice so quiet that Graves struggled to hear her.

"It goes hard when a man struggles with his conscience, Anthony. There are some moments though, when he is apt to empty his heart. They are private moments and I only share them now because the poor man is dead."

Graves held her gaze as he nodded, appreciatively. "Thank you, Flo," he said, gently.

Flo closed her eyes against a tear that had sprung there and took another swig at her glass.

XI: Through The Looking-Glass

Essex Street looked impossibly pretty in the spring sunshine. To its north end, Sir Christopher Wren's St Clement Danes Church stood on its island between Fleet Street and The Strand like a beached berth. One of two 'Island Churches' along with St Mary-le-Strand, its tiered tower was visible from miles around. To the south lay Temple Pier and the River Thames. To protect the residents of the genteel street from the sights and sounds of the wharves and warehouses, a triumphal gateway known as Watergate had been built over the flights of stone steps down to Milford Lane and the river's edge. From Essex Street, it was a grand affair of red brick and fluted granite columns topped with pilasters in the Corinthian style. From the riverside, it was a narrow flight of stone steps beneath a plain brick doorway. It was as if the inhabitants of the street had thrown a screen across the road to spare them from the hoi polloi.

The early morning sun glanced off the walls of the elegant townhouses that lined the street, causing the two detectives to screw up their eyes against the glare. Detective Inspector Simeon Grainger was a bull of a man. Now in his sixtieth year, it was clear from his gait and sheer presence that he had once been a man to reckon with. As he bowled across the cobbles at some considerable street, he propelled himself with the swinging of his great arms, his barrel chest leading the way. If his frame inspired fear, then his face exuded kindliness. It was framed with a pair of white mutton chops that met over his full lips in the form of luxuriant moustaches. Wisps of white hair escaped from beneath his top hat as he walked, and even his unruly eyebrows looked like snowy peaks. Despite his benevolent facade, a pair of piercing blue eyes betrayed him to be a man of keen intelligence. A scar just visible on his skin spoke of an early life among the criminal classes.

That Grainger had spent his youth as a pickpocket gave him, perhaps, a special insight into the workings of the criminal mind. It was an insight that had served him well and seen him rise through the ranks of the Metropolitan Police Force at speed. He had come to the Force late in life and had enjoyed his position of poacher turned gamekeeper. He had clearly seen some things in his time, particularly in his five years spent at Her Majesty's pleasure for repeated arrests for affray. It was not a past he was particularly proud of, but one upon which he was always willing to call should the need arise. He had a network of acquaintances who existed on the fringes of criminal activity. It had proven most useful in his various investigations.

Detective Sergeant George Bowman both admired and feared his superior. The young sergeant had been impressed at first simply by the man's force of character. He had found Grainger to be a stentorian presence at Scotland Yard but his bluster concealed a keen, analytical mind. As he had been assigned to more investigations in his charge, Bowman had grown to like him and even, perhaps, to see him as something of a mentor. Despite his relative youth, Bowman struggled to keep pace with his superior. Advancing in years he may be, the sergeant mused, but there was certainly no decline in his physical faculties.

"We're but a stone's throw from Temple Gardens," Grainger enthused. "Many of these buildings around us are in service to the Inns of Court."

As the weather was so clement, Grainger had decided that the two men should walk from Scotland Yard. It was a journey that had taken them along the Victoria Embankment and past the grand edifices of Charing Cross Station, the Savoy Hotel and Somerset House. Bowman had relished the opportunity of a walk beside the river. The Thames was in full spate, its swollen waters busy with rivercraft of all shapes and sizes. Flimsy ferries plied their trade between the two shores, north and south, while larger steam launches chugged between the piers, groaning with tourists intent on enjoying a day upon the river.

At last, the two detectives had turned onto The Approach at Temple Station, and Bowman had found himself in the most rarefied of streets he could imagine.

"Of course," Grainger continued, "that Watergate once sat upon the very shore of the Thames." He turned to Bowman with a twinkle in his eye. "I remember watching them building the

Embankment that hems in the river. I may even have cut a few purses along this very street as a nipper." A broad, toothy grin spread across his face. "This was before Robert Peel had his way and posted a policeman on every corner. He took the thrill out of life, if you ask me."

Bowman played along. "Has it been a life of boredom since?"

Grainger threw back his head and laughed. "Not since the Lord provided you for my amusement!"

Bowman smirked at the jibe. Grainger had assumed an easy familiarity with Bowman when they first met, a familiarity that had led to many such comments at his expense.

The Detective Inspector turned as they reached their destination. "A man is but the sum of his experiences, Sergeant Bowman, don't you ever forget that. We are here at this moment by dint of Fortune only." Grainger looked suddenly serious, his forehead creased in thought.

Bowman nodded at the sudden turn in the man's expression. He was used to Grainger's habit of sprinkling his conversation with such earnest pronouncements. "I shall remember," he replied, in as serious a tone as he could muster.

"Good." Grainger seemed satisfied that his point had been made. "Now, ring the bell, if you would be so kind."

Bowman had been so enrapt by Grainger's story that he had not even realised they had stopped walking. Looking along the row of houses before him, Bowman could see it was a street designed to attract the wealthy. A straight, treeless thoroughfare, Essex Street seemed to exult in its cleanliness. Turning to the door, he craned his neck to look up at a tall building of five storeys. Its plain, red brick exterior was quite at odds with the exquisite and ornate furniture he could see through the window. Inside, he saw a family consoling a young woman before the fireplace. An older man stood behind her, while two other ladies bent to comfort her. The young woman, no more than a girl, twisted a mob cap in her hands, occasionally dabbing at her eyes with the hem of her apron.

"We're here to help 'em, Sergeant Bowman, not spy upon 'em."

The rebuke was enough to have Bowman reach for the

doorbell, and he heard its gentle chime echo throughout the house.

Within a very few moments they were greeted at the door by a young footman. He presented himself in a fine, traditional livery including breeches and silk stockings. His hair was neatly parted in the middle and his face was youthful and smooth. Bowman noticed he ground his teeth as he stood in the hallway, as if he was fighting hard to present a professional facade. After the necessary identification, Bowman and Grainger were led inside and the door was closed behind them.

The hallway impressed Bowman at once with its tasteful elegance. A staircase wound its way up to the upper floors immediately before them. Bowman knew the servants would have their quarters on the very top floor. With such a small household, perhaps there was only the footman and one other. The floor was laid with tessellated tiles in black and white to make a pleasing geometric pattern. The walls were hung with family portraits in heavy frames. Bowman saw a middle-aged man with a severe look, a woman of similar age with steel-grey hair and a younger lady in a yellow dress. He recognised them at once as the three people he had seen crowding round the young lady in the parlour. A large sideboard stood by the entrance to the lounge, decorated with fine china and an exotic bird stuffed and mounted beneath a glass dome. Sergeant Bowman felt at once that he was in the house of a rather well-to-do family and guessed they were just one of many along the street. The only noise in the house came from the drawing room; the sobs of a young woman and the attendant cooing of those attempting to soothe her. Inspector Grainger nudged Bowman to indicate that he should remove his hat as he swung his own from his head. He saw his superior lick his fingers and use them to smooth his hair and, comically, his eyebrows.

"Detective Inspector Grainger," announced the footman in clipped tones at the door to the drawing room.

Bowman swallowed. It was clear he was not to be introduced.

"And this is Sergeant Bowman," Grainger concluded, obligingly, throwing Bowman a look of amusement as he did so.

The sergeant felt all eyes upon him. He was sure a blush had come to his cheeks and he felt sweat prickle on his upper lip. Perhaps, he thought, he should grow a moustache.

"And about time, too!" roared the gentleman from behind the chair. "Hetty has been worse than useless these last few hours."

Bowman thought he noticed the footman blinking irritably at the remark.

"You are being cruel, Father," the young woman chimed. She stood just out of sight behind her mother at the fireplace. "She has had the most terrible fright."

The older woman with the grey hair moved to greet them. "Forgive us, Inspector Grainger. We have been under much strain this morning, as well you might imagine."

Grainger dipped his head in understanding. "Of course." He cast his keen eyes around the room. "Mrs Mortimer?" he enquired of the lady before him.

She nodded. "And this is my husband, Percival."

Percival Mortimer gripped the back of the chair where he stood. He was clearly irritated by the recent turn of events.

"And this," Mrs Mortimer continued, "is our daughter, Anna."

She moved to one side to reveal a young lady in her early twenties. Bowman was struck by her natural poise and the tumble of chestnut curls that hung to her shoulders. "It was her idea that we call Scotland Yard over this matter."

"And a greater waste of time I could not imagine."

"Father!" Anna chided the man again. She cast Bowman a demure smile and he felt himself blush again. He had the impression of a lively soul behind her concerned eyes.

"And this is Hetty," Mrs Mortimer concluded, "our maid of all work."

"Maid of *no* work, more like," Percival Mortimer puffed.

Once again, Bowman noticed the footman tensing at his employer's remarks. Perhaps Mrs Mortimer noticed it, too. "That will be all, Terence," she barked, and the young man left the room, but not before casting a final glance to the young maid in the chair.

"Might I sit, Mrs Mortimer?" Grainger enquired. Bowman

saw his interest had been piqued.

"Of course," the lady before him purred. She gestured to another, larger chair placed directly before the window.

"Don't get too comfortable, inspector," grumbled Mr Mortimer. "I would have this room to myself in an hour. I have much to do."

"What is your employment, sir?" Grainger enquired, politely.

"I am a court clerk, sir," proclaimed Mortimer with more than a little pride in his voice.

"Ah," returned Grainger, "then you above all else will perhaps appreciate that, for the law to take its proper course, all the facts must be laid before us."

"The law has no interest here, Inspector Grainger." Mortimer stiffened as he spoke. "Hetty has been the subject of a prank, a jape, if you will, and nothing more."

"I have seen both sides of the law, Mr Mortimer," Grainger responded enigmatically. "Believe you me, I know just where its interests lie."

"Perhaps," interjected Bowman, seeking to diffuse the tension in the room, "Miss Mortimer might tell us why she saw fit to call for Scotland Yard."

As Anna Mortimer nodded in assent, Bowman felt glad that she had indeed called upon the detective division. If, as Grainger had asserted on the doorstep just minutes ago, they were here by dint of Fortune only, then Fortune was to be thanked. Sergeant Bowman fought hard to concentrate upon the young lady's words as she spoke, distracted as he was by the swoop of her neck and her almond eyes.

"We have all read reports in the newspapers these past months," she began, "of a diabolical figure who terrorises the city. I refer to the man who has made his presence felt particularly to the young ladies of London, jumping out at them and pawing at them most inappropriately."

Bowman noticed the maid had begun to sob again in her chair. Percival Mortimer rolled his eyes. "He has deflowered two that we know of," Anna continued, "and likely caused the death of another through fright."

Simeon Grainger nodded his head. "You refer to the fellow

the papers have christened 'Jumping Jack' on account of his supposed ability to leap great heights."

"The very man, Inspector Grainger." Anna nodded. "Last night, our own Hetty fell prey to his advances."

Grainger glanced at his sergeant. "Then his grisly work continues apace." Percival Mortimer sighed. Sensing the man's cynicism, the inspector continued. "We are currently investigating two other such reports. One from a tooth manufactory in Angler's Place in Camden, another at St Pancras Old Church."

Hetty's face creased as she sobbed all the more.

"No one was hurt," Percival Mortimer boomed above her moans. "Inspector, I shouldn't wonder you have more pressing matters to investigate."

Anna rounded on the man behind the chair. "Father," she scolded, "I have no doubt that if this incident had involved a man or a crime that you might recognise as incurring financial damage to the victim, you would be the first to call upon the law. You only dismiss it as it involved a young woman."

"But she was not hurt and nothing was taken," her father blustered.

"Her very person was violated and her dignity impugned," Anna countered. "Surely that is as great a crime as any may be committed on a young woman?"

"Dignity?" roared Percival Mortimer. "She is nought but a maid!"

"She is a fine example of God's greatest work, Father," Anna's voice was rising in her passion. "And she deserves our respect for that, if nothing else. Sergeant Bowman," she said suddenly, making Bowman start where he stood, "I consider a woman's body to be no one's possession but her own. Does the law not agree?"

Bowman felt his neck burn beneath his collar. His mouth gaped alarmingly as he fought to furnish her with a response.

"You must forgive our daughter," Mrs Mortimer smiled. "We have sought to bring her up as a young lady who knows her own mind. Perhaps we have rather overstepped our goal."

In truth, Bowman admired her all the more for it. "Not at all," he stammered. "It is most… commendable."

Turning to her again, he noticed that Anna Mortimer had fixed her eyes upon him. It was as if, in that very moment, she was deciding exactly what she thought of him. As the conversation continued around them, Bowman felt the past, present and future collapse upon this moment and they were alone in the room. His heart beat fast against his chest as he stood in the light of her gaze. At last, a subtle incline of her head and a twitch at the corner of her mouth gave him to understand that she was pleased to be in his company. And he could not help but smile back.

"Who is this terrible man, Inspector Grainger?" Bowman heard Mrs Mortimer ask. "Does he find some pleasure in pursuing young ladies in this way?"

"Well, Mrs Mortimer," replied Grainger, teasing his moustache between his fingers. "He is certainly a menace. His crimes for now have been little more than a nuisance." Bowman saw Anna shake her head. "But there is danger that he will grow bolder still." He leaned forward in his chair to address the maid. Bowman, in his fascination with the young lady by the fireplace, had forgotten she was there at all.

"Hetty," Grainger began, softly, "can you tell me what happened last night?" His manner had changed entirely as he spoke to the young girl in the chair, Bowman noticed. Not for the first time, he marvelled at how Grainger seemed to have an understanding of every class of person. In the course of their investigations together, Bowman had noticed Grainger seemed to delight as much in the company of a lowly maid as with the aristocracy. If, as now, he was called upon to help those further down the rungs of society, he would commit himself to the task with as much concern and understanding as he would exhibit in the service of those higher up the ladder. As Grainger was often wont to expound, the law is a spotlight and its glare falls upon us all, no matter what our station.

Bowman forced his attention upon the maid in the chair. She was a mouse of a girl with pale, almost luminescent skin, ginger hair and freckles. She was clearly in much distress, burying her face in her mob cap as she fought to stem her tears. Bowman noticed that her hands shook as she spoke and he felt a spark of pity for the girl.

"I was visitin' me old ma," Hetty sniffed. "She's in service to a family in Farringdon. At about ten of the clock, I was on me way back to Blackfriars." Her voice turned to a barely audible squeak. "And that's when he jumped me."

Grainger gave her an encouraging look.

"I was mindin' me own business, like," Hetty continued, with an effort, "takin' a shortcut, when I saw a gentleman walking towards me."

"A gentleman?" Grainger looked up to Bowman who took a notebook from his pocket.

"He wore a top hat and cape and, at first, he had his head down so as I couldn't see his face. But then he looked up," Hetty's voice broke again, "and I have never seen so horrible a sight." At this, her emotion overcame her and she slumped forward, her head in her hands.

"It's all right, Hetty," Inspector Grainger soothed, kindly. "You are doing well."

"His eyes were ablaze with a green fire!" Hetty bawled, suddenly clutching at the arms of her chair as if in fear for her life.

"It is just as the newspapers have reported the other attacks," Percival Mortimer interjected when she had calmed a little. "Almost word for word," he added, pointedly.

"Mr Mortimer," Grainger replied, testily. "It would be useful if you were to allow me to hear Hetty's story in its fullest form, without fear of interruption." The note of authority in Grainger's voice, together with the reprimanding looks being levelled at him by his wife and daughter were enough to quiet the man. Mortimer took a breath, clearly resolving to be still for now.

"Go on, Hetty," Grainger said.

Hetty steeled herself. "Before I knew it, he was upon me." She dropped her gaze. "He tore at me dress until it was shreds."

Grainger looked up. "Do you still have the dress, Mrs Mortimer?" The lady of the house nodded. "That is well," said Grainger softly as he looked back to the maid. "Much may be learned from the study of evidence."

Bowman scratched dutifully at his notebook.

"His hands were like claws, sharp and cold," Hetty continued.

Percival Mortimer rolled his eyes. "Gloves, perhaps?" he offered, coldly.

Hetty ploughed on in spite of his evident cynicism. "He pushed me to the ground and stopped my mouth with his scarf."

"Did he say anything through all this, Hetty?" Sergeant Bowman asked.

"Not a word." She swallowed. "He went about his work in silence."

Bowman saw Anna's hand lift to her mouth. "And what dreadful work it was," she whispered.

"He took that which I had promised to another!" Hetty collapsed into sobs again while Grainger patted at her hand.

It was clear Mr Percival had heard enough. "If he had hands like claws as you say, Hetty," he breathed, "why is there not a mark upon you."

"There may be any reason why a woman may not fight back under such a circumstance," Bowman heard Anna say. "Shock, fear. Hetty is barely more than a child, you cannot judge her by what an adult may have done, nor a man neither." Her bottom lip trembled with emotion, and Bowman was sure he saw tears in her eyes. He was not used to seeing a young lady being so outspoken, particularly to her own father, but was impressed that it was in defence of another. Despite Mrs Mortimer's earlier protestations, it seemed to the sergeant that she had done well to bring up such a principled young lady.

Inspector Grainger sought to steer the investigation back on course. "Are you betrothed, Hetty?"

"As good as," Hetty nodded through her tears. "Terence and I are on a promise to each other that when we can, we shall marry." The very thought upset her all the more and she was lost to her grief again.

At a glance from Grainger, Bowman nodded. That would explain the footman's apparent discomfort at the turn of events. Clearly, he would rather be the one to comfort his sweetheart, but his station in the household would not permit it.

"You must not blame yourself," Grainger was saying to the maid. "You are no less a woman for what you have lost."

Hetty pulled a handkerchief from her sleeve. Wiping her face of her tears, she found her voice at last. "Thank you, inspector," she said, simply.

"You have not heard the whole of it," muttered Percival beneath his breath.

Inspector Grainger shifted his weight in his chair and fixed the young maid in his gaze. "What more is there Hetty?" he implored. "Did you see the man?"

"I did not, sir," she confessed. "But, when he had… finished…" she swallowed, "he gave the most awful laugh and then he disappeared."

"Disappeared?" Grainger repeated, his forehead creasing in thought.

"Just that, inspector," Hetty replied. "Just like the reports in the papers Mr Mortimer speaks of. I opened me eyes and he was gone in a moment."

There was a silence in the room as she finished her tale. Mrs Mortimer looked at the two detectives expectantly while Anna turned to the fireplace, the better to hide her obvious discomfort. Percival Mortimer merely rolled his eyes again. Suddenly galvanised, Grainger stood and held out a fleshy hand. "Hetty, might I trouble you to show us exactly where you encountered this miscreant?"

"I cannot!" Hetty screamed, suddenly alarmed. "I cannot go back there!" She turned to grab her mistress by the arm. "Please don't make me go back there," she pleaded.

"It's all right, Hetty." Anna was advancing from the fireplace, a kindly smile upon her face. "I shall come with you to see that you come to no harm." She turned to the sergeant with the notebook. "That would be permissible, would it not Sergeant Bowman?"

"Of course," Bowman stuttered. In truth, he was happy to admit of any excuse to prolong his being in her company. From the corner of his eye, he was sure he could see Inspector Grainger smiling, slyly.

"Then, that is settled," Anna smiled. She held out her hands, nodding in encouragement as the maid rose to her feet.

"Thank you, miss."

As the party moved to the door, they were greeted by the imposing form of the footman. Whether or not he had been listening from the hallway, Bowman could not tell, but it was clear he was concerned for his sweetheart.

"It's all right, Terence," Hetty said as she placed her fingers lightly on the buttons of his coat, "These gentlemen and Miss Mortimer are to accompany me to the alley."

Bowman noticed the footman flinch. "Are you sure that's wise, Kitty?" Terence asked, his eyes flitting to Inspector Grainger. "What could be gained by such a visit so soon?"

"It would assist me greatly to see the scene of the crime," Grainger responded, pulling himself up to his full height. "There is no more to be gained from sitting in the drawing room." He turned to Mrs Mortimer. "No matter that it is exceedingly well appointed."

Mrs Mortimer nodded in acknowledgement of the compliment, for compliment it was. Not for the first time, Bowman was impressed at how Grainger could insinuate himself upon anyone of any class without resorting to obsequiousness. He had clearly made an ally of Mrs Mortimer.

The lady of the house turned to her footman. "Terence, would you show them out? I must prepare the drawing room for the morning's business."

Terence gave a curt nod and led the party to the door. As they stepped through the threshold, Bowman noticed a look pass between the footman and the maid that he could not quite understand. Was it a look of warning?

As the sergeant stepped onto the street, he was suddenly aware of how bright the sun was shining. It seemed to hang abnormally low in the sky for the time of year, and Bowman was forced to raise his hands against the light. As Grainger moved away before him, with Anna placing an arm about Hetty's shoulders, the sergeant heard a ringing in his ears. The sun's glare grew ever more intense. He was perplexed to find that, try as he might, he could not move his feet. Inspector Grainger seemed to notice he was not keeping up and turned to chivvy him along.

"The convulsions have stopped," he said in a voice that belonged to someone else. Suddenly confused, Bowman's breath quickened. His habitual frown cut deep into his forehead.

Anna turned to follow the inspector's line of sight. "They were no cause for alarm," she said. Improbably, she spoke with a French accent. "He may be returned to his room."

Just as he was about to give voice to his consternation, Bowman opened his eyes to find he was in the bare brick confines of the Electric Room at Colney Hatch. He was strapped into a chair. Two orderlies busied themselves around him, one wiping the drool from his mouth as the other bent to release the contraption's brakes.

Aristide Aubertin leaned in close, so that, like the light of the sun only moments before, his face filled Bowman's vision. "Welcome back to the world of the living," he chuckled.

As Bowman was wheeled from the room, Aubertin lent to switch off his equipment. He wound the various wires into a coil, deposited them neatly in the box with the battery and decanted the bowls of acidulated water into two large bottles that stood at the table's side. Finally, he gave a satisfied sigh and, his labours completed, reached for his cape and top hat from a hook by the door.

Bowman struggled to make sense of his experience. He felt his head clearing as he lay in his bed, yet still his mind reeled at the results of Aubertin's interventions. It had not seemed like a vision, and yet was too real for a memory. It seemed to Bowman, and he could not pretend to understand the reasons why, that he had experienced a living recollection. Perhaps Aubertin's therapy had jolted his mind into a frenzied state, just as over-cranking an engine might see it run amok. It was a marvel, of that there was no doubt. Bowman had felt the road beneath his shoes, smelt Anna's distinctive perfume as he had entered the Mortimer's drawing room, just as he had all those years ago. With a jolt, he realised he had been afforded the privilege to spend time in her company again. Not as a ghost or vision, but as a memory that seemed as real to him as the orderlies who had helped him to his bed following his return to his room.

Calmed by the cool night air, Bowman wondered why he had been allowed this most precious of gifts. He remembered Aubertin asking if Elizabeth represented a connection to his trauma, if she was linked in some way to the incident that led to Anna's death in Hanbury Street. Bowman had dismissed it, and yet…

Elizabeth had spoken of a man who had leapt over buildings in his escape from George Yard, just as Hetty had described her assailant. Although they were separated by a decade, were the events in Holborn linked to those that had taken place in Blackfriars? Was that the connection that Aubertin had posited? Bowman drifted in and out of a fitful sleep as his mind whirled. What dreams he had were filled with images of a man with blazing eyes and capable of leaping great heights.

He woke with a start at the ringing of the bell. He realised he had kicked the covers off his bed as he had slept. He could feel the cold in his bones. Swinging his feet to the floor, he stripped the sheets from his bed and made a bundle in his arms, ready to deposit them into the laundry chute on his way to the baths. Once there, he was subjected to an examination of his teeth and hair and then the ultimate ignominy of sharing the water with at least a dozen other men.

His ablutions complete, Bowman determined to return to his room to shave before breakfast. As he walked past a line of waiting patients, he felt under scrutiny by patients and staff alike. He saw nudges and sly looks pass between the orderlies. He noticed them dropping their gaze just a little too quickly as he raised his eyes to meet them. And it was then that he noticed. The tremor in the fingers of his right hand, that had been a source of irritation and embarrassment for the best part of a year, had stopped.

The refectory echoed with the sound of chatter. As Bowman carried his porridge to his place at the long table, his thoughts again drifted to his meeting with Elizabeth Morley. She had mentioned calling upon Sergeant Graves with the news of the death at her brother's brewery. Before she could report her concerns, however, Graves had mentioned that Inspector Bowman was to be found at Colney Hatch and, as far as Bowman remembered it, Elizabeth had left at once. So, no one at Scotland Yard knew of the unfortunate man's death at the brewery in Southampton Street, let alone Elizabeth's pursuit of the strangely attired man in George Yard. If Hetty's and Elizabeth's assailant were indeed one and the same man, Graves should be made aware of the fact. Bowman cast his mind back to his previous investigations under the benevolent auspices of Inspector Grainger.

'Jumping Jack' had made his reputation throughout the spring and summer of Eighteen Eighty Two. He had certainly caused much distress to the women he had accosted but, as far as Bowman could remember, he was never suspected of murder. Such a thing seemed to be beyond even his limits. If he had returned, as Bowman suspected, to the streets of London and added murder to his catalogue of crimes, it was certainly a turn for the worse.

Bowman cast his eye around the refectory with a sigh. With its lines of tables and benches stretching the length of the room, the erstwhile inspector felt he was part of some strange reclusive monastery, a sect that held itself remote from the world. A man on the opposite bench chatted to himself inanely as he spooned his porridge into his mouth. His neighbour stared into the middle distance, scratching feverishly at his cheek until it was red raw. If a monastery it was, it was a monastery of madness. How was he to get a message to Graves? He might as well be in another country or another time. As he cast his eyes down in defeat, a thought occurred to him. He leant across to interrupt his babbling neighbour, speaking low so as to avoid the attention of the orderlies.

"What day is it?" Bowman rasped.

His fellow diner paused with his porridge halfway to his mouth, a look of incredulity clouding his features. "I might be mad," he harrumphed, "but I'm not stupid." The man chuckled at his joke. "It's Friday. You can't catch me out." Evidently considering the conversation at an end, the man continued with his wittering.

Unsure whether the man was still conscious of his presence or no, Bowman nodded in thanks anyway, finished his drink of malt and made his way to the library.

XII: In Pursuit Of The Dead

Sergeant Graves leapt from the footplate of the tram as it came to a halt at its designated stop on Camberwell New Road. The morning had brought no let up in the constant drizzle, and so the young sergeant had decided against a hansom cab and availed himself of a tram from Waterloo. This had necessitated a short walk from Scotland Yard to the south bank of the River Thames, but he had walked briskly enough to ward off the cold. Now, as the horse drawn tram slid away towards Camberwell and Peckham, Graves found himself in one of the most notorious areas south of the river. As he walked along Wyndham Road towards Crown Street, he was surrounded by a jumble of houses, all crushed together along the road. A gaggle of children spilled from an open door, their shoeless feet filthy from the pavement. One held out his hand as Graves passed, another cursed him as he walked on by. Each of them seemed to have a pipe in their hand, and the sergeant noticed a bottle of gin being passed between them. A man lay groaning in pain across the entrance by Beckett Street, unheeded by the sorry gaggle of ruffians who fought in their drunkenness further up the road. Knowing that to stop and offer help would be to make himself the victim of an ambush, Graves set his face against the rain and kept on walking. All around him, strange smells rose from the slums. The scent of animal and human ordure assaulted his nostrils and, more than once, he had to step across the road to avoid some ambiguous debris. The rain had made the road a quagmire, but still it teemed with life. Dogs and children ran its length while knots of youths hung on the corners, their eyes narrowing at the approaching stranger in their midst. Graves did his best to avoid their gaze as he turned into Hollington Street.

This seemed hardly the place that a man with an account in his name at the Royal Armitage Bank might call home. Almost every other building was derelict. Broken windows punctuated the filthy walls at intervals, giving Graves something of an insight into the lives that were led within. There was no furniture to speak of in any house that he passed. In one, several sleeping bodies were piled on a ragged mattress. The unmistakable detritus of an opiate addiction littered the floor around them. In another, a child sat bawling on its mother's lap, the woman's glassy eyes staring blankly down at him. The infant was dressed in little more than a filthy sheet even in the cold of an October morning but his mother seemed insensible to his distress.

Graves walked carefully on, passing an alley to his right. He saw that it cut through to the adjacent Sultan Street and boasted a public house on its corner. Its wares, the sergeant mused gravely, were probably the only source of comfort available to the residents of the streets around. Just as he was wondering how he was going to find Golightly's house among the slums around him, he was surprised by a flurry of activity above him.

"Oi!" came a voice. Graves looked up to see a man leaning out of a window, a cheroot dangling from his lips. As far as Graves could see, he was wearing a tattered waistcoat and little else. A procession of poorly drawn tattoos made its way up both his arms. Graves saw a lopsided mermaid and a skull with uneven eyes. "What you want?"

Graves cleared his throat, suddenly feeling entirely ill-equipped to deal with a man of such bearing. "I'm looking for someone," he smiled.

The man nodded. "You won't last five minutes in that getup." He gestured to Graves' smart coat and neckerchief. "You'd better find him quick."

"I'm looking for Thomas Golightly," replied Graves, looking around him for signs of trouble. "Did you know him?"

The man let out a raucous laugh that turned into a rattling cough. "Know him?" he roared. "Golightly was the most hated man on the entire street."

That was some accolade indeed, mused Graves as he looked up and down the rows of battered houses. The rain was running freely from the broken gutters and coursing in rivulets between the bricks. Once on the road, it ran in channels through the mud, mixing the rubbish and such debris as Graves could only guess at into a slop of filth.

"Why?" the young sergeant enquired, carefully. He was usually of a sort that delighted at being out and about. Today,

112

however, he was keen to be on his way and back amongst the comforts of the offices at Scotland Yard.

"He was a thief among thieves," the man confided, "and not to be trusted. I dare say there's no one here that misses him." The tattooed man cleared his throat noisily and let the resultant phlegm fall to the road by Graves' feet.

"Then he was not a man of private means?" Graves could not square how such a man would hold an account at so prestigious a bank.

Another peal of laughter echoed from the window above him. "Private means? I doubt it! If he had private means, then I'm Prince Albert himself." The man cackled as he drew on his cheroot.

Graves nodded.

"John?" came a woman's voice. "Who is it?"

The man turned back into the room. "Someone looking for Thomas Golighty. Remember? He lived over the way, in old ma Crombie's dive."

Graves looked across the road to the house opposite. It was more tumble down than all the rest. From the door that hung off its hinges to the chimney that leaned at an alarming angle upon the roof, it was a picture of dereliction. Barely a single window had any glass in it, and many a pane was boarded up against the elements with scraps of wood and rags. The brickwork was crumbling into the road, and Graves could see an enormous crack spreading across its entire front wall. If old ma Crombie lived in such a place, mused Graves, then her life must be very harsh indeed. He felt a sudden pang of pity for the residents of Hollington Street, but knew their particular circumstances were shared by many across the city. The slums of London were nests of crime, vermin and disease and those that lived among them were subjected to daily horrors. Their brief lives were rounded with fear and ill health such as Sergeant Graves could not imagine.

"How long did he live here in Hollington Street?" the sergeant enquired of the man at the window.

"All my life," the man replied, chewing thoughtfully on his lip. "Until his death some three years ago."

Graves blinked. "Three years ago? Are you sure?"

"'Course I'm sure," the man rasped, suddenly offended. "He died the same year that tram tipped over on Camberwell New Road."

"And what did he die of?"

"Same as most round here, mate. The typhoid got him."

Graves rubbed his chin in thought. The death certificate he had seen at the Royal Armitage Bank had stated Golightly died on the thirteenth day of October. Just under a week ago. Indeed, his Last Will and Testament had been witnessed and signed barely two months before. Graves could come to only one conclusion; that the death certificate had been forged in order to gain access to the bogus account. The sum total of Golightly Holdings' wealth had been left to his supposed physician, the man who had also signed the death certificate. It was in finding Doctor Samson that Graves knew he should now direct his efforts.

As the young sergeant tipped his head in thanks, the tattooed man threw down the sash to his window and retreated back inside the building. Graves felt suddenly vulnerable in such a dissolute neighbourhood, particularly as the fog was starting to drift in from the river. He turned his heels with speed to Camberwell New Road and the tram that would take him back to Scotland Yard.

The journey back to the north bank of the Thames saw Sergeant Graves deep in thought. He would report his findings to Callaghan and perhaps ask for more resources for his inquiries. A constable at least would come in useful. That would mean he could continue in his investigations into the death of Augustus Gaunt as well, despite his having been forbidden to do so by Callaghan.

As Graves crossed Westminster Bridge on foot, he was pleased to see the rain had stopped but now, a blanket of fog had been laid over the city. He cursed as he tripped on a loose stone by the roadside. "Can't see a thing," he muttered to himself. Taking the steps two at a time to the entrance to the building, Graves resolved to keep his findings at The Blackfriar to himself for now, more so his discussions with Doctor Crane. Crane would be bound to mention it to Hicks, of course, but Hicks had seemed so certain Snell was the culprit, Graves doubted he would hurry to discover the doctor's findings. For now, with his knowledge of the wound to the back of Augustus Gaunt's head, Sergeant Graves had the advantage. He would not see Snell go down for a crime he did not commit. As for Snell's assertions that the murderer had simply vanished into the night, well, that was one more mystery to be solved.

The reception hall was busy as usual. Police constables in their uniforms tried in vain to keep a semblance of order, but still the air was full of the hubbub of a restless crowd, with the occasional shout piercing the air. The benches were full of people waiting their turn; a rag-tag collection of different classes, backgrounds and races. Two Chinese men sat patiently alongside a sister of a convent. A young man chatted idly with an elderly gentleman in a top hat. All were hoping to engage the might of the Metropolitan Police Force in their quest for justice.

Graves saw several men and women waving pieces of paper at a distressed Sergeant Matthews. They had no doubt even now hot-footed it from the Royal Armitage Bank in pursuit of reparations. Graves knew they would be disappointed.

Just as he was about to duck through the crowd to the stairs, Sergeant Graves felt a tug at his sleeve.

"Sergeant Graves? Anthony Graves?"

Graves turned to see a young man dressed in a suit of thick tweed. His hair was neatly parted, his shining face was clean-shaven. Graves thought there was something a little *too* particular about his appearance. "I am Sergeant Graves," he confirmed.

The man clasped him even tighter by the arm. Graves could feel his fingers pinching through his sleeve.

"My name is O'Reilly," he announced loudly, his eyes wide. "I have a missive from Inspector Bowman." He pressed an envelope into Graves' hand. "I have lately come from Colney Hatch." He looked around, suddenly ashamed. "I had, of late, made the inspector's acquaintance and he asked that I find you upon my release." O'Reilly swallowed. He had not meant to use the word. "The desk sergeant pointed you out to me."

"Thank you," Graves whispered. He held his breath for a moment to let his heart settle, then looked the young man full in the face. "How is George?" he asked. "How is Inspector Bowman?"

O'Reilly looked away. "He is improving," he said. Graves knew he was either lying or he did not know. He imagined Bowman would most likely keep his own company, much less discuss his progress with fellow patients. He nodded in thanks. It was clear the young man did not wish Graves to lose hope in his friend's recovery.

"Am I to give you something by way of recompense?" Graves reached into his trouser pocket.

"Not at all," O'Reilly shook his head. "I am only pleased to be of use."

The phrase struck Graves as an odd one. "Then am I to send a note in reply?"

"Not by me, at least," O'Reilly stammered. "I hope never to see the place again."

With that, he let go of Graves' arm and weaved his way through the crowd to the exit and the promise of a new life beyond. Graves watched him go with a concerned look. Though O'Reilly had given every indication of being a well-appointed man, it seemed little more than a semblance to sanity. He had betrayed himself with his furtive glances and halting speech. Graves brought himself up short. Which of us, he mused, might not pass for sane if tested?

He was roused from his reverie by the remembrance of the envelope in his hand. Holding it up before him, he could plainly see his name written in Inspector Bowman's distinctive, flowery hand. Looking about him in hopes his meeting had not been noticed, he ducked through a door towards the lost property stores, the better to peruse the contents of the envelope in private. He could not know that, just as he did so, Detective Inspector Ignatius Hicks stepped out from behind Sergeant Matthews' desk. Despite O'Reilly's attempts to contain his excitement, Hicks had heard every word.

XIII: A Patient Writes

My dear Graves,

I can well imagine your surprise at this letter and the manner of its delivery. We did not part on the best of terms, and it must go hard with you that I find myself at Colney Hatch once more due to your actions at Larton. You must rest assured that I thank you for it. Had you been of a mind, I am sure you could have chronicled my condition as well as any doctor here, for you alone saw first hand just how weak my spirit had become. As well as an excellent colleague and a detective of the first order, I am also fortunate to count you as a friend, as I believe you count me as yours. I can only marvel at the fortitude with which you bore my decline and the patience you showed me at every opportunity.

It is to appeal to your undoubted skill as a detective that I write this letter. Some days ago, I received a rare visit to Colney Hatch. In fact, most rare, indeed. You will remember Miss Elizabeth Morley whose father was the victim of a garrotting at his saw mill some months since. Indeed, you told her yourself of my incarceration here, an indiscretion I am willing to bear. I am sure you meant it as a kindness. In point of fact, had you not told her of my condition, Miss Morley might well have told you all she told me; that a strange occurrence at her brother's brewery had brought her to Scotland Yard.

It seems that some time last week, an employee of her brother's was victim to an unfortunate accident at the workshop. On the very night of the accident, Miss Morley herself chanced to pass by the establishment on Southampton Street, Holborn, whereupon she saw a well-dressed man make his way from the shop in haste. Thinking it odd that such a thing should happen at so late an hour, she demanded that her cabbie give chase into Little Queen Street. There, it was discovered that the man had disappeared. It was Miss Morley's contention that he had leapt the nearby buildings to effect his escape, a notion which I initially dismissed as fanciful.

It is here, my dear Graves, that I must beg your indulgence.

117

Since my meeting with Miss Morley, certain cases have resolved themselves in my memory. The fog of Time has been lifted. Some ten years ago, I served beneath an Inspector Grainger, in whose company I investigated the sightings of a man who became known, by the popular Press at least, as 'Jumping Jack'. Throughout the duration of a summer, he preyed upon young women throughout the city and then went to ground. He was described as being of a demonic appearance, with blazing eyes and breath of fire, all of which are, of course, highly improbable. Despite Grainger's best efforts and energies, he was never caught and has not been heard of until this week.

Miss Morely's description could certainly fit the man from my investigations of a decade ago. I feel I owe her something due to my association with her, not least in light of the loss of her father which I am sure has left her somewhat bereft. I should be grateful if you could investigate on my behalf, as indisposed as I am. A visit to her brother at Southampton Street might serve to throw some light upon the matter, but I shall, of course, leave the investigation to your own discretion and your very capable hands.

Sincerely yours,

George

Sergeant Graves had found a chair in the corner of the lost property store and angled the letter into the light from the large window. Surrounded by the shelves of boxes that lined the room, he had felt safe enough to open the envelope far from prying eyes. Having read the letter, he let his eyes wander to the bare trees through the window. Their skeletal branches tapped against the window in the wind, giving the eerie impression that they were trying to get in.

Graves leaned back in his chair and read the letter again. It was the most extraordinary thing to have heard from his erstwhile colleague in Colney Hatch. He could only imagine under what circumstances the letter had been written, and only guess at Bowman's condition at the time. It seemed somewhat rushed, but the details were pertinent indeed. The similarities to Snell's altercation at the printing works and Bowman's investigations with Simeon Grainger were plain to see, with one exception; that Jack had not committed murder before. If his appearances at Ludgate and Holborn were an indication of his return, they were also an indication of an escalation in his ambition. Sergeant Graves was not old enough to remember Jack's previous appearances, but the description seemed similar enough, and with the possibility of his striking at the brewery on Holborn, he had already killed two people in as many days.

Suddenly sensing that time was of the essence, Graves swung himself from the chair and headed for the door, only to be confronted by the mountain of a man that was Ignatius Hicks. Graves noticed he was out of breath, a sure indication that he had been in something of a hurry.

"Ah, Graves!" he panted. "Callaghan wishes to see us in his office."

Clearly in the belief that what his sorry lungs needed most was the influx of noxious smoke, Hicks struck a match against the doorframe and lit the bowl of his pipe. Graves narrowed his eyes with suspicion. Hicks had clearly seen him enter the stores. How else had he known he was within? And, judging from the beads of sweat that sprung from his forehead, he had plainly been somewhere else in the meantime. He hazarded a guess that it was to see Callaghan himself, but why?

"Of course," Graves demurred, cheerfully. "I need to see him myself." He clapped his colleague across the shoulder. "There have been some interesting developments in my investigations at the Royal Armitage Bank."

Inspector Hicks blew smoke about him as he spoke, his great beard bristling. "I am certain he will be most interested," he purred. Stepping aside, he let Graves walk before him through the crowded reception hall to the stairs beyond.

Detective Superintendent Callaghan was, as ever, immaculate. He stood gazing out over The Thames like an eagle in its eerie, ever watchful for prey. The fog that had plagued the city every evening for days was beginning to settle along the river. The lamplighters were out along the Victoria Embankment, although what light they produced was soon swallowed in the muffling gloom. Callaghan rested his hands in the small of his back. His handsome face was granite and his posture gave nothing away. He presented a studied picture of solid immutability. It had taken him years to perfect it. Patting a stray hair into place, he took a breath so deep that his chest strained at the buttons on his waistcoat. He was disappointed in Anthony Graves. The young sergeant had overreached himself. Such behaviour could not be tolerated if the Detective Division was to maintain its reputation as a professional force. It had already been dealt one blow with Inspector Bowman's very public fall from grace. It could not afford another.

There was a knock at the door. Callaghan waited, deliberately, for another knock before he responded.

"Come in," he barked, feigning irritation. In truth, he was expecting the two men who entered.

Inspector Hicks closed the door behind them. For the second time in as many days, Graves found himself in his superior's office, certain that trouble would follow.

"Detective Sergeant Graves," Callaghan began, benignly, still at the window, "I know life for you at Scotland Yard has changed." Graves blinked. "But change," the detective superintendent continued, "is the one constant in life."

Graves was conscious of Inspector Hicks shifting his weight behind him. He could practically hear him breathing. At last, Callaghan turned from the window. Graves saw his features were set more sternly than ever.

"Change, by its very nature," he began again, "can be disconcerting. It may leave us feeling adrift, untethered."

Graves wasn't sure where Callaghan was leading him, but he didn't like the sound of it one bit.

"Is that how you feel here, Sergeant Graves?" Callaghan spat his words as if they had left a taste in his mouth.

Graves looked back at his colleague. Hicks stood with his hands on his hips, attempting to affect an air of nonchalance. The bluff inspector looked around the room at the bookcases, potted plants and fine furniture in an effort to avoid making eye contact.

"No, sir," the young sergeant replied, truthfully.

"Because, you see, Sergeant Graves," Callaghan continued regardless, "Scotland Yard isn't for everybody, and not everybody is for Scotland Yard." Detective Superintendent Callaghan walked slowly towards the young sergeant. Graves was reminded of a cat stalking its quarry. Stopping immediately before him, Callaghan held out his hand.

"The letter, if you please."

Graves heard Hicks cough behind him. The inspector had never been one to hide his discomfort easily. The young sergeant held Callaghan's gaze as he reached for the envelope in his pocket. Smoothing it between his fingers, he held it out for the detective superintendent. Callaghan resumed his place at the window as he read its contents. Graves was certain he noticed his shoulders stiffening considerably.

At last Callaghan turned. He held the letter aloft between a thumb and forefinger. "Most touching," he said between gritted teeth.

Graves stood his ground. "It was an unexpected pleasure to hear from him."

The corner of Callaghan's mouth curled into something approaching a sneer. "Of course, it is not your place to investigate the death at the brewery in Holborn. Your remit lies with the investigation into the Royal Armitage Bank."

Graves nodded, urgently. "And I have much news to that end."

Callaghan raised his eyebrows and lowered himself expectantly into his chair.

"It appears," Graves continued, bravely, "that an account was set up fraudulently in the name of a Mr Thomas Golightly of Hollington Street, Kennington. The real Mr Golightly died some three years ago, yet his death certificate, presented at the closing of the account and the withdrawal of funds, states his death was just four days ago." Callaghan was eyeing him curiously, Graves noticed as he blustered on. "In the meantime, there's many a desperate man fallen victim to a scheme devised to extract the maximum amount of money on the promise of receiving it back many times. Many have got poorer as a result, whilst one man, it seems, has grown richer. I suspect that man is the doctor, one Frederick Solomon, who signed the fraudulent death certificate using the details of a man who died without consequence some years ago." Graves felt he was a train running out of track. As he reached his conclusion, he took a breath to steel himself. In that moment, he thought he saw a flicker of something in Callaghan's eyes. What was it? Recognition?

When at last the superintendent spoke, it was with the tone of a tired tutor to a recalcitrant pupil. "And did your investigations into this case take you to Doctor Crane at Charing Cross Hospital?" Callaghan sat back in his chair.

Graves swallowed. "They did not," he admitted.

"Did they take you to Mr Temperance Snell in the cells at Cloak Lane?"

"No, sir."

Callaghan waved Bowman's letter before him. "And are you now to investigate a death at a brewery in Holborn on the whim of a madman?"

Graves thought carefully before he spoke. "Inspector Bowman has my respect as a fellow detective and my respect as a friend."

Callaghan nodded, thoughtfully. "Just how long have you held the rank of detective sergeant, Graves?" he asked.

"Some five years, sir."

Callaghan was rising now, a threatening tone in his voice. "And, in all those years, how many times have you ignored direct instructions from your superior?"

"Not once that I remember, sir."

"Not once," echoed Callaghan, "until now." Planting his fists on his desk, he leaned forward and threw the letter across the table to the sergeant. "I gave you explicit instructions not to pursue your investigations into the death at Gibson's Printing Works, but rather to leave the matter in the capable hands of Detective Inspector Hicks." As before, Callaghan was careful to emphasise Hicks' rank. "You ignored that instruction, did you not?"

Graves could feel his heart racing.

"In fact, you openly flouted my direction, opting instead to conduct your own interviews with the suspect and the presiding doctor. All unsupervised, and all without authorisation."

"Yes, sir," Graves whispered. So Hicks had told him everything. He flicked his eyes to his companion. Ignatius Hicks was puffing furiously on his pipe, his eyes cast down to the floor.

"Such insubordination might well be grounds for demotion, Detective Sergeant Graves."

Graves flinched under Callaghan's penetrating gaze. The detective superintendent was waiting for just such a reaction and seized upon it as an indication of weakness.

"I need trustworthy men about me, Sergeant Graves," he hissed. "I need men who get results. Are you such a man?"

Graves nodded, slowly. "I am such a man, sir." He remembered how Callaghan had singularly failed to gather trustworthy men about him during his time with the Special Irish Branch. One of the men beneath him, Ichabod Sallow, had proven to be in league with the Kaiser, a gangland overlord not above extortion, blackmail and murder. The experience had burnt Callaghan badly. It was clearly not a mistake he was prepared to make again.

"Then I shall trust you to keep to your course. Leave the investigation at the printing works to Inspector Hicks and direct your attentions to finding this Doctor Solomon. This is the second time I have directed you to do so. I trust I have made myself plain this time."

Graves cleared his throat. "You have, sir."

Callaghan pointed to the letter on the desk. "And I would ask you to bring any further communication with Inspector Bowman to me. He is clearly not in full possession of his wits." Graves heard an ill-tempered harrumph from Hicks. "He is certainly in no position to suggest what my detectives may or may not do with their time."

"Understood, sir."

Callaghan nodded, certain he had made his point. "Now,

Inspector Hicks," he said, turning to the portly detective by the door, "what news from Cloak Lane Police Station?"

Caught unawares, Hicks pulled the pipe from his mouth. A great plume of smoke came with it that drifted to the ceiling like a cloud. "My interview with Temperance Snell went just as I might have predicted. Armed as I was with certain knowledge of his past, I was able to present a full case against him with regard to the death of Augustus Gaunt." Hicks was blowed if he was going to mention the reports, or the strange circumstances under which they had fallen into his possession. "He as good as admitted it."

Graves knew he was lying.

"A confession?" Callaghan looked impressed.

Hicks twisted his pipe in his hands, nervously. "There will be," he said. "In time."

Just as Callaghan was about to congratulate his detective inspector, there came a knock at the door.

"Come in," Callaghan barked, irritably. Hicks stood aside to admit Sergeant Matthews. He clearly sensed an atmosphere in the room.

"Begging your pardon," the desk sergeant began, "but you might want to let your man in Cloak Lane go free."

Hicks' eyebrows raised almost comically on his forehead. "What the blazes?" he blustered.

"There's been another murder overnight," Matthews announced, sombrely. "A man found dead in Farringdon with one witness saying they saw the murderer flee."

"Let me guess," Callaghan sighed. "Did he wear a hat and cape and effect his escape in leaps and bounds?" He reached up to smooth his hair in a gesture Graves felt was entirely designed to hide his distress.

"He did that," Matthews confirmed, "if the witness is to be believed."

Sergeant Graves looked at Hicks. He was blowing his cheeks out in his exasperation at the news, lost for words.

"Yet Temperance Snell has been in the cells at Cloak Lane all night," Graves said, as innocently as he could.

Matthews was still at the door. "Oh, and The Evening

Standard have got wind." He held up a copy of the evening's newspaper. Graves could clearly read the headline, written in large type across the entire front page; 'JACK IS BACK!' Beneath the text was an expert drawing of a demonic figure with blazing eyes. He was otherwise dressed as a gentleman but, improbably, he was pictured as if in flight, the rooftops of London at his feet. 'Yard caught on the hop!' ran the text beneath.

Graves snatched at the paper to read the details, only to be served with a withering look from his superior.

"Sergeant Graves," Callaghan rasped, "I expect you are keen to be about your business."

Graves relented, rolling up the newspaper and sliding it pointedly in his inside jacket pocket.

Callaghan rubbed a hand across his chiselled jaw. "Very well, Matthews," he sighed. "Send Inspector Crouch to question the witness and identify the suspect if he can. He'll need a constable or two, no doubt."

Matthews gave a curt nod and left the room at a brisk pace. Callaghan turned to Inspector Hicks, his lower lip trembling in an effort to control himself. "Inspector Hicks," he began, a strand of hair falling from its place to dangle over an ear, "have Temperance Snell released at once and make your way to the brewery on Southampton Street as Inspector Bowman has suggested." It was as if it hurt him to say the words. "Let's try and join the dots, shall we?"

A rather chastened Inspector Hicks jammed his hat upon his head, took a last draw on his pipe and lumbered after the desk sergeant, snatching at Bowman's letter as he left. Callaghan turned and made his way to the window, deep in thought. A blanket of fog had descended over the river obscuring everything on the furthest bank. With a final look to his superior, Graves reasoned the meeting was over. Thinking the better of saying anything else he slipped quietly from the room, closing the door behind him with a soft click.

XIV: The Chalk Map

George Bowman was feeling restless. To calm his frenzy, he determined to spend some time in the asylum's gymnasium. It was a large, airy room, open to the rafters in the ceiling. Two or three patients were dotted about the place, each attending to their preferred exercise in solitude. Bowman knew that larger classes were also held every day. He had not thought to attend them, preferring instead the rigours of tending to the gardens and allotments in the grounds. He stood at the door for the first time, surveying the scene. Bars and ropes lined the walls and strange contraptions were crowded into one end. Bowman spotted a horizontal inclination machine and resolved to test its capabilities. Sitting down on a large, padded mattress, he reached for the handle in the wall. It was attached to a rope that, in turn, was tied to a weight by way of a pulley that was housed behind a wooden panel. He leaned back to pull at the handle and felt the weight lifting behind the panel. He relaxed, letting the rope pull him back to the wall, then applied himself again. The whole action reminded him of rowing a skiff.

He tired after several minutes and looked around him for some other distraction. In a far corner, a large man was repeatedly lifting a heavy medicine ball above his head. His face grew red each time he did so, and a vein stood out upon his forehead that looked fit to burst with the pressure. Another patient of more slight stature was in the midst of performing a sequence of jumps and squats. Bowman noticed him scolding himself for his performance at the end of each repetition and, alarmingly, slapping repeatedly at his own face.

His head low so as not to make eye contact, Bowman sloped from the hall to pace the corridors beyond. He soon found himself outside the kitchens. Peering round the door, he saw great vats of boiling meat and vegetables bubbling on a long range. A team of kitchen porters, all dressed in the soiled aprons of their trade, stirred and agitated the broth, tasting it with greasy spoons and adding more stock where required.

Bowman looked around him with caution. He knew he had

strayed into an area of the asylum that was ordinarily forbidden to patients, although a handful of the more subdued among them was chosen every week to help with the chores in the kitchens.

Bowman marvelled how he had been left alone for much of his stay. Aside from the requisite treatments he had been subjected to, not once had he been coerced into a daily exercise routine or helping with some mundane task in the workshops. He knew there were teams of men employed every day to weave baskets to the rear of the building. These were sold for use in the markets and shops of the city, and Bowman understood the men were even paid for their labours. Others still were put to work maintaining the building itself. Under guidance from the master of works and his assistant, they might find themselves painting walls or, as Bowman had seen over the past few weeks, even building them. Every day, teams of the most trustworthy patients were cajoled into the grounds and tasked with planting trees or felling them, raking the great lawns of leaves or dredging the pond of its weed.

Bowman had been left to his own devices. It had been much the same during his first stay last year. Coupled with the luxury of having been afforded a room to himself, he couldn't help but think some unseen hand was at work to make his life as comfortable as possible. As a result, he was free to spend his time how he chose. Within these walls and far from the world, he dared to believe he might be recovering from his ordeal at Larton. Perhaps Monsieur Aubertin was to be thanked for that. Could it be that, after only one application, his Galvanic Therapy was proving efficacious?

Bowman left the cooks to their spoiling of the evening meal and made his way back to his room. As he walked, he couldn't help but turn over in his mind the salient points presented by his investigation with Inspector Grainger. The memory had indeed been most vivid, and he felt he could recall it almost perfectly. In particular, he was struck by the location of Hetty's encounter with the masked man. Was there something in it? As a younger detective sergeant, he had been unable to spot the link between Jack's previous appearances and his latest in Blackfriars. Could they have some bearing on the murder at the brewery in

Holborn? Bowman passed a storeroom on his route and peered absently inside as he walked. Sacks of flour, sugar and other comestibles were stacked carefully inside, alongside large chests marked 'Tea' and 'Malt'. A blackboard hung on the wall where each item in the room was listed by weight. Several pieces of chalk lay on a small ledge at the bottom. A sudden thought presenting itself to him, Bowman tripped quietly through the door to retrieve a stick of chalk. He slipped back into the corridor outside just an orderly puffed his way around the corner, a large sack resting on each shoulder. Bowman kept his gaze to the floor as he skulked past, slipping the chalk into his trouser pocket and wiping the dust from his fingers onto his jacket lapels.

As he walked back to his room, Bowman noticed that, despite the day being young, many patients had retired to their beds. The wards off the main corridors seemed almost full. Soon the bell would ring for the exercise hour and the residents would be required to move as one to the airing courts. Bowman knew he wouldn't be missed. With a few hours to spare before his next encounter with Monsieur Aubertin, he was determined to make the best of the time.

There was an aspect of Miss Morley's case that was troubling him. It was a slippery thing and the more Bowman reached for it, the more it eluded him. What further connections were there between Jack's appearance to Hetty the maid in Blackfriars and Elizabeth's confrontation in Holborn? He remembered Grainger mentioning further incidents, too. What linked them all? Bowman opened the door to his room, conscious of the fact that the best place for him to think was currently unavailable to him; his office at Scotland Yard. Closing the door behind him, Bowman drew the stick of chalk from his pocket. If he couldn't go to his office, then he must bring his office here.

Carefully moving a small table to the centre of the room, Bowman stood and faced the blank wall before him. This, he mused, would have to do. He closed his eyes. Slowly, he moved his hands in the air before him, trying to engage the one thing a good detective must possess; his imagination. Seemingly satisfied, he suddenly snapped his eyes open and approached the blank wall before him. With wide sweeps of his hand, he drew two wavy lines across the entire length of the room. Running parallel to each other, they meandered their way from left to right. As they approached the furthest end of the wall, so they diverged a little, the space between them now measuring several inches. Bowman stood back to admit his handy work. The distinctive loops and basins were a perfect representation of the River Thames as it ran through London. Next, he marked the bridges from east to west; from Tower Bridge and London Bridge to Southwark, Westminster and Chelsea Suspension Bridge to Battersea, Wandsworth, Putney and Hammersmith. With a swoop of his chalk, he marked the great stations; Euston, Waterloo and Paddington, and the lines that ran between them and from them in a web around the city.

He closed his eyes again, imagining himself at Scotland Yard. He was in his office, facing the map on his wall. He could practically smell the wood panelling on the wall behind it, feel the sun on his back from the window. He let his mind's eye fall upon the map, its landmarks and edifices. With a sudden burst of energy, he transcribed them onto the wall in chalk; Trafalgar Square, St Paul's, Covent Garden and the Palaces of Westminster. He willed them into existence before him. He filled in the roads and the smaller lanes that ran from the main thoroughfares. Every alley and shortcut, each yard and cul-de-sac, all were represented. The larger thoroughfares were shaded, the Victoria Embankment to the south, Euston Road to the north. Even individual buildings were included. The great churches he knew, of course; Southwark Cathedral, St Martin in the Fields, St Mary-le-Bow, St Dunstable and All Saints, but he also marked the locations of Public Houses, workhouses and factories. Some roads that he knew well were divided into discrete dwellings with outbuildings and gardens. Some streets were represented with such detail that Bowman could almost imagine himself walking down them. The great London parks were filled in with blocks of colour and even particular trees were remembered; a line of elms that grew in St James' Park, an impressive oak that thrived on the banks of the Regents Canal. Finally, he marked the sites of recent investigations;

Highgate Cemetery, St Saviour's Dock, Hampstead Heath, St John's Wood.

Bowman had been so intent upon his task, that he had not noticed the shadows moving around his room as the afternoon progressed. The sum total of his exertions was that, as he stood in the middle of the room, his sleeves rolled up to his elbow and his collar undone, he was faced with as near a representation of London as could be imagined. Bowman smiled and scratched at his head. Only now could he apply himself to the investigation at hand. Stepping forward again, he marked the locations he could remember Grainger mentioning in Essex Street all those years ago. Thanks to Aubertin's application of electricity, they were now at the forefront of his memory. Reaching up, he made a cross on the map at Angler's Place in Camden and another at St Pancras Old Church. Both were sites where, a decade ago, Jack had made himself known. Lastly, Bowman placed another cross in Holborn, just west of the viaduct. Southampton Street. The location of Roger Morley's brewery where, just three days ago, Jack had returned.

Seemingly pleased at his afternoon's work, Bowman lay what was left of the chalk upon the table and clapped the dust from his hands. He was sure the answer lay on the design before him but, for now, he could not see where. He had once thought of the map on his office wall as a tyranny. Now, he thanked the hours that he had spent before it. If the whole of London could be held within the confines of this little room at Colney Hatch, he mused, perhaps the city could be tamed. And perhaps Jack could be caught.

Lost as he was in his reverie, Bowman was suddenly startled by the door to his room being thrown open. Two orderlies stood in the corridor outside, bemused looks upon their faces. They stared at the improvised map on Bowman's wall, clearly in thrall to its detail.

"It is time to meet with Aubertin," said one. He stood aside to reveal the contraption to which Bowman would be secured for his journey to the basement. Casting a glance back at his map, the inspector nodded in submission. He was missing a few details in Hetty's confrontation with the fiend at Blackfriars. If

Aubertin's therapy could reveal the precise location of the attack upon the maid, it could then be marked upon the map and, perhaps, bring Bowman one step nearer to enlightenment.

XV: Trouble Brewing

Boulter's Brewery was a small, ornamental edifice of dark red brick. Its crenelated walls and gothic styled windows marked it out among the more utilitarian properties around it, giving it the appearance of a building much older than its thirty years. In all that time, it had been a brewery. Its fortunes had risen and fallen as the taste for old fashioned porter had declined, such that many of its outbuildings had been sold off for workshops. The workforce had shrunk by some forty or so employees since its heyday, leaving just a dozen or so to man its equipment. Boulter's produced dark, mild ales. The grain was received each morning, then placed in tuns to steep with water to make a mash. The resultant mild ale was kept in barrels made on site and sold in turn to the surrounding public houses.

"I thought I had bought myself a going concern," Roger Morley announced as he led Inspector Hicks around the brewery. "I had not considered that the previous owners might have been a little less than honest on their balance sheet." He nodded to the portly inspector, knowingly. "My lawyers have matters in hand."

Morley was an upright man with a condescending stare. He looked at the world through hooded eyes that nestled beneath a pair of beetle brows. With his smart coat and silver-tipped cane, he gave every appearance of being the successful businessman.

It hadn't taken Hicks long to forget his initial reticence at being sent to Holborn. An hour spent at a brewery seemed to him the perfect way to spend the time.

"And this is where your unfortunate employee was found?" he asked.

They had stopped before a great wooden vat covered in metal hatches. Hicks breathed deep of the sweet, malty air emanating from the mash within.

"Quite so, inspector," Roger replied, "though I must say it seems to me nothing more than an unfortunate accident."

"But your sister - " Hicks began.

"My sister," interrupted Roger Morley, "has something of a

vivid imagination. A fact to which anyone who has spent more than a moment in her company will attest."

Hicks nodded as he smoothed his great beard with a fat hand. "Is that why you did not report the death?"

"I did not wish to have Scotland Yard involved, Inspector Hicks." Morley shrugged. "I see it is too late now."

"You saw nothing suspicious in the death?"

Morley shook his head. "Suspicious?" He gave a sardonic laugh. "Inspector, forgive me. I have spent the last three years in the Princely state of Pudukkottai in India. Life hangs by a thread in such places. One acquires a special understanding of the fragile nature of things."

Inspector Hicks narrowed his eyes. Morley leaned in.

"I saw such things in those three years, inspector, that would freeze your very marrow." He clapped the inspector on the back with a laugh. "In short, I have spent much time in a country where death is commonplace and accidents such as this, unremarkable." He leaned across to lift one of the hatches on the mash tun. "We exist at the fortunate end of the scale, inspector. We have become soft. We have forgotten that, as comfortable as we may be at the heart of the Empire, accidents still happen." Reaching up to a shelf, Roger plucked an earthenware jug from a hook and plunged it into the vat before him. Scooping up the mash, he held the steaming jug before him with a look of pride, then waved it under Hicks' nose.

"The mash is heated here, inspector. The resultant wort will then be boiled with hops in the copper." Hicks dipped a finger obligingly into the jug and licked at the sticky liquid. It had a musty, malty taste that was not altogether unpleasant.

Replacing the jug, Morley slid open a large wooden door and led Hicks through to another room dominated by a row of large copper vessels. They rested on bases of ceramic tiles, wherein Hicks could hear the roar of a hot fire. "Finally, the yeast is added and the wort will be left to settle before being aged and conditioned in the casks you see around you." He turned to wave to a line of barrels stacked along one side of the room. "The result will be ambrosia from the very heavens."

As interesting as all this was, Hicks was keen to direct the discussion back to the death of the man in the mash tun.

"Why was he left to work here alone?"

"He wasn't." Roger Morley sighed. "There were others in the building, but they were at work in other areas. One in the cask workshop, two in the grain store and one in here with the coppers."

"Then," replied Hicks, "the entrance to the brewery was left open?"

"Of course, inspector," Morley laughed. "I am not in the habit of making prisoners of my employees!"

"And no one saw a thing?"

"Worsnip discovered the poor man afloat in the vat. It was quite a temperature too, so you can guess at the state of the body."

Hicks suddenly coughed at the taste of the mash in his mouth. He hoped the tun had been cleaned since. Morley held up a finger and beckoned to a small, stringy looking man in felt trousers and a waistcoat.

"Yes, Mr Morley, sir?" The man looked up at his employer from beneath the brim of his cap in much the same way, noted Hicks, that a puppy might look at his master.

"This is Inspector Hicks from Scotland Yard, Worsnip. He is looking into Tobias Dankworth's death."

Worsnip wiped the sweat from his forehead and tugged at his cap in deference. Hicks noticed there was something hesitant in his manner as he spoke.

"He was found there, sir, in the mash tun. Boiled like a kipper, he was."

Even Hicks blanched at the image. "How long had Dankworth worked here, Worsnip?"

"Couple of months, no more," Worsnip stammered. "Just passing through as far as I could see."

"Passing through?" Hicks narrowed his eyes.

Worsnip dropped his eyes to the floor. "There was talk among the men that he was a fella with a past."

"What kind of past?" Hicks was about to lean a hand against one of the huge kettles when he felt the heat of the copper and thought better of it.

"Gossip only, I am sure, Inspector Hicks," Morley interjected. "Pay no heed to the idle tongues of the men."

Hicks ignored him, pointedly. "Go on, Worsnip."

Worsnip looked around him and lowered his voice to a whisper. Quite who he thought might be listening, Hicks had no idea. "Word was he was on the run from the law, having got into trouble a few years back, Shoreditch way."

Hicks sniffed, thoughtfully. "Did you see anyone else in the brewery or hereabouts that night, Worsnip?"

Worsnip seemed to lose himself in thought, as if he was wrestling with some great conundrum. Finally, he lifted a finger. "I did not," he announced.

Morley had clearly heard enough. "Thank you, Worsnip. Let us not keep you from your work."

Worsnip tugged at his cap again and backed away in almost comical deference to his employer.

"So," blustered Hicks, "it would seem Dankworth received nothing more than his just deserts."

Morley rounded on the inspector. "Is Scotland Yard now in the habit of believing everything it hears, including idle tittle tattle?"

Hicks reached for his pipe. "Mr Morley," he began, "could you tell me where you were on the night of Dankworth's death?"

"I was at my late father's house, Inspector Hicks. I hesitate to call it home." Morley looked suddenly downcast.

"Of course," Hicks mumbled, guiltily. "You have my condolences." He had read Bowman's letter in the cab to Holborn.

"It is quite one thing to lose a father, Inspector Hicks," Morley said, sadly, "but to lose him in such a way…" He turned from the inspector as if to hide the emotion in his face. "I will leave you to look around, Inspector Hicks. Ask what you will of whomsoever you choose. I shall be in my manager's office." He gestured towards a door in the corner of the room that led into a room with a fine view of the brewery floor.

"Very well," Hicks replied. "I shall be sure to let you know when I am on my way."

Morley waved in acknowledgement as Hicks turned his attentions back to the thin man in the cloth cap.

"Mr Worsnip," he called. "Might I trouble you for a word?"

Worsnip took a breath and gestured that the inspector might join him through a door to the workshop beyond. As Hicks ambled into the room behind the man, a new scent assaulted his senses; the smell of wood. Piles of shavings littered the floor at his feet and stacks of a pale wood were arranged on shelves around him.

Worsnip busied himself at a work bench, tightening a metal belt around a small wooden barrel.

"You make the casks here?" Hicks asked in surprise.

"I'm a cooper by trade, sir," Worsnip replied. "Part of Mr Morley's drive to reduce costs." He spun the barrel before him, checking each join for cracks. "If he has the casks made here, he doesn't have to pay some other man for the effort."

Hicks had reached out for a piece of wood from a shelf and held it up before him.

"Trouble is," continued Worsnip, "he's cuttin' corners with the wood."

Hicks raised his eyebrows, questioningly.

"It's inferior quality, sir." Worsnip shook his head, sadly. "And it'll taint the beer something terrible."

Satisfied with his work, he swung the cask to the floor and, rather irritably Hicks thought, snatched the lump of wood from the inspector's hands. He placed it in a clamp on his workbench and, after bending to look carefully along its length, reached out for a plane from a set of tools on a shelf. Hicks looked the man up and down. There was something about him that he did not trust. It had been there in his reticence to speak at the mash tun and his unwillingness to look the detective in the eye.

"Mr Worsnip," Hicks asked, slowly, "why did you not tell me it was you that found Dankworth's body?"

Worsnip suddenly stopped mid-task, his plane poised just above the length of wood before him. "I had nothing to do with his death," he insisted suddenly.

Hicks leaned in. "Then you have nothing to fear," he said, simply.

"But I am afraid," Worsnip admitted, his lip trembling. "I make a living here that keeps me, my wife and children. It gives me a roof above my head and a place I can call home." He eyed Hicks. "Though nothing a detective would call grand, I 'spose. I cannot afford to lose it, nor be tainted by a crime I did not commit."

Hicks leant on the table. "No one is accusing you of anything." He took a breath. "Yet," he added, pointedly.

"I've heard about you Scotland Yarders," Worsnip snivelled, "and I don't approve of your methods."

Hicks raised his eyebrows. "Methods?"

Worsnip gave full vent to his misgivings. "I know of too many who have found themselves in the wrong place at the wrong time and hanged as a result."

Unusually, Hicks was lost for words.

"So, you are right, Inspector Hicks. I am afraid. I am afraid that telling you I found the body makes me a suspect."

"What preposterous nonsense," blustered Hicks. "Where on Earth did you hear that?"

Worsnip rolled his eyes. "Your reputation precedes you," he sighed.

Hicks struggled to regain his composure. "Mr Worsnip," he said with exaggerated politeness, "if you know anything of Tobias Dankworth that might assist me in my investigations, you must declare them." He cast his gaze to the office in the corner, just visible through the door to the workshop. "Or, indeed," he added, carefully, "of Roger Morley."

Worsnip seemed to hesitate a moment before acquiescing. Brushing the sawdust from his trousers, he walked to the door and slid it slowly shut.

"Boulter's brewery is in trouble," he said, quietly.

"How so?" Hicks replied.

Worsnip removed his cap and wiped the sweat from his forehead with the back of his hand. "We cannot compete with the bigger breweries," he sighed. "They operate at such a scale they have cornered the market in the best materials." He waved his hand around the room as he spoke. "This wood is the best we can get, but it ain't good enough. Same goes for the grain and the hops." He lowered his voice still further. "Business is falling as a result, and I do not think we can survive the week."

Hicks nodded. Despite appearances, it seemed Roger Morley wasn't quite the successful businessman he presented himself to be. The inspector blew air between his teeth as he considered the implications of Worsnip's remarks.

"That might explain why Morely was reluctant to call upon the Yard."

Worsnip nodded. "Such a scandal might well put paid to Boulter's for good. Its reputation would be lost."

Hicks saw the enormity of the brewery's predicament in Worsnip's eyes. "Would you not find employment with the larger breweries?" he asked in all innocence. "You know your trade, after all." He cast his eye around the workshop at the array of tools that seemed to adorn every surface. There were hammers and saws, of course, but other, stranger tools whose use Hicks could only guess at.

"They're all my own," Worsnip announced, proudly. "That set of awls belonged to my father and his father before him." He gestured to a set of wooden-handled tools that rested in a rack at the furthest end of the bench. Each had a metal spike of varying lengths protruding from its base with a tip that was sharpened to a point. Hicks noticed the burnished handles shone with a patina that spoke of generations of use. "But labour is plentiful, inspector. And there are men far younger than me nipping at my heels."

Hicks reached instinctively for the pipe in his pocket. "What does the state of Mr Morley's business have to do with the death of Tobias Dankworth, Mr Worsnip?"

"That, Inspector Hicks, is a matter for Scotland Yard." With that, Worsnip rached for an awl and proceeded to score a mark in the wood before him. Hicks nodded to himself. The interview was clearly at an end.

Inspector Hicks filled the bowl of his pipe as he watched Worsnip at work. Having scored the wood, the cooper took a hand drill to make a hole. At this, Hicks took a final, redundant look around the workshop and turned on his heels. As he made his way back through the brewery to the entrance, he was certain he caught a glimpse of Roger Morley through the glass of his manager's office. He did not look a happy man.

XVI: Remembrance Of Things Past

The Watergate made for a grand egress from Essex Street. Almost as one, the small party raised their eyes to appreciate the scale of the monument. Even Anna Mortimer, Bowman noticed, though she had surely passed beneath its arch many times, tipped her head to take in its majesty. In doing so, she afforded Bowman with a view of her exquisite neck. For a moment he was lost.

"I never tire of it, Sergeant Bowman," Anna declared as they emerged into Milford Lane. "Though not for its architectural glory." Bowman noticed she had a pleasing cadence to her voice. He was in thrall to her. "It is a reminder to me of just how divided we are. That such a thing was built simply to shield the better off from the poor should give us pause, don't you think?" She turned her clear eyes upon him.

Bowman swallowed. He felt his neck burning beneath his collar. "I had not considered it," he stammered, awkwardly.

"And why should you?" She seemed almost disappointed. "Much of our society is built around division. You yourself are a beneficiary of such a system."

Bowman struggled to follow her argument. "In what way?" he panted.

"In that you are a man, Detective Sergeant Bowman. A woman's lot is a very different one indeed."

"There is a woman upon the throne of England," chided Bowman, gently.

Anna nodded. "And is it not telling that the only way a woman may attain such a lofty height is by accident of birth?" She swept her hair from her face. "It is that and that alone that decides a woman's fate."

Bowman flicked his eyes to the young maid who walked silently beside them. She took small, faltering steps as she led them along Milford Lane to the location of her assault. It was clear she was in some discomfort at her predicament. Bowman noticed several passers by eyeing her with suspicion, wondering no doubt just what company the maid had found herself in.

Glancing ahead to where Detective Inspector Grainger was striding out, his coat tails flapping behind him, his great barrel chest leading the way, Bowman was not surprised. Grainger had a habit of muttering to himself when in thought, a habit that he indulged all the more in the open air. Even from a distance of several feet, Bowman could discern the occasional burst of speech to no one in particular. More than once, his babblings were misconstrued as attempts at conversation, and one or two pedestrians stopped mid stride to engage with him.

"Forgive me, madam," Bowman heard him say on one such occasion, "But I am about important business." The poor lady passed on, nonplussed, as Anna cast Bowman a look of bemusement.

"What drives a man to be a detective, Sergeant Bowman?"

Bowman thought. "A desire to bring solace," he said.

Anna smiled. "Then it seems we are driven by much the same thing."

They had, by now, passed onto the wide boulevard of the Victoria Embankment. It was busy with traders and businessmen; the former crying out their wares as they walked, the latter trying to avoid them. A man stood roasting chestnuts on a brazier. Bowman noticed his skin was burnished as brown as the chestnuts in his pan. Every now and then, he would toss them into the air to turn them with a practised skill. He caught the eye of a young nanny and her charge and engaged her in an easy conversation about the weather. The River Thames rolled in full spate behind them. It was busy with craft of every size. A pleasure boat was pulling away from Temple Pier, bound for the Tower Of London and Greenwich beyond. A young lad stood on the deck, waving to any who might notice. Beneath her bows, a couple of rowing boats bobbed in agitation. Bowman noticed one was piled with produce upon which, rather incongruously, stood a handsome pig. His owner sat at the oars trying to maintain his heading against the wash from the pleasure boat. Detective Sergeant Bowman shook his head. London never failed to surprise him.

To the party's left lay the environs of Temple Gardens. Home to many a barrister's chambers and the very fulcrum of the legal profession; it had stood on this site for almost three hundred years. The green spaces beyond the lines of cherry trees on its perimeter were not generally open to the public. Rather, they were the preserve of those who practiced within the Chambers and wished to sit among their formal gardens in the contemplation of the Law and all its complexities.

At the Royal Hotel, the party turned away from the river at Hetty's bidding and proceeded north. As they passed William Street, barely two hundred yards away from the north shore of the Thames, the maid suddenly buckled with grief. Huge sobs escaped her.

"What is it Hetty?" Anna soothed, doing her best to quiet the girl. Bowman noticed they were now the subject of many sideways glances from passers by. "Is this the place?"

Bowman looked around him. The London Chatham and Dover Railway loomed overhead. It seemed to leap the river in one bound to Blackfriars Goods Station on the south bank, the arches of the bridge plunging down into the murky depths beneath. New Bridge Street stretched away to the north and was a bustle of activity.

Hetty nodded. "This is where he grabbed me." She sank suddenly to her knees and screamed.

Galvanised, Inspector Grainger ran to her side and offered his hand. "Hetty," he breathed, "let me help you."

"Get off me!" Hetty struck out with her fists, her blows seeming to land with little consequence on Grainger's wide expanse of chest.

"Now, now," he coaxed, tenderly.

"She all right, mate?"

Bowman turned to see a newspaper seller at his stand. "We're from Scotland Yard," the sergeant expounded. He felt suddenly foolish.

"Ah," the man replied, knowingly. "That'll explain it."

"Where did he take you, Hetty?" Anna was crouching beside her now, her skirts ballooning around her into the mud.

Taking great gulps of air, the young maid pointed down William Street.

"It's all right, Hetty," Bowman heard Anna say. "You're safe
142

now. But the gentlemen need to see where he took you."

At last, Hetty calmed herself. Nodding in understanding, she rose to her feet again.

"Lean against me," Anna commanded. Gingerly, Hetty hooked her arms through Anna's and leaned her weight against her mistress. Bowman was touched by the bond that seemed to exist between the two young ladies. Anna seemed to have an easy way about her such that the gulf between them, that of a mistress and her maid, was as nothing. It seemed wholly in keeping with the young lady's character, and Bowman admired her all the more for it.

Hetty walked with more confidence now, grateful for Anna's support. She led them through William Street and into the dogleg at Water Street. Here, the road veered to the right to continue its course before joining Tudor Street at its furthest end. The buildings rose around them as high as any escarpment. Bowman could only imagine how Hetty must have felt as she was pulled through these brooding streets in the dark.

"Down here," Hetty panted, suddenly rubbing at her wrists at the memory. "He had me so tight I couldn't run, and a hand about my mouth such that I couldn't even scream." Tears welled in her eyes as she recounted her story.

"You are doing well, Hetty." Grainger loped at her side, his eyes glancing all around him as they walked into Dorset Street. Bowman was struck by how quiet it seemed. Even at this busy hour, not a single person was to be seen. The two public houses which stood back from the street were boarded up, their windows hidden behind hastily erected shutters fashioned, it seemed, from old pallets. The houses adjoining them appeared devoid of life. The street seemed as if it had been forgotten, the very picture of neglect. The clatter of traffic along New Bridge Street could barely be heard. He nodded to himself. Whomsoever had snatched Hetty, he surely knew the area well. It seemed he had chosen the place with care.

"This is where he took me," Hetty announced as she stopped by the opening to an alley. "He dragged me in there and had his sport with me."

Bowman swallowed. Before him, a narrow passage led into a

dark courtyard. Even at this time of day, with the sun at its height, no light was admitted.

Grainger was looking around him. "Are you sure, Hetty?"

"As sure as I'm standing here now," she sobbed. "Though I wish to God I weren't." She buried her face into Anna's sleeve, and Bowman noticed her mistress lift a hand to stroke her hair.

Grainger was by her side now, his face creased into an expression of concern. "Did he take you further into the alley, Hetty?"

Hetty shook her head. "He took me here," she whispered. "Against this wall."

"And you say he then disappeared?"

"If it was Jumpin' Jack, as I've been readin' in the papers, I can only imagine he leaped over them buildings at the end."

"But you didn't actually see him do so?" Grainger was clearly fighting hard to keep the cynicism from his voice.

"I saw him run down there, and there ain't no other way out." Hetty could sense she wasn't being believed.

"Could he not simply have come out the way you had gone in, Hetty?" Bowman asked, quietly.

Hetty suddenly stamped her feet. "Why ain't you listening?" she wailed. Bowman could feel a flush coming to his face.

"It's all right Hetty." Anna smoothed her hair again. "Just tell the detective what you know." Hetty's eyes were wide with defiance. "I *know* he didn't come this way, because when he'd finished he struck me to the floor and he never stepped over me. I *know* he went that way, and I *know* the only way out of this alley is over them buildings."

At a gesture from Inspector Grainger, Bowman sidled down the passage to the small courtyard beyond. Suddenly in shade, Bowman felt a chill seep through the fabric of his coat. The alley branched off to the left and right but, ultimately, led nowhere. Turning up his collar against the cold, he glanced upwards. All around him, tall, greasy walls rose to the sky, punctuated only by the occasional window. There was indeed, no exit to be had this way.

"Dead end," he announced as he rejoined the party on the street.

"Then it must be as I said," Hetty announced in a fit of pique. "He must've jumped those walls to get away."

A flash of cobalt blue suddenly filled Bowman's field of vision. He felt a tingling in every sinew of his body. His muscles tensed. He looked in turn at his companions, but they seemed ignorant of his predicament. He opened his mouth to speak, but no sound would come. As the scene around him began to fade, he had the presence of mind to look up at the street sign that hung on the corner to the alley. He knew, somewhere, somehow, that it was of the most tremendous import. Just as the shadow of the passageway seemed to stretch along the ground to pluck him back to the Electric Room at Colney Hatch, Bowman caught a glimpse of the sign and resolved to remember what was written there; 'Dorset Court'.

XVII: Family Ties

The Silver Cross was filling up nicely. At this time in the morning, Graves knew, he would soon be joined by workers and traders seeking to fortify themselves for their day's labours in the chill October air. Grateful for a warm hearth and even warmer beer, their spirits would soon lift higher than their voices as they readied themselves for the day.

Graves had arrived at The Silver Cross just as the last of the overnight fog was lifting over the city and the morning sun lent a golden glow to the rooftops. Having ordered his breakfast, he cast an eye over to the hearth where the usual chairs were arranged. He couldn't quite bring himself to sit in the one closest to the fire, opting instead to pull the furthest chair a little closer to feel the benefit of the guttering flames. Slinging his coat over the back of the chair, he reached into its pocket to remove the edition of The Evening Standard Matthews had presented at Scotland Yard the day before.

The young sergeant smoothed the newspaper out on the table before him and read the headline again. 'JACK'S BACK!' it screamed. Graves felt stung as he read the subheading; 'Scotland Yard caught on the hop!' It had Jack Watkins' touch, for sure. If only Callaghan had allowed him a freer rein, mused Graves in bitterness, more might have been learned. Just as he turned over the page to read the details of the report, Harris, the landlord, slid a plate of devilled kidneys across the table.

"I suppose we should be grateful it weren't the other Jack," Harris sighed as he read the headline over Graves' shoulder. "I remember the last time Jumping Jack was about." He rubbed his stubbly chin with a gnarled hand. "Don't recall him being quite so deadly, then."

Graves nodded, his blue eyes seeming to sparkle in the fire. "I'm not convinced the two men are one and the same, Harris," he said.

Harris nodded. "The first man never killed, though he was devil enough." He lowered his voice, conspiratorially. "Literally, if some are to be believed."

Graves laughed. "I think the Devil might have more important things on his mind than the taking of a few souls in London." He chose not to mention that Augustus Gaunt had been despatched with a sharp-pronged instrument.

"Perhaps he's taking a piecemeal approach." Harris leaned in so close that his lank hair fell across his eyes. "Little bit here, little bit there." With a shrug and a ghastly leer, Harris shuffled back to the bar and left the sergeant in peace. Graves couldn't help but smile at the landlord's performance.

"Should have caught him last time," came a voice from the bar. It was owned by a tall man in an even taller top hat.

"There's too many such men getting away," interjected another from the window, a glass of porter in his hand. "But then, if this is where the detectives of Scotland Yard spend their time," he gestured at the saloon bar around him, "perhaps that is no surprise."

"Is a man not allowed his breakfast?"

Graves turned to see the impressive girth of Detective Inspector Ignatius Hicks filling the doorframe. Lumbering to the fireplace, he flung himself into Bowman's usual chair with no consideration for niceties. Nodding to Harris at the bar, Hicks smoothed his great beard with his fat fingers. "The usual, if you will, Harris," he boomed, fixing the man in the top hat with his gaze. "And another pint of porter for my friend, there."

Suddenly disarmed, the man at the window smiled weakly and nodded in gratitude. "I dare say even detectives must line their stomachs," he muttered.

"What are we to make of it, Sergeant Graves?" Hicks nodded towards the paper.

Graves was wary. "According to Detective Superintendent Callaghan," he said slowly, testing the waters, "I am to make nothing of it at all."

Hicks nodded, his great beard bristling as it tumbled across his chest. "That's as maybe," he said as he reached for his pipe and tobacco pouch, "but Superintendent Callaghan doesn't know you as I do."

Graves watched as the bluff inspector filled the bowl of his pipe with shreds of golden tobacco. "And how's that?" he

147

asked.

Hicks narrowed his eyes. "I know that you are a man to be listened to."

Graves was unsure what to make of Hicks' manner. In his experience, any change in the man's demeanour was usually as a result of expediency. If it was of any gain to Hicks to change his mind, then he would. Perhaps he had been struggling in his investigations into the mysterious assailant?

Hicks was drawing hungrily on his pipe as he held a match to the bowl. The tobacco flared as he puffed and soon the table was enveloped in as thick a fog as any to be found on the streets.

"What are we to make of his third victim?" Hicks nodded again at the newspaper. Conceding Graves flicked to the page that bore the details of Jack's latest deadly escapade.

"The detectives at Scotland Yard are floundering again," he read aloud, "as Jumping Jack continues his reign of terror amongst the streets of London." Graves rolled his eyes at the hyperbole. "Where were the Scotland Yarders earlier this week when Tobias Dankworth was found at Southampton Street? Where again when Augustus Gaunt was discovered beneath the press at Waithman Street? And where last night, when Auberon Farley met his end on Hosier Lane, Farringdon? It is no wonder that the only witness to the aftermath of this dastardly crime came first to The Evening Standard." Graves raised his eyebrows and puffed out his cheeks in exasperation. "Mr Benjamin Franks was walking home to Holborn when he saw the fiend at work in Hosier Lane. He is described as wearing a top hat and cape and has eyes which blazed. Upon discovery, the demon knocked Mr Franks to the floor and made good his escape with a ghastly cackle. By the time Mr Franks had quite recovered himself, the devil had disappeared, leading Mr Franks to suppose that he can only have leapt the very walls around him." Graves threw a glance to Inspector Hicks who sat, inscrutable, puffing on his pipe. "He then found Mr Auberon Farley, who was known to him, dead upon the ground, his head crushed beneath a barrel from a nearby public house. Mr Farley had recently started work as a porter at Smithfield Market where he had made Mr Franks' acquaintance. He is the third victim in almost a week to suffer at the hands of this diabolical tormentor. All of London cowers beneath the grip of this mysterious man with blazing eyes."

Graves folded the newspaper carefully in half and laid it back on the table.

"Let us admit to the fact that Temperance Snell did not kill Augustus Gaunt at the printing works," said Hicks airily. "No more than the man who discovered the body at the brewery killed Tobias Dankworth."

Graves sighed at the man's gall. He reached for his plate of devilled kidneys. They were pleasantly spiced, he noticed as he took a forkful, with the effect that Graves felt as much warmth from the eating of them as he did from the flames of the fire.

"No more than this Benjamin Franks," Hicks continued, "must be held responsible for the death of Mr Farley at Hosier Lane."

"But in each case," interjected Graves between mouthfuls, "they were the first to find the body." He stared at Hicks, pointedly, as he spoke. "Does that not make them each the chief suspect?"

"Not at all," Hicks replied, oblivious to Sergeant Graves' barbs. "That is an old-fashioned idea," he blustered, "that will get us nowhere."

Graves held his tongue.

Hicks tapped the bowl of his pipe on the table as Harris appeared with a jug of foaming ale.

"I have a fine duck pie," he breathed salaciously at Hick's shoulder, "that I thought to save for you, Inspector Hicks."

Sergeant Graves was sure he saw Hicks' eyes grow to twice their size in contemplation of Harris' offer. "Perfect," the inspector nodded, smacking his lips in anticipation.

Harris placed Hicks' ale before him and reached to collect Graves' empty plate. "I hope you'll be at the piano soon, Sergeant Graves," he winked. "Business is never better than when there's entertainment."

"I'm sure I will find my way there eventually," Graves twinkled. "But for now - " he paused.

"Oh," Harris exclaimed suddenly, feeling the sergeant's eyes upon him. "Of course. I shall leave you to your work."

Hicks chuckled as Harris left them. Once the landlord was at the bar, he turned to his companion and, suddenly, adopted a serious tone. "What connects each of these men, Graves?" He pointed a chubby finger at the newspaper on the table. "Save the fact that they were murdered by a man who styles himself as a creature of myth?"

"A myth is a powerful thing," Graves asserted. "It cuts straight to the heart." He leaned forward on his elbows. "He has wrapped himself in the cloak of an enigma, but we must remember that he is a man. And, as a man, he is fallible."

Hicks nodded, then looked down his nose at the young sergeant. "What did you discover from Doctor Crane?"

Graves shrugged. "No more than you I should expect. That Augustus Gaunt was killed not by the printing press but by a blow to the back of the head with an instrument."

"Do you not think it pertinent that Auberon Farley was crushed by a barrel in Hosier Lane? Or at least, that his head was crushed?"

Graves nodded. "It might go some way to disguise the real manner of his death if he died in a similar way to Gaunt."

"And the man at the brewery." Hicks was warming to his theme. "Dankworth. He was pulled from the boiling waters of a mash tun. By all accounts he was unrecognisable, such was the bloating effect of the liquid within."

"Might that have disguised the true manner of his death?" Graves was thinking hard.

"It is certainly a possibility." Hicks expelled a lung full of smoke in Graves' face.

"If that is the case," the sergeant spluttered, "then perhaps the manner of their death is not all they share."

Hicks stroked his beard, absently. "Go on," he breathed.

Graves lowered his voice as he spoke. "There was more to Augustus Gaunt than Snell knew." Hicks raised his eyebrows, expectantly. Graves continued. "I've learned that he had some criminal dealings in the past."

"Where did you learn this?" Hicks growled.

Graves thought back to Big Flo in The Blackfriar. "Let's just say I heard it from one who knows." He remembered Flora's story of Gaunt's pillow talk, the ramblings of a man troubled by his conscience. "Gaunt was part of a bungled robbery in Farringdon some years ago. It resulted in the death of a police constable and the owner of a jewellery shop." Hicks was leaning in, the better to hear over the growing hubbub in the inn. "He drifted for a while, living in Holborn and Camberwell before settling in a doss house in Fleet Street."

"Ah!" Hicks nodded. It was as if a thought had just that moment occurred to him. "Dankworth also had a criminal past."

"Indeed?" whispered Graves.

"I was at Boulter's brewery yesterday." Hicks seemed inordinately pleased with himself. "Rumour has it that Dankworth had escaped from custody having been charged with the murder of his own daughter."

Graves lifted the folded newspaper before him. "Then what's the betting the latest victim also had a criminal past?"

"So, just who is Jumping Jack?" Hicks sat back as Harris delivered him his plate of steaming duck pie. "A vigilante? A bringer of revenge?"

"He's more than that," offered Harris, unsolicited, as he slipped Hicks' plate before him. "The people say he is not of this world."

"Then the people are not to be listened to," Graves sighed.

Harris stood up and folded his arms across his chest. Graves noticed the leathery skin on his forehead shining in the light from the fire. "Then how to explain the fiery eyes? And the bounding across buildings?"

"From what I have read," Graves expounded, patiently, "there is not one single witness to him actually having bounded such great heights."

"But - " Harris protested.

"In fact," Graves continued, heedless of the interruption, "I believe that those that have claimed to see him do so have fallen prey to some mass delusion."

Hicks looked sceptical. He chewed thoughtfully on a stray shred of tobacco that he had picked from the table. "Is such a thing possible?" he asked through the side of his mouth.

151

Graves nodded. "Eminently," he enthused, eager to expand upon the matter. "There is many a case of people exhibiting strange behaviour due to some collective mania. Sometimes, a great many people. Those with more impressionable minds are all too easily influenced." Luckily, Inspector Hicks missed the sidelong glance afforded him by Sergeant Graves as he spoke. "Folklore is littered with such cases," he continued, "from witch trials to the sighting of strange beasts."

Harris rubbed his chin. "You think Jumping Jack is just such a beast?"

Graves leaned back on his chair. "I think whoever is pretending to be Jumping Jack is making good use of our predilection to embroider our experiences with a good dose of imagination."

Even Inspector Hicks looked impressed. "And of his already existing in the minds of those who remember him from his last appearances," he offered.

Graves' eyes danced in the firelight. "Precisely. Those that don't are provided with the details via the pages of our more salacious daily newspapers." He stabbed at the headline on the paper before him. "The public has been whipped into such a frenzy that the more gullible of them see what they expect to see." Graves nodded, enigmatically, his blond curls bouncing in his eyes. "It becomes a self-fulfilling prophecy."

As Graves drained the last of his drink, he mused how much he wished for Bowman's company. He missed seeing the moment in the inspector's eyes when a case became clear, the sudden flurry of activity as he readied himself for action. Graves eyed The Evening Standard as he lowered his empty glass to the table. Bowman had clearly taken an interest in the case from Colney Hatch. Perhaps there was some detail in the reports that would aid him in his investigation. Graves gnawed at his lip. He daren't risk visiting Colney Hatch himself. If Callaghan knew Graves was pursuing his own interest in Jack's activities, let alone corresponding with Bowman, there would be hell to pay. As he stood to push his chair away from the fire, he knew exactly how to get the information to the inspector in the asylum. It would mean a short excursion to the streets of

Hampstead, and making the acquaintance of a certain wily young lad.

Just as Graves turned to leave, however, his attention was drawn to a clatter at the door. A swirl of leaves and dust heralded the arrival of a demure young lady with a subtle cleft to her chin. She pulled at the fingers of her gloves in agitation as she looked around her.

"Miss Morley!" Graves exclaimed moving to her. From the reaction of the assembled drinkers, it was clear that the sudden appearance of a lone young lady was enough to be of interest. That she was a lady of a particular station turned heads all the more.

Elizabeth's eyes fell upon the sergeant and, almost immediately, they filled with tears.

"What on earth is the matter?" Graves asked, softly. Aware that Hicks was clearly unwilling to give up his seat, Graves steered Elizabeth towards his own, glaring pointedly at his bluff companion as he did so. Hicks, distracted by the contents of his pie, seemed blissfully unaware of the slight, content to offer a curt nod by way of a greeting. It was only when Sergeant Graves called for a brandy that he seemed to take notice, gesturing to Harris that his own glass was in desperate need of a refill.

"The sergeant at Scotland Yard said I should find you here," Elizabeth breathed at last. "I was so upset he offered to escort me." She dabbed at her eyes with a handkerchief. "Such kindness." She sipped at her brandy to fortify her nerves. "Sergeant Graves, I am at a loss," she sobbed.

"You must tell us what has happened, Miss Morley," said Hicks, a note of impatience in his voice "or else we cannot be of assistance."

"You are right." Elizabeth took a breath and another sip of brandy. "Sergeant Graves, my brother has quite disappeared."

"From the brewery?"

Elizabeth nodded, sadly. "He did not return home last evening, and he has been out all night." She sobbed again. "Even at breakfast, there was no sign of him."

Graves knelt by her side and to look at her reassuringly. "When was the last time you saw him?"

153

"Yesterday morning, just as he left for the brewery."

Hicks swallowed a mouthful of gristle and cleared his throat. "I can vouch that he got there," he belched. "Saw him there meself, yesterday afternoon."

Graves nodded. "How did he appear to you, Inspector Hicks?"

Hicks thought for a moment. "Troubled," he said, at last. "Miss Morley," he continued, turning to the young lady in the seat opposite the fire, "there was talk at the brewery of the business being in trouble."

Elizabeth shrugged. "There is no secret there. It is a miracle that it has kept afloat for so long. I passed the way of the brewery this morning in search of him, but the gates and shutters are closed." She reached into the folds of her coat to produce a printed note. "This was pinned to the door."

'The Bankruptcy Act, 1869,' the note proclaimed in a heavy type. 'On The Matter Of Proceedings of Liquidation by arrangement or Composition with Creditors, by Roger Morley of Kennington, owner of Boulter's Brewery of Southampton Street, London. Notice is hereby given that a First General Meeting of the creditors of the above named person has been summoned to be held at the office of Mr John Bertram, No. 13, Elm Way, Solicitor on 28th Day of October, 1892, at eleven o'clock in the forenoon precisely ~ Dated this day, 19th October, 1892.'

Hicks placed the note back on the table. "Might that explain your brother's disappearance?"

"I do not think there has ever been a time when he has not been troubled by money or his lack of it." She gave a weak smile as she reached again for her brandy. "I cannot think that that alone would cause him distress."

"How long has he had the brewery?" Graves turned to the nearest table and pulled a chair from beneath it.

"Some three months," Elizabeth replied. "He heard of the opportunity whilst in India." Graves gestured that she should continue.

"He has been at Pudukkottai these last three years," Elizabeth explained. "He was a military man during the wars and, with his commission over, applied for a post in the service of the young

154

King of the Province."

"In what capacity?" Graves was enthralled.

"As part of the King's personal guard. He was only eleven years of age when he ascended to the throne and rules in name only."

"Was your brother employed as a mercenary?"

Elizabeth shifted in her chair. "As I have said, Sergeant Graves, I do not remember a time when my brother was not troubled by a lack of money. He had made some bad investments while serving in India and saw an opportunity. Our father was none too pleased and told him so, but Roger has ever followed his own counsel before others."

Hicks paused at his breakfast, charmed by her tale. "Then why did he not come home in possession of means?" he asked, mopping a dribble of the gravy from the table with his fingers. He gazed at Elizabeth in anticipation.

"He was dismissed from the boy King's service in disgrace," Elizabeth admitted, quietly. "He was caught taking bribes from those who wished to have the King's ear. Roger would arrange clandestine meetings where they might beg his intervention in a dispute or business opportunity. Naturally, he would charge a fee for his services."

"But the king was no more than a boy," blustered Hicks, brushing crumbs from his beard.

"And it is that very fact which was to prove my brother's downfall. He was discovered by the king's Diwan who ruled in his stead, stripped of his possessions as punishment and drummed out of the country."

Elizabeth looked at the two detectives who sat, aghast, beside her. "I have fought often and hard with my brother," she continued, "to convince him of the futility of pursuing Earthly wealth when true happiness lies beyond our realm."

"Realm?" echoed Hicks, suspiciously.

Elizabeth gave a smile through her tears. "This may prove difficult for you to believe, Inspector Hicks." Graves noticed she was looking the portly inspector straight in the eye as she spoke. "If my brother has been killed, I should be happy for him." Hicks opened his mouth to protest, but Elizabeth cut him short. "Happy that he now resides in the world of the spirit, where true happiness and enlightenment may be found." She raised her handkerchief to her face again. "It is the uncertainty which causes me grief."

Hicks was unsure how to respond. Thankfully, Graves came to his rescue. "Miss Morley, if your brother came home with nothing, how did he afford his interest at the brewery?"

Elizabeth stiffened. "He took a loan from a bank. Another thing of which father would never have approved."

Graves leaned in closer. "A loan secured against what?"

"Oh, he said he was to come into some money soon," she waved her hand, airily. "Quite a sum by all accounts."

"Do you know how he was to come by this money?"

"Some scheme or other, no doubt," said Elizabeth, nursing her brandy glass between her hands.

Graves nodded, thoughtfully. "Where is home, Miss Morley?" He asked.

"I live at my father's house in Kennington. My brother joined me there upon his return from India and has taken the ground floor for himself."

Sergeant Graves approached his next question with care. "Did not Mr Morley gain from your father's will?"

Elizabeth shook her head. "Father left the house to us both and I will not sell. His interest in his sawmill in Southwark he left to the Church, together with a small, personal fortune." She heard Hicks harrumph from his chair. "He was a Godly man, Inspector Hicks, and I would have expected nothing else." Chastened, Hicks looked away, pretending a sudden fascination with the flames in the fire.

Graves stood to shake the feeling back into his legs. "Rest assured, Miss Morley, that I shall put the best men on the case at once." He smiled, reassuringly. "Scotland Yard shall not rest until he is found."

"Then I can expect no more." Elizabeth rose from her chair and dipped her head in thanks.

"Where shall I find you if there is news?" asked Graves as he led her to the door.

"I shall be at home in Kennington, Sergeant Graves. The desk sergeant has the address."

Graves opened the door before her and watched her walk slowly into the street beyond. In amongst the careening traffic and hustle of the crowd, he noticed, she looked quite lost.

"I will return to the Yard and start the search," Graves announced, turning to his companion by the fire.

"I shouldn't worry," Hicks blustered, returning to his food. "He'll turn up soon enough."

Graves' eyes widened with incredulity. "How can you be so sure?"

Hicks shrugged. "Men like him always do," he explained, simply. "Like bad pennies. Besides," he added, raising his already empty glass, "I can feel it in me water."

Graves sighed to himself, certain that Detective Inspector Ignatius Hicks was more beer than water.

As the young sergeant swung his jacket about his shoulders, he turned suddenly. "Inspector Hicks, just why did you go so hard on Temperance Snell?"

Hicks stopped with a forkful of food halfway from his plate. The inspector seemed not to notice the gravy running down his beard. "Certain information came my way," he mumbled, evasively.

"Information?" Graves arched an eyebrow.

Hicks chewed as he thought. At last, he relented and dropped his fork back to his plate. "I was delivered of an envelope to this very table," he sighed. "It contained several reports concerning Snell's work practices." Graves noticed the inspector couldn't meet his gaze. "I thought it was enough to incriminate him in Gaunt's death." Hicks looked suddenly uncomfortable. "I was wrong," he whispered.

Graves nodded. "Who delivered the envelope?"

"That I do not know," Hicks admitted. He licked his lips, awkwardly. "I was distracted for a moment and did not see."

Graves frowned as he took a breath. "I will speak again with Doctor Crane. He might well confirm the means of death for Dankworth and Farley." Oblivious to the urgency in his colleague's voice, Hicks resumed his meal with a nod.

His duck pie finished, Graves knew the portly inspector would go straight to Callaghan and present the sergeant's theories as his own. No matter, thought Graves as he nodded goodbye to his companion. So long as the fiend was apprehended, he cared not who took the credit.

Hicks caught his eye as he turned for the door and raised a hand. "Graves, I am very much afraid that I have mislaid my wallet." He patted his pockets, as if the very action would confirm his claim. "Would you be so kind?"

Graves rolled his eyes as he made his way to the bar, then rolled them again as he realised he would also have to pay for the gentleman by the window who, even now, raised his glass to him in gratitude.

XVIII: A Diminutive Messenger

"It is entirely possible," announced Aristide Aubertin, "that the therapy has opened a door to your inner mind where the memory resides." Aubertin stood with his arms folded across his chest, his Adam's apple bobbing alarmingly at his throat.

Bowman nodded. "Is it able to reactivate memories long forgotten in the finest detail?" he asked, tentatively.

Aubertin stroked his chin in thought. "Peut-être," he mused, almost to himself. "The workings of the human brain are little understood, Monsieur. The memory even more so." He leaned against his trolley, toying absentmindedly with the instruments that lay upon it. "However," he continued, "it is my strong belief that everything we experience in life is filed away in the cabinet of the mind." He raised a bejewelled finger before him. "If we but had the key we could recover every minute detail of our lives."

Bowman felt excited at the prospect. "Monsieur Aubertin," he began, "your treatment has, on two occasions now, enabled me to relive an event that occurred a decade ago." His moustache twitched with excitement. "In truth, it has brought me much comfort. However, I did not relive it as in a dream or a simple reminiscence, but as a real event with all attendant sensations."

"Mais, oui!" Aubertin nodded his head, furiously. "That would, indeed, make much sense. In this particular drawer in the cabinet of your mind, would reside every feeling connected with the event you have experienced. Your emotional and physical state would be filed away as surely as you file away your correspondence." He chuckled at the analogy. "Did you feel hot or cold? Tired or refreshed? Hungry? Morose? Did you feel the movement of the wind upon your skin? All this and more would be recorded there." He rubbed his chin again. "Perhaps the application of the electric current provided the key to the lock?" To drive home the point, he mimed the turning of a key in its casing.

Bowman stood at the door to the Electric Room. Having passed the most restful night's sleep he could remember enjoying for quite some time, he had determined to talk the matter over with Aubertin. As he had sat at his breakfast, Bowman had been struck by the clarity with which he saw the world. Even the drab, municipal surroundings of the refectory had seemed suddenly full of colour; from the vibrant red of the hair of the man who sat opposite, to the bright green of the apple he had been offered as he collected his bowl of oats from the counter.

"The sensations were as real to me as those I feel right now," Bowman continued as Aubertin listened, intently. "In my dreams, I am more often than not an observer, conscious of my being outside the events as they play before me." He fought for the right words. "The reality of my dream is often exaggerated or expanded upon so that they very quickly become terrors." He shivered as he remembered some of the delusions to which, only days before, he had been subjected; the horses, the speeding bullet, the head on the block. "The events I experienced while under the influence of your therapy were different. Not just memories, nor delusions, but the reliving of an actual episode in my life."

Aubertin looked inordinately pleased with himself. Bowman noticed him patting the battery on its shelf with something approaching pride. "This is a most remarkable incident," the Frenchman announced, suddenly. "Perhaps there is a benefit to reliving past events. Perhaps they may bring a peace of mind." With a sudden burst of movement, he snatched a notebook and pencil from a shelf and proceeded to scratch at the pages. "Monsieur Bowman," he panted, "I shall write a most celebrated paper on this!" He checked himself and looked guiltily to the inspector by the door. "With your permission, of course," he added.

"It is the least I can do," Bowman replied with a genuine smile. He was both amused and impressed by the eccentric Frenchman and his methods.

"Bon!" Aubertin exclaimed. Snapping his notebook shut, he suddenly adopted a more sombre tone. "Mais," again, he waggled his finger before him. Bowman marvelled at how Aubertin's rings sparkled even in the intermittent light of the spluttering gas lamps on the wall. "Do not be complacent. Just because you feel well today, this does not mean that you are well all together."

"I understand," Bowman nodded, solemnly, although he couldn't help but think that Aristide Aubertin might just be wrong. A renewed vigour had come to Bowman's spirits and, with it, an ability to view his condition calmly and objectively.

"We will, of course, continue with the Galvanic process," Aubertin announced, perhaps wary of Bowman's misplaced confidence. "To stop now might prove a calamity, n'est pas?"

Bowman nodded. "Then I will see you this evening, Monsieur Aubertin." The inspector turned to go, then stopped. "But there will be no need to restrain me tonight."

Aubertin nodded in understanding.

When the bell rang for the morning's exercise, Bowman felt of a mind to walk in the air. Grabbing at his regulation felt coat from a line of hooks by the door, he joined the throng of patients who were intent on availing themselves of the airing courts. Some were led, shuffling, by the orderlies, their eyes vacant and their faces a blank. Others walked alone with more confidence, but looked furtively about them as if they felt themselves in peril. Bowman saw one elderly man divesting himself of his trousers until gently directed by a smiling orderly to dress himself before joining his fellows outside.

There was a chill in the air, and Bowman sensed the imminent arrival of a cold autumn. The horse chestnuts and maple trees competed with the rowan trees in the grounds to present the most beautiful colours; from russets and purples to deep, vibrant reds. As the majority of the patients were shepherded to the great airing courts where they might exercise in safety, Bowman turned his heels to the allotments. Navigating his way through the neat flowerbeds that lined the paths, he noticed the summer roses, peonies and oxeye daisies had fallen victim to the first frosts of the year, withering where they stood as if in defeat. Bowman turned to look back at the building he had never thought to know so well. Colney Hatch sprawled to the left and right, a motley collection of outbuildings huddling against its austere, grey stone walls. Wood smoke rose from chimneys to join the fog that fought valiantly to retain its grip on the morning. Squinting into the sky, Bowman saw the pale disc of the sun waiting patiently behind the haze, as if confident it would win the day. He anticipated a fine afternoon and determined to use the time in contemplation of the future. It was a feeling that took Bowman by surprise. He had spent so much time a prisoner to the past, that he did not think he should ever think of the future again.

Reaching the allotment at last, the inspector pushed his sleeves to his elbows and bent to clear some weeds. As he pulled at the more stubborn roots, his mind returned to Elizabeth Morley and the case she had presented to him only days before. In truth, it felt like weeks ago and Bowman mused at how much happier he would be to see her now. He wondered, too, if Sergeant Graves had received his letter and if it had been of interest. Might it have seemed the ramblings of a madman? Perhaps, despite the friendship Bowman believed existed between the two men, it had been discarded and ignored. Through the lifting fog, Bowman could see the smudge of the city on the horizon. Not for the first time, he felt remote from the world. How was he to tell Graves of his discoveries? Elizabeth's experience of the mysterious man in George Yard mirrored almost exactly that described by Hetty in Dorset Court, separated though they were by ten years. Finally, as he cleared the earth of stones, Bowman considered the map drawn in chalk on his wall. He had marked the location of Dorset Court upon it as soon as he had been returned to his room. Finding where he had marked the location of Scotland Yard, he had traced the course of the River Thames eastward along Victoria Embankment to the Temple Gardens. There, he had placed a cross and marked it with a neat hand, 'Essex St.'. Then, following the route he had taken with Hetty in the company of Inspector Grainger and Anna with his finger, he had turned off New Bridge Street and placed another cross with a circle around it. Here, he had written the words, 'Dorset Court'. Bowman had felt the eyes of the orderly upon him as he stood back, the better to view the results of his labours. There had been something in the pattern of the locations he had marked. From Angler's Place to the north, through George Yard to Dorset Court further south, there was a line that seemed evocative of... *something*.

Bowman shook his head as he tended his plot. The map on his wall seemed to him as an incomplete picture. As unfinished as it was, he feared it would not last long. Taylor would undoubtedly order its removal, convinced no doubt that it was the feverish expression of a chaotic mind. But Bowman knew better. He knew that the map, in fact, represented something that his life had lacked of late; order. The map was not merely a representation of the streets of London in chalk, but a symbol of Bowman's grasping the world and pulling it to him. Of him, finally, making sense of his predicament. "For what other reason do we employ a map," Bowman muttered as he worked, "other than to show us the way?"

"It's the first sign of madness, y'know."

Bowman looked up, startled by the sudden intrusion.

"Talking to yourself," the voice came again. "It's the first sign of madness."

Bowman looked around for the source of the interruption, his eyes finally alighting upon a young boy straddling a branch of a nearby cedar tree. With his jaunty cap and well-worn trousers, the inspector recognised him at once.

"Detective Sergeant Robert Tompkins," the boy announced, mischievously. "At your service." He gave a smart salute, playfully pretending to knock himself out with the force of his hand against his forehead.

"Robert Tompkins!" Bowman stood aghast in the dirt, his moustache twitching on his upper lip. For a moment he feared he had been subject to yet more delusions. Tompkins was just as Bowman remembered him, save perhaps a little chubbier round the face. It was a stark reminder that time had continued to pass in the outside world whereas, within the walls of the asylum, it had appeared to stand still.

"How the devil did you get in here?" the inspector spluttered. Robert Tompkins would be the last person he would expect to see at the allotments at Colney Hatch, even on the best of days.

The boy laughed. "You don't become a detective sergeant

163

without learning to climb!" He nodded over to where one of the higher limbs of the tree dropped down to the perimeter wall. "It was simple enough," Tompkins sniffed. Bowman noticed a tear in the fabric of the boy's jacket, just above the elbow. He smiled. That detail alone gave the lie to the boy's tale of an easy climb.

The inspector looked around him. The other men working on the allotment were some distance away and were either not aware of Tompkins' arrival or choosing to ignore it. Still, Bowman knew there would be implications if he were caught, not least from the superintendent who would, no doubt, be very interested to know just how easily the perimeter wall had been breached.

"I don't think much to your new office," Tompkins beamed, gesturing to where the forbidding walls of the asylum rose against the horizon.

Bowman couldn't help but smile again. "It is a temporary accommodation," he said.

"It's a madhouse, ain't it?" the lad asked, directly.

"It is that, Robert," Bowman nodded.

"How long you been here, then?"

Bowman scratched his chin with his dirty fingernails. "Long enough to grow these marrows," he replied, nudging the bloated cucurbits with a foot.

Tompkins thought for a moment and then smiled again. Like all children, mused Bowman, he seemed to possess the ability to accept strange and new circumstances at once, quickly adjusting to the situation at hand.

"What are you doing here, Robert?" Bowman squinted up at the tree. "And how did you find me?"

"Sergeant Graves sent me," Tompkins replied, simply. "Nice chap, ain't he?"

"He is, indeed," Bowman concurred. So, Graves had received the letter, after all.

"He told me you were here and bid me come find you." Tompkins reached into his pocket to pull out a handful of change. "He gave me funds," the boy grinned. "Expenses, he called them." He pocketed the money again. "Got meself a cab, didn't I? On police business."

Bowman was confused. "But how did he know where to find you?"

Tompkins shrugged. "Turns out he remembered you mentioning me with regard to the garrotting in Hampstead. He read your report to get me address."

"Dove Street, near the workhouse." Bowman nodded. He needed no Galvanic Therapy to remember those details. His investigations into the death of Sartorius Milne in Hampstead had taken place just five months ago. For all that the memories seemed fresh in his mind, they might as well have happened a lifetime ago.

"You acquitted yourself well, Sergeant Tompkins," Bowman said with a wink.

"Thank you, sir!" Tompkins swung his cap from his head to reveal a mop of unruly hair, then bowed as low as he could while retaining his balance on the branch. "I had a good teacher, sir."

Bowman took a breath and sighed. This was a strange meeting indeed, but one that he was enjoying tremendously. Then, suddenly, he thought to ask the one question he should have asked all along.

"Why did Sergeant Graves send you to me, Robert?"

The boy's eyes narrowed as he raised a finger. "Aha!" he exclaimed, reaching for his jacket pocket. After a pause that was almost theatrical, he pulled out a rolled up newspaper and let it drop at Bowman's feet.

"Read all about it!" he chimed.

A deep frown cut into Bowman's forehead. Puzzled, he bent to retrieve the newspaper and unfurled it. It was a copy of The Evening Standard, its front page bearing the striking headline, 'JACK'S BACK!', in large, capital letters. Keeping one eye on Tompkins in his eerie, Bowman turned to the appropriate page to read the report. His heart was thumping hard against his chest.

"Sergeant Graves said you would realise the sifinance." Tompkins' attempt at the word raised a smile from the inspector, even as he read.

"I do, indeed, Detective Sergeant Robert Tompkins," he breathed, excitedly. "I do, indeed."

As Bowman scanned the page before him, the details of Jack's more recent appearances jumped out at him. The glowing eyes, the jumping of tall buildings, all were redolent of the cases he had investigated, in vain, with Inspector Grainger all those years ago.

"There have been more," Bowman hissed. But what, beyond the more hysterical details, linked the cases of the past and present? The inspector could sense that a pattern was forming, he just couldn't see where.

"Ever played with a jigsaw puzzle?" he asked, absently, peering up to where the boy was perched.

"'Course I have," Tompkins scoffed. "Fiendishly difficult when you can't find the missing piece."

Bowman nodded slowly, another smile spreading across his face. "Well, Sergeant Tompkins," he beamed, "it looks like you've found it."

Having instructed Tompkins to remain where he was, Bowman ran with unpractised speed back through the gardens. Clutching the newspaper to his chest as he sprinted ungainly back to the building, he didn't even notice the leaves from the sycamore whipping at his face as they fell around him. He splashed through puddles and slid through mud in his eagerness to get back to his room. His haste did not go unnoticed by other patients in the grounds and, when he reached the high fence surrounding the airing courts, he found that one or two of the more excitable inmates were keeping pace with him behind the wire. Flinging his coat towards the hook by the door, he did not even wait to see if it had found its mark before skidding round the corner and past the dormitories. Passing one of the wards for more troubled patients, Bowman slowed his step as he caught the matron's suspicious eye, before regaining his speed once out of her sight. As he rounded the corner to his room, Bowman was surprised to see the door ajar. Sensing trouble, he grabbed at the door jamb to slow himself. There, kneeling on the floor beneath his chalk map, sat an orderly with a cloth and bucket by his side.

"Stop!" shouted Bowman as he pushed the man away. Whirling round, he saw that a good third of the map had already been removed. The whole of the west of London from Chiswick to Green Park was just a smudge. The River Thames and its bridges had been reduced to a chalky smear.

"Doctor Taylor," droned the orderly, "says that the wilful damage of property is not to be tolerated."

"I have damaged nothing," Bowman seethed. "Please, just give me a minute."

The orderly rolled his eyes. "Mine is not to reason why," he sighed, brandishing the cloth again, "but to obey."

Bowman was thinking fast. His hands a blur, he unfurled the newspaper on his bed and reached for the chalk.

"Waithman Street," he read, muttering under his breath. "Waithman Street." The orderly raised an eyebrow at the repeated phrase. "Waithman Street," Bowman said again, "there was another murder in Waithman Street." Moving to the map, Bowman lifted the chalk before him and closed his eyes. "Waithman Street." It sounded so familiar. Bowman was sure he had passed it once or twice in a cab, or perhaps even on foot. "Waithman Street!" he exclaimed, suddenly, his eyes snapping open. "Ludgate Circus!" Tracing an imaginary line along Fleet Street to Ludgate hill, he dropped his arm an inch or two and made a cross on the map. Drawing a circle around it, he labelled the position in as neat a hand as he could manage; 'Waithman Street'. Beneath the orderly's gaze, Bowman sprang back to the newspaper on his bed. "Southampton Street, I have already marked," he panted, pointing back at the map behind him. "The sight of the murder at Mr Morley's brewery. But…" He closed his eyes again. "Hosier Lane, Farringdon," he whispered. "Hosier Lane…"

Once again, he was back at the map, his chalk before him. "Hosier Lane."

"You'd better hurry up, mate," barked the orderly. "Doctor Taylor himself will be here any minute. There'll be trouble if this map's still up."

Bowman quietened the man with a finger to his lips and a

shake of his head, then closed his eyes again. Hosier Lane was proving difficult. He knew he had passed it in the course of his investigations, but where?

Suddenly, Bowman was sat in his leather, wing-backed chair at his desk in Scotland Yard, facing the door, the window behind him. He forced himself to feel the leather at his back, to smell the faint tang left in the air by Hicks' tobacco smoke. Bowman let his mind's eye drift along the walls to the bureau where a decanter stood in wait. With a start, he realised he had not had a drink in weeks. Nor, he was startled to find, had he missed it. "Hosier Lane," he heard himself say again as he focussed his attention on the map above the bureau. He followed the course of High Holborn eastwards towards the viaduct. There was the tobacconist he had visited during his investigation into the Holborn strangler. There, just off the viaduct, was Plumtree Court, where his first victim had been found. Bowman moved on, over the viaduct towards the city. He could almost hear the traffic rattling past. Something in the inspector's memory bade him turn north onto Giltspur Street and he saw Smithfield Market before him.

"Of course!" Bowman exclaimed, taking the orderly so much by surprise that he clutched at his breast in alarm. "Hosier Street, Farringdon." Bowman raised his stick of chalk to the wall. "It is but a stone's throw from Smithfield Meat Market!" With the memories of another investigation swirling about his head, and the sights and sounds of the meat market calling to him, Bowman brought his chalk down on the wall and made the sign of a cross with a circle around it. 'Hosier Lane', he wrote next to it.

Bowman threw the chalk to the floor in triumph and recovered his breath. He stared at the map intently, and at the locations he had marked over the last two days. Angler's Place, Camden. St Pancras Old Church. Dorset Court. The locations of Jumping Jack's previous manifestations. And then, his latest appearances. George Yard, Holborn. Waithman Street, Ludgate. Hosier Lane, Farringdon. Bowman stared. With a sudden flash of inspiration that caused the orderly to jump again, Bowman reached for his chalk and drew a straight light, equidistant from each location, from Camden to the north bank of the River Thames. And, finally, it was apparent. The last piece of the jigsaw.

Bowman's jaw dropped and, for a moment, he let his head hang. Just as the orderly was about to enquire after him, Bowman laughed. Throwing the chalk to the floor, he jumped over the bucket on his way to the door.

"What shall I do with the map?" the orderly shouted after him, exasperated.

"What you will," Bowman called over his shoulder as he ran. "I have no further use of it!"

The orderly watched the inspector take a corner off the corridor at speed. Shaking his head in disbelief, he rubbed his face in his hands, bent for his bucket and reached for his cloth again.

The library was empty, as usual. With O'Reilly back in the world, there had not been one patient who had taken the time to sit amongst the books. Everything was just as it had been the last time Bowman had seen it. Even O'Reilly's newspaper was just where he had left it. As the inspector skidded into the room at speed, he disturbed the motes of dust that hung in the air. They danced about him as they sparkled in the light from the huge windows. The silence afforded the room an air of reverence, like a church or temple and, for a moment, Bowman felt guilty at the frenetic manner of his arrival. Smoothing his moustache between a finger and thumb, he walked smartly to a bookcase by the grand fireplace. The grate was loaded with logs but they remained unlit. Whether the lack of a fire was as a result of the paucity of patients interested in visiting the library or the cause of it, Bowman could not tell, but he rubbed his hands together as he stood, looking intently along a particular shelf marked, 'Geography'. Tracing along the shelf with a finger, he muttered each title under his breath, tilting his head to one side to read the text on the spines. "The Universal Geography with Illustrations and Maps. A Handbook for Travellers in Turkey. Bradshaw's Continental Railway Guide." It was certainly an eclectic collection and sorted into no particular order. At last, Bowman found the book he was searching for. "The Cartographical Study Of The Ancient Rivers Of London," Bowman whispered.

Plucking the book from the shelf, he walked to the nearest table and flung himself into the creaky chair beside it. He opened the book to read the frontispiece. There, he saw an enigmatic dedication written in a flowery hand. 'Presented to Martha Goodman with best wishes for her travels'. The book, Bowman noticed, had only been published some four years previous to finding itself upon the shelf at Colney Hatch, so Martha had clearly found little use for it. Bowman flicked over the first few pages in search of a table of contents. At last, he came upon a list of chapter headings, each pertaining to the lost subterranean rivers of the capital city; The Walbrook, The Tyburn, Hackney Brook, Muswell Stream. His finger came to rest upon the fifth entry down. Bowman couldn't help but say the words out loud. "The River Fleet."

Thumbing the pages excitedly, Bowman came to rest at a two page pictorial representation of the Fleet and its course through London. 'The River Fleet,' the text ran beneath, 'rises in Hampstead Heath where it is dammed into the two Hampstead Ponds. From here, it runs south to the north bank of the River Thames at Blackfriars. To the casual observer, however,' the text continued, 'it is almost entirely invisible for its whole length, submerged as it is beneath the teeming streets of our Metropolis. Clues may be found, however, as to its course beneath our feet, if only we are of a mind to stop and notice them'. Bowman's eyes flicked to the lithograph above. Pressing down upon the book to smooth its pages across the spine, he placed a finger upon the locations he had marked with chalk on his wall, north to south. Angler's Place, St Pancras Old Church, Hosier Lane, George Yard, Waithman Street and Dorset Court. With a start, he realised he had been right. Each of those locations was but a hundred yards from the subterranean course of the River Fleet. Whomsoever was now masquerading as Jumping Jack had clearly looked to his previous appearances, made the same deduction and literally followed in his footsteps. It was clear to Bowman that, far from leaping buildings to effect his escape, the entirely misnamed Jumping Jack had descended below the streets to make his getaway. The fog and people's imagination had done the rest.

The sound of Bowman snapping the book shut echoed around the room, serving to rouse the inspector to action. If Jack was to be caught before he killed again, Bowman had to inform Sergeant Graves of his findings. Jumping to his feet, he made for the door at speed, hoping against hope that his diminutive messenger was still hiding in the branch of a cedar tree, just where he had left him.

XIX: Connections

Doctor John Crane, MRCS slid his spectacles down his nose. "This seems to be becoming something of a habit," he purred. "Is Detective Inspector Hicks aware of your visit this time?"

"He is," Graves nodded, sheepishly.

"And Detective Superintendent Callaghan?"

There was a pause while Graves thought what best to say. "Less so," he admitted, at last.

Sergeant Graves had spent the last twenty minutes standing alone in Doctor Crane's dissecting rooms. He had discovered the doctor at work, cleaning the tools of his trade in a large porcelain sink in the corner. Graves had arrived just as he was attaching an Indian rubber hose to a riser tap on the wall. He had stood for a few moments at the door before interrupting him. The doctor had not taken his request at all well. Clearly hoping that his day's work had been completed, Doctor Crane had listened with a growing ill temper to Graves' suggestion that he fetch two bodies from the mortuary. At last he had acquiesced, though not with particularly good grace. Indeed, Graves was sure he had heard the doctor mutter beneath his breath as he left the room. He didn't care to imagine what he might have been saying.

Alone in the dissecting room, Graves had let his gaze wander across the walls. The quiet in the room was beyond silence. He could hear his own breath as it escaped from his body. If he concentrated hard enough, he fancied he might hear the thump of his heart. He had cleared his throat and, strangely, had to fight an impulse to laugh. He had felt wholly out of place in this temple to death.

Finally, Doctor Crane had returned with first one, and then another cadaver. He placed the first at the furthest end of the room with an irritable announcement. "Tobias Dankworth." Graves nodded. That was the man, according to Hicks, that had been found in the mash tun at Boulter's brewery. Crane had then left the room to fetch the other body as requested. This time, Graves had not felt so alone. The figure beneath the sheet by the furthest wall had seemed to hold him in its thrall. The detective sergeant had been in the presence of many a dead man before, but never alone in such particular surroundings. Just as he had thought Crane might never return, the doctor had pushed another trolley through the door. This, he had placed alongside the first with an equally obstreperous pronouncement. "Auberon Farley." Graves had given another curt nod. This was the man discovered in Hosier Lane.

Now, Crane invited Sergeant Graves to join him with a flick of his hand. "It is of no matter to me who you have told, Sergeant Graves," he began in his clipped Scottish brogue. "I do not answer to Scotland Yard." He took a breath. "Though sometimes it would seem they believe so." He stretched up to his full height which, Graves noticed, was actually rather tall. "I dance to nobody's tune but my own," he said.

"Quite right, too," Graves twinkled. "And I am grateful to you for accommodating me."

Crane flashed him a suspicious look but contented himself with a barely audible growl of discontent.

"Shall we take a look?" Graves pulled his notebook and pencil from his pocket in readiness. "Let's start with Dankworth, shall we?"

The doctor, rather alarmingly Graves thought, flexed his hands to crack his knuckles, then reached for the white sheet covering the first body. "It is as well this man had no family to claim him," he snapped as he pulled back the sheet, "or he would have been taken by now."

Graves peered closer at the man on the trolley. His flesh seemed red and bloated, particularly around the torso and legs. The eyes, barely contained behind red-raw lids, bulged from a fleshy face. His tongue protruded ghoulishly from his mouth whose lips themselves were pink and swollen.

The young sergeant swallowed. "Has he been - "

"Cooked, Sergeant Graves?" Crane interjected. "Certainly. Boiled, more like." He pointed to the various parts of the poor man's torso. "You can see the fattier parts of the body, in particular, have swollen. This is partly the result of swelling of the tissue in response to heat, and partly the retention of water."

Graves let the air whistle through his teeth. "To be boiled alive. What a dreadful end."

"I did not say he had been boiled *alive*," the doctor said, matter-of-factly.

Graves threw him a questioning look.

"Sergeant Graves," the doctor began, "would you assist me in turning the man?"

Graves blinked. It was the same command Crane had issued with regard to the body of Augustus Gaunt just a few days ago. Then, it had been to present the wound that had done for the man. Not the action of the printing press against his skull, but a blow to the back of the neck with a heavy instrument. Had Crane discovered just such a wound on Dankworth?

"As you can see, Sergeant Graves," Crane confirmed, "he suffered a similar fate to your man at the print works."

Crane extended a bony finger to the sight of a wound on the back of the man's neck. "Once again, it was made with a sharp instrument and, once again, it resulted in the snapping of the man's neck between the top two vertebrae, the atlas and the axis."

"Before he was thrown in the water?"

The doctor shook his head. "In this case, it is impossible to ascertain. But, given this body exhibits exactly the same wound to the neck as shown by Augustus Gaunt, and we know he received that very same wound *prior* to being placed in the printing press," the doctor took a much needed breath. "I should say it was likely. Wouldn't you?"

Graves said nothing, but scratched at his notebook.

"And then, there's this fellow." Crane turned to the second cadaver beside him.

"Auberon Farley," Graves breathed. "He was discovered on Hosier Lane in Farringdon the night before last."

"His head crushed by a beer barrel, I am told." The doctor was almost smiling.

Graves knew what was coming next. With all the theatrical timing of an actor upon the stage, Doctor Crane pulled the sheet from Farley's body. Graves saw that it was pristine, save for some bruises about the knees and an horrific gash to the top of his head.

"The bruises are as a result of him falling forwards to the floor."

Graves was thinking fast. "Yet that welt on his head is at the front. Surely he would have fallen backwards from the force of that blow."

Crane opened his eyes wide with pleasure. There was something approaching pride in his voice as he spoke. "Very good, Sergeant Graves."

Graves followed his thoughts to their natural confusion. "So, once again, Farley must have received a blow from behind."

"A fatal blow!" Doctor Crane proclaimed in triumph. He twisted Farley's disfigured skull to one side. Once more, Graves saw the unmistakable signs of a wound to the back of the neck. "Let me guess," he breathed, excitedly. "The atlas and the axis?"

Crane raised a pale finger before him. Graves couldn't help but notice how long, and how clean, his fingernails were. "Precisely!"

"So that blow, which would have undoubtedly killed him, sent him falling to his knees."

"The body was then turned and a barrel dropped upon it," the doctor concluded.

Graves nodded. "It was another attempt to disguise the true method of the man's death." He tapped the end of his pencil against his cheek, absently. "Just as Gaunt was placed in the press and Dankworth thrown in the mash tun."

A deep silence returned to the room as Crane allowed the young sergeant to enjoy the moment. He knew that, to a man like Graves, the moment of discovery was sweet, indeed.

"But," the sergeant continued, suddenly, "if you knew all this, why did you not declare it to Scotland Yard?"

Crane was suddenly officious. Throwing the sheets back over the two bodies with a series of swift movements, he made clear his distaste at the implications of Graves' question.

"As I said, Detective Sergeant Graves," he sniffed, haughtily, "I dance to nobody's tune but my own." He waved his arm about him. "Until now, no one from Scotland Yard has bothered to enquire as to the deaths of these two men. The details are, of course, contained in my reports to the coroner, but it would seem that, as far as the Yard is concerned at least, minds have already been made up."

Graves gnawed at his lip as the doctor straightened the sheets about the bodies. "Now, Sergeant Graves," he barked, irritably, "I have two bodies to deliver back to the mortuary, then I am to give a lecture on the symptoms of Porphyria."

Sergeant Graves was glad of the October air as he ascended the steps to Agar Street, not least because it afforded him the opportunity to clear his lungs of the smell of formaldehyde that had hung about him in the dissecting room.

"Charing Cross Hospital at four of the clock, just as you said."

Graves broke his stride. Spinning round, he saw a young lad in a cap sitting nonchalantly at the kerbside.

"Tompkins," the sergeant called with a grin. "Did you meet with success?" Graves squatted on his haunches, the better to speak with the boy.

"I did that," the boy nodded.

"You spoke with Inspector Bowman?" Graves could scarcely believe it.

"And I gave him the paper just as you said."

Graves pulled the boy's cap over his eyes, playfully. "You'll make a Scotland Yarder, yet!" he beamed.

Robert Tompkins pulled a meagre pile of change from his pockets. "Not on these wages," he winked, mischievously. "Two cab rides there and back have eaten into me expenses."

"Tell you what, Tompkins," Graves guffawed, "tell me what Bowman said, and I'll make sure you've got enough for a pie or two."

Tompkins thought for a moment, then nodded. That seemed enough to settle the matter. "Right you are," he said, springing to his feet.

XX: The Lion's Den

The Strand was a quagmire. Successive years of neglect had seen one of the main thoroughfares across the city reduced to nothing more than a series of potholes, ruts and fissures. The pavements had worn away so much that it was difficult to know just when one was walking on the road and when beside it. As a result, mused Sergeant Graves as he darted between shop awnings, the walk from Trafalgar Square to Fleet Street was akin to taking one's life into one's own hands. Raising a fist at a particularly errant brougham, he would certainly have been of a mind to appraise the cabbie of his position at Scotland Yard, if such a disclosure had not been enough to tempt the driver to have another go at him. Wiping mud from his trouser hems, Graves crossed the road bravely and stood before the offices of The Evening Standard.

Bowman's reply to his letter, so expertly delivered by Robert Tompkins, had sent his mind into a whirl. It was not enough for Graves that the subterranean River Fleet was the only connection between the killings. He kept recalling a remark that Hicks had made at The Silver Cross just that morning. What was it he had called their mysterious assailant? A vigilante. A bringer of revenge. Graves pursed his lips. Perhaps there was something in that. If so, he reasoned, he must know more of the victims and their past. With that thought uppermost in his mind, he shook the drizzle from his curls, reached out a hand and pushed open the door.

Graves could hear the clatter of Watkins' typewriter as he ascended the stairs, to say nothing of the smell of cigar smoke that wafted from the open door on the landing. The sergeant had had dealings with the editor of The Evening Standard many times in the course of his duties, but he had never yet seen inside his office. A knock at the door provoked a curt "Come!", and Graves attempted an entrance. Pushing at the door, he found it heavier than expected. It was only when it was halfway open that Graves noticed the impediment. A stack of books and discarded papers had been piled up on the floor, spilling onto the faded rug as the door was opened. Looking around, he saw that the rest of the room was entirely in keeping. A mess of debris littered the floor and the many shelves that graced the room. Here and there, maps of the various districts of London had been perused and discarded. Graves saw an expenses sheet on the windowsill. Notebooks and loose leaves of paper lay on the furniture, some so dangerously close to the fire, that Graves was sure they might catch alight at any moment.

The man behind the desk was just as dishevelled. Jack Watkins seemed to exist in an atmosphere of his own. The smoke that escaped his cigar, the remnants of many more squashed into the ashtray on his desk and the colour of his fingers spoke of a man for whom tobacco was a necessity. Even the hair on his head and the whiskers on his face reminded Graves of the shreds of golden tobacco Inspector Hicks would press into the bowl of his pipe. Watkins sat at his typewriter with his waistcoat undone and the ends of his cravat untied. His weasel face was a mask of concentration.

"Detective Sergeant Anthony Graves of Scotland Yard." He barely looked up from his work as he spoke, the cigar seemingly clinging to his lower lip by force of will alone. "What an unexpected pleasure." The tip of his cigar glowed crimson as he drew upon it. "If you are about to suggest an addition to this evening's copy, you are too late."

Graves shook his head, attempting to ignore the stinging sensation the smoke was bringing to his eyes. "I am after no such thing," he beamed.

Watkins' eyes narrowed as he typed. "Are you here to take issue with any of our coverage?"

"Not at all." The young sergeant was content to play the editor's game.

At last, Watkins paused in his work. Looking up at Graves for the first time, he took the cigar from his lips and leaned back in his chair. "Ah," he breathed. "Then you are here to crave a boon."

Graves nodded. He was rather enjoying himself. "There you have me," he admitted, cheerfully.

Watkins eyed him between puffs of smoke. "And, as ever

178

Sergeant Graves, when faced with such a proposition I must ask, what's in it for The Evening Standard?"

"No quid pro quo this time, Watkins," Graves cautioned. He could well remember how giving too much leeway to Jack Watkins had fair near scuppered Inspector Bowman's previous investigations. "I offer nothing more than an opportunity to act in the public good."

Watkins laughed, a short piggish snort. It gave Graves a fine view of his brown and yellow mottled teeth. "Are you to lecture me on the public good?"

If he had ever had control of the conversation, Graves realised at once that, in that moment, he had lost it. "I would do no such thing," he replied, quickly.

"I am very glad to hear it, Sergeant Graves." Watkins leaned forward and rested his elbows either side of his typewriter. "Looks like Jumping Jack has been giving the Yard the run-around," he said, slyly.

Graves nodded, feeling he was being toyed with. "It is early days. We are making progress."

"Progress?" boomed Watkins. "Three men dead in a week and no sign of an arrest, and you call that progress?"

Graves swallowed. Beyond Inspector Bowman's revelations from Colney Hatch, little progress had been made. He daren't, however, tell Watkins that. "We are hardly floundering, Watkins."

Watkins chuckled. It was the very word he had used in his report.

"This third murder," Watkins continued, stubbing out his cigar. "The one in Hosier Lane."

Graves nodded.

"There was a witness, I understand." Graves noticed Watkins smirking openly as he spoke.

"Yes," the sergeant confirmed. "A Mr Benjamin Franks."

"Mr Franks, yes." There was a pause. "Is it not rather telling, Sergeant Graves, that Mr Franks would rather come to The Standard with his story than go to the police?"

Graves was momentarily at a loss. It was true the Metropolitan Police Force was very often the last institution to be trusted by the public, alongside members of parliament and lawyers. "It will not be The Evening Standard that catches this man, Mr Watkins," Graves smiled at last. "Nor any other newspaper that I can think of."

"Perhaps," hissed Watkins as he reached for his humidor. "Yet many have lost faith in Scotland Yard. One need look no further than our letters page to see it."

Graves was at a loss. "We do not, at Scotland Yard, have recourse to salacious headlines. We must deal with the facts and follow due process in our investigations."

Watkins seemed impressed. "I see George Bowman has taught you well," he sneered. "How fares the detective inspector?"

It was all Graves could do to control his temper. "Inspector Bowman continues to recover," he said, simply.

"I'm sure our readers will be delighted to hear it," Watkins leered. The strange power play at an end, Watkins clearly felt he had asserted his authority over the young sergeant. "Now, what would you have me do?" He lit another cigar. "For the public good?"

Graves considered it time to speak plainly. "I require access to your archive." He swallowed again. "As part of Scotland Yard's investigation into Jumping Jack."

Watkins spread his arms wide in mock supplication. "Of course, Sergeant Graves," he grinned, fixing a spare cigar behind his ear. "What's mine is yours."

As they descended the stairs to the basement, Watkins delighted in telling Graves all about The Evening Standard's unique indexing system. "It is a living history," he enthused. "More comprehensive and more concise than anything you'll find at Scotland Yard." They passed through an entire room of men hunched at desks, scratching at ledgers or tapping at typewriters. A fog of pipe smoke hung in the air.

"I want that story on the Battersea barge by tomorrow morning," Watkins barked to a sullen reporter at a desk. The man nodded back "And don't forget to look into what was going on at the Royal Armitage Bank yesterday." Graves held his tongue. "The Evening Standard as you know it," Watkins droned as he walked, "has been with us since Eighteen Fifty Nine, but it was a morning paper for some thirty years before that."

Having reached the basement, Watkins drew a set of keys from his pocket and opened a door before them. "Behold," he grinned, "our repository of knowledge."

Graves couldn't help but whistle at the sight. The length and breadth of the room was given over almost entirely to an array of wooden filing cabinets. They stretched very nearly to the ceiling, each with a label on every one of its compartments.

"Every copy of The Standard is to be found in this room," announced Watkins with pride, his cigar clamped firmly between his yellowing teeth. "And every name and place ever mentioned in any article is filed in these indexes." He patted the nearest cabinet, Graves noticed, in much the same way one might pat a horse.

The sergeant was impressed. Such a system would serve Scotland Yard well. He knew full well even the new building on Victoria Embankment was lacking in space. It looked like Watkins had himself a system that could save the Force many wasted man-hours and space besides. "I am after three names, Watkins," Graves declared.

"Name them." The editor of The Evening Standard was clearly in his element.

Drawing his notebook from a pocket, Graves licked his finger to flick through its pages.

"Augustus Gaunt," he announced.

Watkins' eyebrows rose at the name. "The man discovered at the print works at Ludgate?"

Graves nodded in confirmation. "Quite so."

Watkins shrugged and moved along a line of cabinets. At each, he stopped to look up, reading the labels on each drawer aloud. "A to C, D to E." He stopped. "F to G." Walking to a corner, he retrieved a set of wooden steps such as Graves had seen in a library and set them up by the cabinet in question. Climbing two or three steps, he teetered dangerously to open a drawer. "GA, GA," he muttered to himself as he flicked through an array of colour-coded slips of paper. "GAUNT,

AUGUSTUS!" Pulling out the piece of paper in triumph, he read the information printed in it. "Arrest and acquittal, twenty-fourth November, Eighteen Eighty Seven."

Graves looked on as Watkins descended the steps with care and walked to a line of deeper wooden drawers on the far side of the room. Finding the right year above a cabinet, he squatted on his haunches to open one of the lower drawers, then fingered through its contents. "Twenty-fourth November, Eighteen Eighty Seven!" he announced at last, pulling an old newspaper from the drawer. "Next?"

Graves referred back to his notebook. "Dankworth," he replied. "Tobias Dankworth."

Watkins puffed knowingly on his cigar. "Am I to suppose," he began, slyly, "that the third name on that list is Auberon Farley? The man found at Hosier Lane?"

"Correct," said Graves.

"Then you are looking for information on the three of Jack's victims. Do you suppose the next two, like the last, have had a criminal past?"

Graves smiled. He could tell he had piqued Watkins' interest and, perhaps, even earned a little of his respect.

"Let's see shall we?"

As Jack Watkins set about retrieving the next two newspapers, having first made reference to his index cards, Graves leafed through his copy to find the pertinent article concerning Augustus Gaunt.

"Here we are," he said at last, folding the page before him, the better to read it in the meagre light. "Police have been thwarted in their attempts to charge a known miscreant in the case of the Farringdon jewellery robbery and murders. It is to be lamented that the jeweller and a police constable called to the scene fell victim to the burglar; the first held hostage until the latter's arrival. Detective Inspector Callaghan - ", Graves paused to read the name again before continuing, "who led the case against Augustus Gaunt, expressed his disappointment at the verdict handed down at The Old Bailey this morning. Detective Inspector Callaghan claimed that Gaunt, though found innocent of all charges, was a dangerous criminal who might kill again."

Graves lowered the newspaper. "Detective Inspector Callaghan?"

Watkins was at his side. He handed Graves another newspaper, already opened at the correct page. "Tobias Dankworth," he breathed through a cloud of tobacco smoke. "Seventeenth of June, Eighteen Eighty Five. The man discovered at Boulter's Brewery."

"It is the sad duty of this newspaper," the young sergeant read aloud, "to report upon the discovery of the mutilated remains of a young girl, Ada Dankworth, in Shoreditch. It is surely an indictment upon our benighted city and those who profess to care for the fate of all children that she lay in an abandoned house on Bateman's Row for some three days before discovery. The police officer charged with finding her killer, Detective Inspector Callaghan - " Graves stopped again. He felt suddenly aware of the lack of air in the room. A cold sweat chilled his spine. He continued; "Detective Inspector Callaghan, pledged that the might of his whole division at Scotland Yard would be brought to bear in the pursuit of the girl's father, Tobias Dankworth." Graves' mouth was dry.

Without a word, Watkins passed him the final newspaper.

Graves' voice was a whisper now. "A young man fighting to clear his name has implicated one of Scotland Yard's own detectives in the case which saw him stand before the judge at The Old Bailey charged with murder. Auberon Farley, a railway labourer from Broad Street, was cleared this week of any complicity in the death of Maggie Brent, a stallholder of no fixed abode. Speaking on the steps of the criminal court, Mr Farley opined that his character and reputation had been besmirched beyond repair by the investigation, led by - " Graves paused. "Detective Inspector Callaghan." The young sergeant was aghast.

Not even Watkins' smoke could penetrate the tangle of thoughts that taunted him.

"Looks like your new superior had a run of bad luck," breathed Watkins, shaking his head in disbelief.

"He investigated every one of these men for crimes past," Graves mumbled, almost to himself. "And every one of them got away."

One by one, Graves' thoughts settled in the semblance of an order. "Watkins, I need one more name from you," he said at last.

Watkins dropped the stub of his cigar to the floor in readiness for action.

"When I last spoke to Callaghan it was in connection with the scandal at the Royal Armitage Bank."

Watkins' eyebrows rose. "Go on," he entreated.

"In the course of my investigations there, I have discovered a fraudulent bank account was set up in the name of Thomas Golightly." Graves was speaking quickly now, eager to get to the nub of the matter. Watkins blinked comically as he tried to keep up with the sergeant's train of thought. "In fact Golightly died some three years but a fraudulent death certificate was produced to close the account. It was signed by the doctor who presided at Thomas Golightly's supposed death. When I mentioned the name of the doctor to Detective Superintendent Callaghan only yesterday, I saw a fleeting glimpse of something in his eyes. I dismissed it at first, but now I wonder." He turned to face the editor of The Evening Standard, his eyes alight with the thrill of the chase "Was it recognition?"

Jack Watkins shrugged. "What was the name of this doctor?"

Graves was at his notebook again, turning the pages furiously. "Frederick Samson," he said at last, stabbing at the page with a finger.

"Samson," Watkins echoed as he loped back to the wooden filing cabinets. He was so absorbed in his mission that he had completely forgotten to light another cigar. Instead it remained jammed behind his ear in readiness. He turned the name over and over to himself as he scanned the drawers and the labels written on them. "R to S," he said at last, and slid the steps across to the correct cabinet. Climbing the rungs to the very top, Watkins opened a drawer and flicked through the index cards. "Samson," he called down to Graves, "Frederick. Thirteenth of July Eighteen Seventy Eight."

Graves whistled as he searched the larger cabinets under Watkins' guidance from the steps. That was fourteen years ago.

Graves suddenly doubted he would find any connection to Callaghan at all. "Clutching at straws," he hissed to himself as he searched through the drawer for the correct edition. "Clutching at straws."

At last, he found it.

"Thirteenth of July," he announced, flicking the newspaper from its place in the drawer. In truth, Graves was losing heart. Walking to a nearby table, he smoothed the paper before him and began to turn the pages. Watkins shuffled alongside him. He had, by now, remembered his cigar. Sergeant Graves was grateful that for now, at least, it hung from the editor's lips, unlit.

The sergeant paused over an inside page. It contained a line drawing of India with a circle placed as an indicator around its southern tip. Graves read the headline aloud. "Doctor Of Death escapes custody in Pudukkottai!" The sergeant stopped for a moment. That was the second time he had heard of that particular Indian town. Watkins leaned in closer to read over the Graves' shoulder.

"Self-styled doctor of medicine, Frederick Samson, has absconded from police custody in a Princely province of India," the sergeant read aloud. "It is believed he benefited from the presentation of fraudulent wills following the deaths of three men in his care at a military hospital near Pon Nagar. Upon being charged with the offences, Doctor Samson was held at Sakthi Nagar by the Military Mounted Police under the auspices of…" Graves' voice faded to a whisper. "Staff Sergeant Patrick Callaghan." He exchanged a look with Watkins, then read on. "Staff Sergeant Callaghan was on duty the night Samson escaped, and now faces an investigation into his possible dereliction of duty." Graves' eyes were wide. "In the meantime, Doctor Samson remains at large and nowhere to be found."

"Then Detective Superintendent Callaghan knew each of the men murdered this week." Watkins chewed on his cigar.

"And Solomon, too." Graves remembered Hicks' remark again. "A bringer of revenge," he breathed.

"How's that?" Watkins asked.

Graves licked his lips and swallowed. "Callaghan failed to

185

prosecute these men for past crimes."

Watkins shrugged. "Looks like they were all innocent anyhow."

Graves nodded. "But perhaps, in Callaghan's mind, they were the ones who got away."

Watkins stared, suddenly aware of the implications. "In which case - " he began.

"Now Callaghan knows of his existence," concluded Graves, "Doctor Frederick Solomon might well be next."

XXI: Behind The Mask

Detective Inspector Ignatius Hicks was nothing if not predictable. Just as Sergeant Graves had known he would, he had finished a leisurely breakfast, downed his pint of porter and made his way to report his findings to Detective Superintendent Callaghan. No matter that Graves had done most of the donkey work, it was the result that counted. And Callaghan, if nothing else, wanted results. Hicks could lay before his superior all Graves' findings into two of Jack's victims and their past. The rumours of Gaunt's bungled robbery and Dankworth's involvement in a murder would surely be enough to convince Callaghan that progress was being made. Hicks had been impressed at the Detective Superintendent's trust in him. It was only right, he thought, as he climbed the steps to Callaghan's office, that he, as the superior officer, should head the investigation. He knew Sergeant Graves to be a capable man, but had often found him a little too eager, a quality that Hicks had no doubt had been encouraged in him by George Bowman. Well, thought Hicks as he paused for breath on the landing, with Bowman out the way, Sergeant Graves would have to sink or swim on his own merits. He would like to see how the sergeant coped then. It was about time that his own talents and ideas were appreciated. Hicks climbed the next flight of stairs, pulling at the banister to help him shift his bulk from step to step. Catching his breath again, he knocked at the door and awaited an instruction to enter.

Nothing.

Hicks cocked his ear to the door but could hear nothing. No conversation, no shuffling, no noise at all. He knocked again, harder this time, only to find the door swinging open of its own accord. Hicks waited, uncertain what to do. Still, there was silence from within. He cleared his throat loudly enough to be heard and knocked gingerly again. The door swung open a few inches more. Bravely, Hicks placed a foot over the threshold and leaned into the room. As far as he could see, it was unoccupied. The potted palms stood untended either side of the fireplace. The fire was unlit in the grate. Aside from a single leaded glass door hanging slightly ajar from a bookcase, Callaghan's office was just as it had been the last time Hicks had set foot inside; immaculate. There was an illicit thrill to entering Callaghan's office like this. Expecting Callaghan to appear at any moment from the door to his inner office, Hicks thought best of intruding any further. He stood for a while at the door, looking about him. An open book lay face down on Callaghan's desk. Aside from the sound of the passers by on the Embankment below, there was a deathly hush.

"Superintendent Callaghan?" Hicks called. "Patrick?" Hicks felt a rush at having dared to use the Superintendent's Christian name but, in truth, Callaghan had been pleased for Hicks to use it at one of their more recent meetings. It had given the inspector a feeling of belonging that he had enjoyed. Hicks cocked his head to listen all the more carefully. There was definitely no sound at all coming from the door to Callaghan's inner office. For a moment, the inspector froze, unsure of what to do. Then, finally, giving into an impulse he could no longer ignore, he took a step into the room. His eyes darting furtively around him, the inspector made his way gingerly to the window to stare out over the Thames. He was doing nothing out of the ordinary, he reasoned. Simply awaiting Callaghan's arrival so he could make a report. And the door had been open, after all. Turning back into the room, Hicks wondered if he should ever have an office so grand. He marvelled at the tasteful furniture, each piece positioned just where it would be of the most use or the most pleasing to the eye. Callaghan's portraits seemed to stare from the wall, reproachfully. Hicks had to steel himself beneath the gaze of the young man in the military uniform and his older counterpart seated behind the mahogany desk. Daringly, Hicks ran his finger along the leading edge of the very desk from the picture. The wood seemed to speak of authority. Hicks sighed. Perhaps one day he would attain such lofty heights himself, especially with a superintendent on his side. He'd like to see the look on Inspector Bowman's face then if, indeed, he ever saw him again. Lifting his eyes, Hicks happened to glance through the open door into Callaghan's inner office. The door had always been locked on the previous occasions Hicks had been admitted into the room, so he could not help but be intrigued. He would only be a moment, he mused. Just a quick look. Treading as gingerly as his bulk would allow, Hicks made his way across the Persian rug beneath his feet to peer inside.

There, he saw a porcelain jug and bowl sitting on a washstand beneath an ornate mirror. A long wardrobe stood along the length of one wall, its door ajar. Inside, Hicks could just see the superintendent's coat on a hook. It was clear, then, that he hadn't gone far. Perhaps, thought Hicks, he should leave in case Callaghan came back. Just as he was thinking better of his escapade, his eye fell upon a large metal safe, half concealed in the shadows of the wardrobe. He took a step closer to see if it was locked.

"Inspector Hicks!"

The interruption was enough to send Hicks reeling back against the wall. Guiltily, he prepared to make his excuses.

"The door was open - " he blustered.

"It's all right, Hicks," came the voice again. "It's me."

Startled, Hicks looked up to the door. There stood Sergeant Graves, his blue eyes bright with excitement.

"Graves," Hicks panted, clutching at his chest. "You'll be the death of me."

"I think Detective Superintendent Callaghan would be the death of you if he found you in here."

Hicks joined the young sergeant in the main office, his eyes flicking to the door as he spoke. "I was merely curious," he began. "I meant no harm."

"Hicks," Graves breathed, urgently, "I have come from Jack Watkins at The Evening Standard."

Hicks' eyes narrowed at the mention of the name. The last time he'd had any dealings with Watkins, he had found himself rubbing up against Inspector Bowman and his investigations into the head in the ice. Hicks had not been able to help himself, divulging perhaps a little too many details of the investigation to the prying editor. He had, of course, been only too happy to publish them.

"What could you possibly want with Watkins?"

189

Graves spoke quickly. "Hicks, we need to know just what links the victims."

"Agreed." Hicks was concentrating hard.

"Watkins showed me to The Evening Standard's archives where I was able to search through everything it has reported on since its foundation."

Hicks' eyes widened. He was clearly impressed.

"All three of Jack's victims committed crimes that were investigated or pursued by Callaghan."

"What?" Hicks flustered, his great beard bristling.

"Detective Inspector Callaghan was at the forefront of pursuing all three men through the courts." Graves held up his fingers before him to count off the victims. "Augustus Gaunt escaped a charge of murder brought by Callaghan. Tobias Dankworth was thought to be responsible for the death of his daughter. Callaghan was never able to bring him to justice. Auberon Farley was accused of the murder of a woman. He claimed to have been much maligned by Scotland Yard and the detective in charge of the case. Detective Inspector Callaghan."

Hicks looked as if he might fall. Suddenly gasping for breath, he lowered himself carefully into Callaghan's chair, all thoughts of being discovered by the superintendent suddenly irrelevant.

"Callaghan investigated all these men?"

Graves nodded. "And, in each case, they escaped justice."

Hicks took a moment to settle himself, then looked his companion squarely in the eye.

"Just what are you saying, Graves?" he wheezed.

Graves chose his words with care. "That, if you found yourself in a position of authority and with the means at your disposal to right the perceived wrongs in your career, perhaps the temptation to take the law into your own hands might prove too much."

Hicks was at a loss. "But, what of Jumping Jack?"

"A convenient screen," suggested Graves, "as mysterious and impenetrable as the fog." He flicked his eyes to the window where the city was already succumbing to its nightly shroud.

"The legend of Jumping Jack provided Callaghan with the perfect distraction. And the perfect means to escape his victims."

Hicks shook his head. Sergeant Graves was going much too fast for him. "Means of escape?" he stuttered.

Graves took a breath. "I have been corresponding with Inspector Bowman in Colney Hatch regarding this case."

"Against Callaghan's explicit instructions?" Hicks roared, aghast. "I would tread more carefully, if I were you."

Graves held the inspector's gaze. "I rather think we are beyond such considerations now, Hicks. Don't you?"

Hicks patted his pockets in search of his tobacco pipe and smoke.

"As a young detective sergeant," Graves continued, "Bowman worked with an Inspector Grainger, investigating Jack's last appearances a decade ago."

Hicks shook his head as he packed the bowl of his pipe with tobacco. "Before my time," he replied. "I was still a constable in Cambridge."

Graves blinked. He had never considered Hicks to have been a policeman anywhere other than London and in no other force but the Metropolitan. He was sure there must be a story or two to be told there.

"From Colney Hatch, Bowman was able to see just what connected the previous cases and those that we are investigating today."

Hicks leaned forward in his chair, his match flaring just an inch from the end of his pipe. "And what was that connection?"

"The River Fleet."

Hicks drew upon his pipe, thoughtfully. "And yet we have witnesses who say Jack leapt over buildings."

Graves shook his head in earnest. "No. They saw what they thought they should see. They saw a figure they remembered from the news reports of a decade ago, the top hat and cape, the blazing eyes, and their imagination did the rest."

"A collective mania," Hicks said.

"Quite so."

Hicks tapped his fingers on the desk. His eyes fell again upon the book that lay face down on the mahogany, it's spine clearly cracked from repeated misuse. Suddenly reaching for it, Hicks snapped the book shut in his chubby hand, perused the cover and finally with a look of astonishment on his face, held it up for Graves to see.

"A Cartological Study Of The Ancient Rivers Of London," Graves read aloud. He bit his lip. "Callaghan made the same connection as Bowman, and used the very same means of escape as Jack."

Hicks placed the book back on the table, flicking to the pages which detailed the course of the River Fleet through the capital. "In the public's mind, the fiend of Eighteen Eighty Two and the villain who killed those men this week are one and the same."

"And that's just what Callaghan was counting on." Graves' eyes suddenly flicked to the open door to Callaghan's inner office. "Just what did you find in there, Hicks?" he asked, quietly.

Hicks sighed and shook his head. Pushing his chair back from the desk, he loped to the anteroom.

"This," he said pointing at the safe in the wardrobe as Graves joined him. It was a large strong box which stood upon sturdy iron feet that had been fashioned into the claws of a lion. A handle and dial adorned the outside, along with the name of the manufacturer; Arthur B. Curtis of Cincinnati.

"Is it locked?"

An attempt to twist the handle confirmed that it was. "We'll never get in," Hicks panted. "We could never guess the combination."

Graves' eyes twinkled at the challenge. Looking around the small ante room, he saw that it was practically bare save for a washstand with a basin and jug. "There must be some clue as to the number he might choose."

"It could be anything," grumbled Hicks, not unreasonably. "A birthday, an address or just some random numbers."

Graves shook his head as he walked back into the main office. "Callaghan doesn't work like that," he muttered to himself. "He has an orderly mind." Graves' eye fell upon the pictures on the wall. "He also, it seems, revels in his own idea of himself."

Hicks ambled up behind him as he spoke. "How's that?" he breathed.

Graves nodded to the pictures. "He has led quite the life," he said, quietly. "I think he's rather proud of just how far he has come."

"Quite right, too," Hicks concurred, watching as Graves leaned in closer to the pictures on the wall. "Although many have made the journey to Scotland Yard via a career in the military." He gestured to the portrait of Callaghan astride a horse.

Graves had noticed a faded label stuck to the bottom of the picture. "Staff Sergeant Callaghan," he read aloud. Suddenly, he froze. "Inspector Hicks," he said urgently, "I have some numbers for you."

"What?" Hicks' eyes were wide open.

"Callaghan's service number is printed here, at the bottom of the picture."

"You think that may be the combination?"

Graves turned to him. "I think it's entirely possible. Get back to the safe!"

Hicks practically fell over himself. His arms flailed about him as he lumbered back to Callaghan's inner office and fell to his knees. Cracking his knuckles in anticipation, Inspector Hicks shouted back to his companion. "Ready!"

"Five," came Graves' voice from the main office, "Four, Oh, Seven - "

Hicks turned the dial to each number in turn. As he reached the fourth, he heard a gentle click from the mechanism within. "Stop!" he called. Reaching for the handle, he gave it a smart pull down, and the door swung slowly open.

Graves rushed to join him, crouching by his side to peer inside the safe. "What is it?" he asked, impatiently.

As Hicks leaned in closer, he noticed a small brown bottle with a brush lying next to it. Reaching the bottle, the inspector held it up so Graves could clearly read the label. "Phosphorus paint."

"It is common enough at the theatre," Hicks was explaining. "And may be used to produce a glowing effect wherever it is painted."

Sergeant Graves let the breath whistle between his teeth. "The blazing eyes of the legend," he mused aloud. "Brought to life with a cheap theatrical trick."

Just as the two men walked back to the main office in silence, they were startled by a noise at the door. Turning as one, they saw Sergeant Matthews leaning in, a surprised look upon his face.

"There you are, Sergeant Graves," he said, suspicious of the scene before him. "I have been looking for you."

"Then you have found me," Graves replied, hiding his hand and the bottle within it behind his back. "What is the matter, Matthews?"

Matthews felt clearly uncomfortable in Callaghan's office. Looking about him for any sign of the superintendent he reluctantly took a step forward. "It's Mr Hackenburg, sir, the director at the Royal Armitage Bank. He presented himself at the desk earlier today with some details concerning a Doctor Frederick Solomon."

"The doctor who signed Golightly's death certificate," Hicks remembered.

"He gave an address for Doctor Solomon at Clerkenwell," Matthews continued. "Seeing you were out about your business, I left it with Superintendent Callaghan, and wondered if he had passed it on."

Graves' eyes grew wide with alarm. "Callaghan has the address?"

"Why should that be a concern?" Hicks asked, puffing at his pipe.

Graves turned to his portly companion. "I asked Watkins for any past crimes committed by Solomon that might also be connected to Callaghan."

"Why?" Hicks coughed. "What possible connection could there be?"

"When I first mentioned Solomon's name in this office, I noticed a fleeting look in Callaghan's eye." Matthews looked on uncomprehendingly as the young sergeant continued. "I could not think what that look might be Hicks but, in Watkins' basement I wondered if it might have been recognition."

"Recognition?" Hicks had a tremor to his voice.

"I asked Watkins to search for Solomon in The Evening Standard's Archive."

Hicks was positively bursting. "And?" he boomed, his whole body tensed in anticipation.

"Doctor Frederick Solomon was accused of murdering patients for profit whilst in India." Graves was pacing now, as if the action would lend some order to his thoughts. "While at Sakthi Nagar, he was held in the police station by a representative of the Military Mounted Police of Pudukkottai; a Staff Sergeant Patrick Callaghan."

Hicks felt his legs giving way again. His face a mask of shock, he lowered himself back into Callaghan's chair.

"Sergeant Graves," chimed Matthews from the door, "might I ask - "

"Did you say Pudukkottai?"

Graves was confused. "Inspector Hicks, do you not understand? Callaghan pursued Solomon for his crimes. The doctor escaped justice, just like the others, and Callaghan was disciplined for it."

"But," Hicks mouth was opening and closing almost comically. "But, Roger Morley was at Pudukkottai," he whispered.

Graves nodded. "There must certainly be a connection."

Matthews had clearly heard enough. "Sergeant Graves, might I ask just what is going on? And why are you in Superintendent Callaghan's office?"

"Clerkenwell!" Graves suddenly exclaimed. "Doctor Solomon is in Clerkenwell!"

"That's right," stuttered Matthews. "Corporation Row, as I remember it. Ascot House."

Suddenly galvanised, Graves leapt for the book on Callaghan's desk. "Clerkenwell," he murmured as he flicked through its pages. Suddenly, he stopped and turned the book to face Hicks so that he may see the page on which he had landed. It was a pictorial representation of the course of the River Fleet through London. "Clerkenwell is on the Fleet," Graves hissed. "And Callaghan knows that Solomon is there."

XXII: Just Deserts

The fog was as thick as it had ever been. So much so, that the cab proceeded at a speed no quicker than walking pace. Roger Morley grabbed at the wooden flap over his legs with impatience. The few people at large in the streets loomed at him through the fog, as seemingly insubstantial as ghosts. Many had chosen to stay at home, but still there was the evening traffic to contend with. Carts and cabs processed slowly along High Holborn, as if part of some cortège. Lamplighters struggled with their rods. Shopkeepers threw up their arms and threw down their shutters, convinced they'd see no further trade that day.

Morley pulled down his hat against the biting autumnal air, moisture from the brim dripping down his hand and into his sleeve. He shivered. His head throbbed mightily on account of a night ill-spent. He had awoken late in the day in a doss house on the south bank of the Thames. In truth, he was not entirely sure how he had got there. It was a condition with which he was almost painfully familiar.

Morley had been a drifter for most of his life and, he knew, a thorn in his father's side. Joseph Morley had hoped a stint in India might instil in his son the same values with which he had lived his life; sobriety, perspicacity and hard work. Perhaps, thought Roger as he sunk down into his coat, it was as well his father had not lived to see how that had turned out. Pudukkottai had been a disaster. Rather than prove the making of him, Roger's time in the subcontinent had led to debt and an even greater instability. "No fibre," his father would have said. Well, thought Roger as the hansom turned off the main drag at Holborn Circus to head north on Farringdon Road, perhaps he would be right.

Joseph Morley, as he had been fond of telling anyone who would listen, was a self-made man. He had known want and hardship as a young boy, but had succeeded in raising himself to a position of respectability throughout his life. The sawmill beside which he had been found garrotted at the beginning of the year was his crowning achievement; a solid, bricks-and-mortar symbol of just how far he had come. Joseph Morley's name had been written in the largest possible letters on the gates.

Roger knew he could never live up to that. He had spent much of his life running away from any duty or obligation and now, as the cab rattled into Bowling Green Lane, he was doing it again. The brewery had been a terrible investment, made in haste as all his investments had been. It had been as a result of several connections he had made whilst in Pudukkottai. Doctor Frederick Solomon had been another. It was to Doctor Solomon that Roger now turned for salvation.

The cab came to a shuddering halt at the junction with Corporation Row. After paying the driver, Morley stepped from the carriage onto the greasy pavement and peered into the fog. Having only been here once before, on the night he had thrown himself at Solomon's mercy, he took a while to get his bearings. The lights from the school were just visible as dirty smudges on the opposite side of the road. Ascot House stood in a corner plot behind a high, forbidding wall. Morley had to practically feel along the bricks to find the gate. Feeling the latch through gloved hands, he made his way into the tiny garden that sat to the front of the property. The building rose before him in the smog at the end of the terrace, tall and narrow. Disconcertingly, Roger could see the windows were devoid of light. Suddenly worried, he banged at the door. He knew Solomon kept no staff, and so waited for the doctor himself to answer. Peering through the window proved fruitless, but for all that he could see in the murk, there was no movement within.

Cursing beneath his breath, Morley moved round the corner of the house towards the rear entrance. Several times, his feet became entangled in the unruly undergrowth and he was forced to kick his way through the nettles and brambles that clung to the house. Finally at the back door, Morley tapped furiously at the glass to no avail. The house was clearly empty and Fredrick Solomon gone. Morley leaned against the wall for a moment to consider his predicament. With another failed business behind him, creditors at his back and no money, Solomon's scam had been his last hope. He had been promised a sum for acting as secretary to the Golightly estate, recruiting those gullible enough to part with their money for a meaningless promissory note. It would be enough money to enable Morley to flee once again and set up home abroad, far from the reach of the bailiffs. He was sure Elizabeth would be glad to be rid of him. Without her recalcitrant brother about, she would be free to pursue her childish fantasies unhindered. Morley knocked the moisture from the brim of his hat and resolved to wait for the doctor's return.

Looking up the path to the back gate, he thought he heard a noise from the alley beyond. It sounded like a frantic scuffle.

"Solomon?" Morley called, suddenly wary.

Walking gingerly up the path, Morley put his hand on the gate. Swinging it quietly open, he stepped into the passageway. There, he was confronted by the sight of a nightmare made flesh. A fiendish figure was hunched over a body in the middle of the alley, dressed incongruously in a top hat and cape. Morley felt his mouth dry. His head began to swim. As he lowered the body to the ground, the figure looked up to meet Morley's gaze. A pair of demonic green eyes blazed from their sockets. Morley felt his legs begin to buckle at the sight. Looking down to the ground in disbelief, he saw Doctor Frederick Solomon lying still in the dirt, a slick of blood oozing from the back of his neck. Having been interrupted at his gruesome work, the creature turned its attention on Morley. With gloved hands outstretched, it moved towards him. Morley was so much in thrall to the ghastly vision before him that he couldn't move. The figure raised a hand before him and Morley saw a flash of metal. A scream caught in his throat. Lifting his hands, too late, in a futile attempt to protect himself, Morley held his breath. Then, almost improbably, he heard a whistle. A shot rang out.

The sound split the air and rebounded off the walls, rending the air in the alley with a crack. Morley saw the creature recoil and clutch at his shoulder. Looking round for the source of the bullet, he saw two men standing in the gloom at the entrance to the passageway, one with a lamp, the other with a revolver.

"Stop, or I'll fire again!" came a voice, low and resonant. "Get back, Morley!"

Still gripping his shoulder, the figure barged down the alley towards the men, flashing metal flailing before him wildly as he ran. Another whistle pierced the air.

"Stop him!" came a younger voice, and another shot ran out. Morley heard the bullet embed itself into the wall near his arm, and the fiend ran on. Barrelling into the two men, he sent them flying to the flagstones at their feet and emerged into the street beyond. The soles of his shoes skidding on the wet cobbles, the strange apparition darted at speed towards the Thames.

"See to Solomon," roared Inspector Ignatius Hicks to his companion as he turned on his heels, ready to give chase.

"You'll never catch him!" came Graves' exasperated response.

"I gave you an order, Graves," came Hicks' disembodied voice through the fog. "I am the superior officer."

"But I am quicker," Graves replied, to no avail. Hicks was already gone. Graves ran down the alley towards Morley. He held his lamp before him as he bent on the road to tend to Solomon.

"He's dead," Morley rasped, his voice thick with emotion.

Graves squatted on his haunches and turned the poor man over. Seeing a deep wound on the back of Solomon's neck the young sergeant knew that, like Gaunt, Dankworth and Farley before him the doctor had fallen victim to a self-styled agent of vengeance. Graves looked up at Morley just as two constables came skidding down the alley in response to his earlier whistles.

"Escort Mr Morley here to Scotland Yard," Graves commanded, his eyes narrowing. He could hear windows being thrown open in response to the furore.

"Hey!" came a voice in the fog. "What's going on?" Graves could see onlookers starting to gather in the entrance to the passage.

"Have this body moved as quickly as possible," Graves continued as another constable arrived to hold back the crowd. "And close this alley off for further investigation."

As Morley was led away and the constables went about their business, Graves' thoughts turned to his fellow detective and his pursuit of the man in the mask.

Detective Inspector Ignatius Hicks stumbled in the dark, panting, his gun waving redundantly before him. The fog was even thicker now as he waddled down Farringdon Road, his eyes to the ground. He was following a trail of blood that appeared at intervals on the street. The wound that Hicks had inflicted upon the man, though not enough to stop him immediately in the alley, had surely done him substantial damage. The portly inspector rested against a lamppost to catch his breath. He clutched at his chest. These exertions were getting the better of him. Untying the rag of a scarf from his neck, he mopped the moisture from his face. He drew deep of the cold October air in an effort to settle his racing heart. It stung his lungs and induced a coughing fit so violent that, for a moment, he lost his balance. Staggering to the middle of the road, he looked around him for any sign of his quarry. It was then that he felt a hand clutching at his leg.

Graves was panting hard. He knew from the book he had found in Callaghan's office that the River Fleet was running directly beneath him, submerged and subsumed into the great sewer system that ran beneath London's streets. Once among the greatest rivers to run through the city it was now put to work below ground to convey the capital's waste and run-off water to the Thames at Blackfriars. It provided the perfect means of escape for Callaghan, just as it had for Jumping Jack.

Graves stopped by a lamppost and looked around for any sign of Hicks. Few people were on the streets in the fog, and even the usual bustle of traffic had abated. There was an unusual quiet. As the blood settled in Graves' ears, he became aware of another sound. Interrupted by the occasional passing carriage, it was the unmistakable sound of running water. Graves cocked his head to better get a sense of the direction from which it came, then dropped his gaze to the road. Hicks' tattered scarf lay, trodden in the mire, next to a manhole cover in the street. 'T. CROAKER, SANITARY ENGINEERS,' the writing on it proclaimed, proudly, 'MARLBORO' WORKS, CHELSEA'. Having stepped into the road, Graves was close enough to read the legend on the iron cover. He was also close enough to see that it was loose.

Reaching down, he hooked his fingers beneath the heavy drain cover and slid it to one side. The rush of water was more clearly audible. Stuffing Hicks' scarf into a pocket and taking a firm grip of his lamp, Sergeant Graves reached a foot over the edge. Feeling for the uppermost rung sunk into the side of the shaft, the young sergeant took a breath and lowered himself down.

XXIII: In Death's Dominion

The wide brick arches that spanned the River Fleet were a sight to behold. Strong enough to support the roads above, they had been a feat of engineering second to none. It was said that Boudicca fought the Romans on the banks of the river and that the Vikings had attempted an invasion from its innermost reaches. It had been entombed in stages from the Eighteenth Century, the last stretches having last seen the light of day just twenty years before.

As Graves dropped from the shaft, he found himself up to his knees in a torrent of water. Preferring not to give too much thought to where it might have had its origins, he set his face to the darkness and held his lamp high. The sound of the water echoed from the curved tunnel walls as he walked, folding back upon itself again and again until Graves thought he might well have been walking beneath Niagara itself. Soon, he reached a fork in the sewer's course. Leaning into both forks one after the other, he peered into the gloom. Just as he was about to choose the left fork, there was a glint in the shadows. The light from his lamp had reflected off something in an alcove set back from the deluge. Wading closer, Graves gasped as the shadows resolved themselves into more substantial forms. Detective Superintendent Callaghan, his mask and hat discarded, was holding a terrified Inspector Hicks before him, a length of tapered metal at his neck. Graves could see Hicks' eyes bulging as Callaghan pulled the metal tighter to his throat.

"Let him go," Graves pleaded, holding out a hand in what he hoped was a conciliatory gesture.

Callaghan's blue-grey eyes flashed. When he spoke it was not in any voice Graves recognised. It was primal, devoid of the artifice that Callaghan had been wont to hide behind. "He's going nowhere," he hissed. "I will not reward failure."

Graves noticed Callaghan's breathing was erratic. He held his body at an awkward angle, clearly in pain from the shot that Hicks had fired.

"That wound needs attention," the sergeant called above the

tumult.

Callaghan gave a dry laugh and pulled the metal bar tighter against Hicks' neck. Hicks lay half submerged in the water, his great beard a matt of debris and saliva. His eyes looked wildly about him and he snatched each breath as if it might be his last. He reminded Sergeant Graves of a trapped animal.

"Why?" rasped the portly inspector, reaching up with a hand to grab at Callaghan's sleeve. "Why did you kill them?"

"I will not have any man escape justice," Callaghan said, simply.

"Their guilt was not proven," Graves called. "Gaunt was acquitted, Dankworth never stood trial and Farley was found innocent and claimed you had besmirched his name."

"I do not care what the law has to say on the matter, Sergeant Graves," Callaghan roared. "It is plain they are all guilty."

"But you made a mis-step," Graves proclaimed, bravely. "Striking at Farley whilst Temperance Snell was in the cells absolved him of any guilt in the matter."

Callaghan shrugged. "It did not matter," he smirked. "I knew Hicks would soon find another suspect."

Graves saw Hicks wince in shame. "You took it upon yourself to become judge, jury and executioner." The sergeant was moving slowly closer to Callaghan and his captive, struggling to keep upright in the torrent. "Justice is not yours to apportion. It is the result of due process."

Quite unexpectedly, Callaghan threw back his head and laughed. "I hear Inspector Bowman talking," he scoffed. Graves could see Hicks trying to extricate himself from the detective superintendent's grasp, using the rush of water to his advantage. Distracted, Callaghan was gradually loosening his grip on the metal bar.

"I would be proud to think so," Graves replied. "Confined though he might be, it is to George Bowman that I turned in my pursuit of Jumping Jack." Graves' voice was quivering with emotion, his blue eyes blazing. "Even in his current state, a state from which I am certain he will recover, it is thanks to his investigations that I stand here now."

Hicks looked a defeated man. Callaghan had clearly shown

him much favour of late, and Hicks had revelled in it. What did it mean for him now that his champion had been exposed as a murderer, the very antithesis of the upholder of law?

"Let Hicks go," Graves repeated, slowly.

Callaghan glared down at the portly inspector. "He will face justice in his own way." His voice had affected a curious sing-song quality. "This man is not fit to call himself a detective." Feeling Hicks slipping from his grasp, he heaved him back into position in the alcove, the metal bar pressing hard against the fleshy folds of the inspector's neck. "It was my mistake to rely so much upon his lack of acumen."

Graves could tell the words had stung. Hicks blinked wildly in panic, suddenly afraid of the man's intent.

"You put him on the case knowing he would not look so closely as he should," Graves nodded in understanding. "And you kept me on the Armitage investigation."

Callaghan gave a dry laugh. "I could not risk the attentions of Bowman's golden boy."

Graves was thinking fast. Did Hicks still have his revolver? He would surely have used it if he had. Perhaps it had been lost to the water when he was captured.

"Give yourself up, Callaghan," he entreated.

"To what?" the superintendent sneered. "Justice?" He winced at a spasm in his shoulder. "It is nothing more than a pretence. A subterfuge to beguile the populace. I would hang while the men I pursued went free."

"You will have your day in court," Graves soothed. He was almost within reach of Hicks. If he could get that bar from his throat...

Callaghan was almost delirious. "D'Israeli said 'Justice is truth in action'," he boomed above the tumult, spittle flying from his mouth. "I am become Justice!"

With a flick of his wrists, he brought the metal to bear upon Hicks' throat and, even above the rush of water, Graves heard a ghastly snap.

"Hicks!"

Callaghan launched Hicks' bulk at the young sergeant. Graves stumbled beneath the inspector's dead weight, falling for a moment beneath the seething morass. Holding the lamp above water, he grappled with Hicks' body as best he could, struggling to keep it from being washed from his grasp.

"Hicks!" he screamed again, his voice hoarse. With an effort, he hauled the mass of flesh and clothing back into the alcove. The inspector's sodden coat was twisted around him, his wet beard plastered over his face. Shaking the water from his eyes, Graves studied Hicks intently for signs of life, only to find none at all. The portly inspector lay half submerged, his great belly protruding from the water, his head bobbing in the current. Graves propped him against the wall as best he could and folded the man's hands across his chest. Lifting his lamp high, he took a breath and swallowed his grief.

It would be impossible to fight against this current, he reasoned. Callaghan must have travelled down towards the Thames. His face set into a mask of determination, he set off in pursuit. Steadying himself against the slimy brick of the tunnel around him, Graves glimpsed a halo of light ahead; the outlet to the River Thames, the final destination of the Fleet. If Callaghan had made it that far, he might yet escape. Bracing himself against the heaving water, Graves fancied he could feel the pull of the mighty river beyond. One slip, and he might well be pulled into its forbidding currents. Squinting into the light, he could see the iron stanchions of Blackfriars Bridge spanning the river to the south bank. Scanning ahead desperately for any sign of Callaghan, Graves reached up to wipe the water from his face.

Suddenly, the man was upon him.

With a ferocious roar, Callaghan rose from the water and grabbed at the sergeant's neck. Graves dropped his lamp in surprise and reached for his throat. He could feel Callaghan's hot breath upon his face as the superintendent pushed him back into the water. They writhed and twisted together beneath the torrent, the inexorable current sweeping them towards the Thames. Graves felt his breath escape as they fell and now, as the sound of water hissed in his ears, he felt his lungs begin to burn. Callaghan tightened his grip around his throat. Graves could feel the man's nails digging into his skin. Clawing desperately at Callaghan's face, he sunk his thumbs into his assailant's eyes. Callaghan loosened his grip and, even below the water, Graves could hear a roar of pain. Struggling for purchase against the floor of the sewer, the sergeant struggled to find footing enough to stand. He at last got his head above water and took great gulps of air.

Just as he had recovered his wits he felt himself being hauled up by his lapels. Callaghan stood before him, the water surging around his waist. He held Graves in one hand now, the other reaching high above him. With a sudden panic, Graves saw it held the strip of metal that Callaghan had used so cruelly on Hicks. The superintendent's face was contorted in his effort as he brought the cudgel down on Graves' head. The pain of the blow coursed across his skull and the sergeant's vision blurred. He opened his mouth involuntarily to scream, only to feel his lungs flood with water. He felt his gorge rise. Choking on the tide that threatened to engulf him, Graves looked on in horror as Callaghan brought the metal bar down upon his jaw. With an effort, he turned his head away as the metal made contact, but still the resultant blow was enough to make his cheek sing with pain. Graves could feel his strength failing. The effort of fighting the water was proving too much. He could feel himself slipping beneath the frenzy. Then, Callaghan seemed to stop for breath. He clutched at his shoulder as he raised his hand again. Even as his face slipped beneath the waves, Graves could see the slick of blood that seeped across Callaghan's chest. He was clearly weakening. The sergeant summoned all his strength to raise his legs against the current. Twisting them around Callaghan's waist, he tumbled in the water, throwing the superintendent off balance. Graves clutched at his arm as he fell and dug his nails into the wound on his shoulder. Callaghan gave a roar. With a single deft movement, Graves grabbed at the metal bar in Callaghan's hand and swung his body down towards the water. The superintendent clawed the air as he fell. His body slapped against the water, his head making contact with the brick wall of the tunnel as it curved beneath him. Graves felt his body go limp. Suddenly losing all strength in his hand, he felt Callaghan slip from his grasp. As Graves stood panting, he watched as Callaghan's body gave itself up to the current and floated, face down, into the Thames.

XXIV: *Coda*

"It was both the murder weapon and the method of escape."

Sergeant Graves stood at Bowman's side in the grounds of Colney Hatch. He watched as several of the patients tended to the allotments. A bonfire blazed, fed by the bundles of fallen branches they had collected. As the flames reached up into the afternoon sky, Bowman let his gaze follow the rising embers into the heavens as they danced in the currents of the air.

Graves held the metal bar before him. Glancing down, Bowman could see it was perhaps a foot long and tapered to a point at one end. The other was curled into something resembling a handle.

"He used it both to despatch his victims," the sergeant was saying, "and to find his way into the sewers, levering the flagstones or manholes aside to gain access."

Bowman was silent. He watched as another branch caught in the fire, the sap from its leaves bubbling and spitting in the heat. He turned to Graves. The sergeant's face was bruised. The skin around his left eye was a burnished purple.

"I could not, Sergeant Graves," Bowman said, seriously, "hold you in any higher esteem."

Graves held Bowman's gaze as long as he dared then looked away, his eyes glistening.

"Hicks," said Bowman, softly.

Graves nodded. It was the only response he could give. Turning to stare into the bonfire, the sergeant let the silence speak for him. At last, as the eddies in the air drew the flames skywards, he found his voice.

"Callaghan used him," he said, quietly, "knowing he, perhaps, would not be so thorough in his investigations. He gained Hicks' confidence by seeming to prefer him, knowing it would enable him to continue his pursuit of justice."

Bowman nodded. "Hicks' sister has been told of his death?" He remembered the sickly bird of a woman he had encountered at the Hackney Union workhouse.

"She has," Graves sighed. "It was the least I could do to tell her myself."

Turning away from the fire, the two men walked in silence to a narrow terrace overlooking the grounds. Bowman leaned against the marble balustrade and let his eyes wander to the horizon. There, the city crouched as if in waiting, a smudge of smoke rising into the cold blue sky.

"The Yard is in a state of upheaval," Graves said at last. "There are questions being asked of the commissioner himself. The Evening Standard is being the most tenacious of all."

Bowman allowed himself a wry smile. Of course it was. "And Miss Morley's brother?"

Graves puffed out his cheeks. "Roger knew Callaghan's last victim, Doctor Frederick Solomon, from his time in India. He had agreed to act with Solomon in the fraud at the Royal Armitage Bank, recruiting victims in return for a share of the proceeds." Graves rubbed at the bruise around his eye. "It is not clear if Solomon ever intended to pay. Certainly, he made himself scarce the evening Mr Morley came to call." His voice had faded almost to a whisper. "He walked straight into Callaghan in the passage behind his house."

Bowman's eye was caught for a moment by a jackdaw on the lawn. It stood perfectly still, its head cocked to one side, its gimlet eye glinting in the sun.

"How did Callaghan find his victims so readily?" he asked. "Some had escaped him for years."

Graves nodded. "One can only suppose that, as a man like Callaghan rises through the ranks, he gathers many useful men around him. Informants who are only too happy to tell all they know in return for a little protection."

Bowman's frown cut deep into his forehead. "So Callaghan passes into legend with Jumping Jack," he said. "Perhaps that's just what he wanted."

Graves sighed. "I think the people of London were happier in thrall to the supernatural. The idea that a man of flesh of blood - and in such a position - might have carried out such deeds is uncomfortable."

Bowman couldn't help but agree. "The Yard might never recover."

With a tip of its head, the jackdaw stretched its wings and

launched itself into the air. Flying over the cedar that had become Bowman's favourite tree, it soon had the whole of the world within its compass. How Bowman envied it.

"And you, Graves?" he asked as he turned to face his sergeant. "How are you?"

"Oh, you know me, sir," Graves said, sadly. "Indestructible." He flashed Bowman his most disarming smile. The inspector clapped his companion on the back and steered him back to the sprawling building behind them.

"And you, sir?" Graves asked as casually as he could.

For a while, the only sound to be heard was the crunching of gravel beneath their shoes. Just as Graves thought he might receive no answer at all, Bowman cleared his throat.

"I am well enough to be released," the inspector said. "My treatment is complete."

Graves stopped in his tracks, a look of disbelief upon his face. He noticed the inspector tugging his cuffs over his wrists.

"I have been subject to the most unorthodox of medication," Bowman said, slowly. "But, it has been most effective." He met Graves' eye to reassure him of his sincerity, then frowned again. "But one thing has puzzled me."

"Oh?" responded Graves as they resumed their walk.

"During both my stays here, I have found myself the recipient of certain beneficial treatment." He noticed Graves smile. "I have been afforded my own room and certain liberties about the buildings and grounds." Bowman squinted as he looked up at the building before him. The sun was glancing off the white Portland stone around the entrance and windows. "I am at a loss to explain it," he concluded.

Graves stopped again. "You should know, sir, that Doctor Taylor is my brother in law."

Bowman's eyes were wide. He had seldom heard his sergeant mention his family.

"He met my sister when he treated my father for a disease of the nerves."

Bowman swallowed hard. "Here?" he asked.

Graves nodded. "I was not able to visit you myself," he said apologetically, "but I was able to prevail upon the good doctor to extend to you certain privileges."

Bowman let the thought settle in his mind. "I am most grateful," he said, at last, his moustache twitching on his lip.

As they reached the entrance, Bowman drew his hands from his coat pockets and turned to face the sergeant at his side. "I am eager that you be recognised for your part in this investigation, Graves," he said. "That is why I shall be recommending your advancement to detective inspector upon my release."

Graves' eyes seemed to dance at the news. A broad smile spread across his face. "Then you are to return to Scotland Yard?" he enthused.

"That is my intention," Bowman nodded. "I may well have a fight on my hands," he continued, "but with the help of your Doctor Taylor, I believe it is a fight I may win."

Graves could barely contain himself. "It is certainly a poorer place without you," he grinned.

Their conversation at an end, Bowman extended a hand in thanks. Graves shook it firmly and met the inspector's eye. "I shall make sure your office is ready for you, sir," he said.

With a final look of thanks, Graves turned towards the long swooping drive to the gates. His blond curls whipped about his head as the wind rose and Bowman was sure he could hear the young sergeant laugh as he was propelled along, his coat tails billowing behind him.

Inspector George Bowman smiled ruefully as he turned back to the building that would, for just one more night, be his home. Smoothing the hair on his head with the palm of his hand, he lifted his foot to the bottom step to enter the asylum for the last time. As he did so, his eye was caught by a reflection in the window by the entrance. It appeared that, just behind him, a young woman in a yellow dress was watching him as he stood, a smile upon her face. Bowman resisted the urge to turn, shifting his weight, instead, to the other foot. The reflection resolved itself into that of a tree as he did so, its yellowing leaves fluttering gently in the breeze.

End Note.

As far-fetched as it may seem, Jumping Jack is based on a real Victorian legend, that of Spring-Heeled Jack. He was active between 1837 to 1904, spanning the reign of Queen Victoria almost exactly. His first victim was an unfortunate servant, Mary Stevens, who was attacked by the creature on her way through Clapham Common. After leaping out from an alley, he proceeding to paw at her and tear her clothes with claws that were "as cold and clammy as those of a corpse". At his victim's screams, he ran off into the night, only to strike again just twenty-four hours later. This time, he jumped in the way of a carriage causing it to lose control and crash. The injured driver then claimed, along with other witnesses, that the strange apparition made his escape by jumping over a nine foot wall, cackling as he went. Soon, the press had named the assailant 'Spring-Heeled Jack'. The following months saw more appearances, including to a young lady, Jane Alsop, who opened her door one night to be confronted by a cloaked figure. Removing his cowl, he revealed "a most hideous and frightful appearance". The man was said to vomit blue and white flame from his mouth and his eyes were "red balls of fire". As with his first appearance, he then proceeded to paw at the woman with claws that were of "some metallic substance". This modus operandi was repeated just over a week later when, again, he was reported as spurting "a quantity of blue flame" in a young lady's face. Spring-Heeled Jack was never identified, and there are many theories as to who this strange creature was. Many claimed it was simply a case of mass hysteria, others that it was a series of pranks performed by successive practical jokers.

The Victorians had a fascination for the new, including the seemingly infinite uses for electricity. Appearing at the first World's Fair at the Crystal Palace, London, in 1851, Isaac Pulvermacher's 'hydro-electric belt' soon became a talking point in fashionable drawing rooms across the world – with 50,000 people a year reportedly plugging in. It was a simple enough device comprising a belt of small batteries connected to electrodes. These in turn could be applied to any part of the body to provide a titillating electric current. Pulvermacher's belt spawned a generation of similar devices which were soon put to use in the treatment of various ailments, most notably those of the mind. Doctor Newth of the Sussex Asylum employed a battery and some basins of acidulated water into which the patient's hands and feet were immersed. In 1873, he described the effects of the therapy upon a female patient where all else had failed. "Electricity was applied 26 times, positive pole to head, negative to hand. At first, she could only bear a very few cells, six or eight, and it seemed to make her head ache; however, she was afterwards able to bear more. The result has been very satisfactory. She appears much brighter, converses rationally; employs herself skilfully in needlework; has no desire for self-destruction. Both she and her friends acknowledge the benefit that has resulted from the treatment, and she has since been discharged recovered."

Richard James, April, 2020

SUBSCRIBE TO MY NEWSLETTER

If you enjoyed the fourth book in my Bowman Of The Yard series, why not subscribe to my newsletter? You'll be the first to hear all the latest news about Bowman Of The Yard - and I'll send you some free short stories from Bowman's Casebook!

Just visit my website **bowmanoftheyard.co.uk** for more information. You can also search for and "like" Bowman Of The Yard on **Facebook** and join the conversation. I would love to hear your thoughts.

Finally, I would appreciate it if you could leave me a review on Amazon. Reviews mean a lot to writers, and they're a great way to reach new readers.

Thanks for reading!
Richard